RISING RELEVANCE OF BIS

Quality Control

& BUREAU OF INDIAN STANDARDS

RISING RELEVANCE OF BIS

Quality Control

&

BUREAU OF INDIAN STANDARDS

Himanshu Tewari

Assisted by:

Abhinay Kapoor | Joseph K. Antony

Published by
OakBridge Publishing Pvt. Ltd.
M 35, 1st Floor, Old DLF, Gurugram, 122001, Haryana, India
Tel.: +91 124 4305970, E-mail: info@oakbridge.in
www.oakbridge.in

ISBN: 978-93-95764-16-2

Printed and bound at: Saurabh Printers Pvt. Ltd.

Disclaimer:

The contents of this book are Author's own view on the current status of BIS law and regulations in India. It is not intended to be a source of business or legal advice. Making any business decision and/or compliance strategy should only be undertaken after referring to the BIS website at www.bis.gov.in and any further consultation.

‘If I am to speak ten minutes, I need a week for preparation; if fifteen minutes, three days; if half an hour, two days; if an hour, I am ready now’.

— *WOODROW WILSON*

प्रमोद कुमार तिवारी, आई ए एस
PRAMOD KUMAR TIWARI, IAS
महानिदेशक
Director General
दूरभा T/Phone : +91-11-2323 7991, 2323 6980
फैक्स/Fax : +91-11-2323 5414
ई-मेल/E-mail : dg@bis.gov.in
वैबसाईट/E-mail : http://www.bis.gov.in

भारतीय मानक ब्यूरो
(भारत सरकार)
मानक भवन, 9, बहादुरशाह जफर मार्ग
नई दिल्ली - 110 002
Bureau of Indian Standards
(Government of India)
Manak Bhawan, 9, Bahadur Shah Zafar Marg,
New Delhi – 110 002

FOREWORD

Growing economic influence and increasing level of integration of economy with global value chain requires greater focus on quality and standards. India is at the critical threshold of passing through a quality and standards revolution and mainstreaming of debate on quality and standards. Aspirational economic growth targets and the need for accelerated engagement with global consumers are natural triggers for wider adoption of quality standards. Quality has to become a mission for all stakeholders in the Indian economy and it is in this context that the book seems to be timely and relevant. The book aims to complement the Government's effort encapsulated in Standards National Action Plan (SNAP) by taking the message of transformation to the boardroom of businesses engaged with Indian economy

BIS is leading the mission of building capacity and capability around quality standards, and it welcomes the academic effort in the form of this book to mainstream the key elements of the national quality and standard mission. Given the relevance of the subject, I am delighted to write this foreword underlining the message of how quality standards will redefine the ways of doing business in India and, with India.

I am happy that the book provides an overview of India's quality control superstructure and its role in boosting India's trade capabilities. Standards play a significant role in generating high-quality items and supporting us in achieving the Indian government's goal of developing India in its journey through the 'Amrit Kaal'. Indian standards also aid industry and business in establishing a self-sufficient India by ensuring the creation of only the highest quality, safety, and dependability products and services.

When we look at the history of industrialized countries, we can see those countries who accepted the term "Quality" early in their growth cycles followed a steep growth trajectory. These countries were able to engage with the rest of the world from a position of strength, instilling the spirit of having high-quality products, goods, and services, which led to a high-quality lifestyle for the people.

Recently, on January 6th, 2023, BIS celebrated its 76th Foundation Day. For the last 75 years, the Bureau of Indian Standards (BIS) has overseen the country's standardization activities. As the National Standards Body established by the BIS Act, 2016 and the protector of the national standardization system, BIS recognizes the value that standards can give to the nation, its economy, and society at large.

I would like to state that BIS has been striving to raise awareness and improve readiness among all stakeholders across the board, from planning through enforcement. The goal is to assist stakeholders in working together to build a standards ecosystem in India based on quality, safety, and good regulatory principles. Indeed, there is compelling need to publicize BIS's remarkable work in the Indian quality ecosystem.

The Author has compiled an easy-to-read and understandable collection that touches on essential parts of BIS quality control regulation in India and its interplay with the way of doing business in India. I appreciate the Author's efforts in fusing professional and industrial experiences with the quality control regulations framework and supporting it by case studies relevant to Indian context. The fact that the Author undertook sincere efforts in churning out this insightful book is a source of pride and happiness. I want to express my gratitude to Mr. Himanshu Tewari for ideating and completing this book. I am convinced that this book will be a helpful primer for a sizable target audience, which includes regulators, policymakers, industry specialists, exporters, importers, lawyers, and other participants in the global trade scenario.

Pramod Kumar Tiwari

MESSAGE

Standards and their engagement with trade policy and administration are undergoing a fundamental shift in India. We see a strong correlation between economic growth and an increase in the relevance of standards and quality control in the economy. This correlation becomes stronger as the country moves up the economic ladder from developing to developed, as is evident from the comparative data on mandatory standards in India and the US.

India, as a $3.5 trillion economy that aspires to be a $10 trillion economy by 2030, is on the verge of a new trade policy framework in which the importance of quality standards will increase rapidly. While India develops policy and administrative capabilities, it is critical for businesses to align with this policy shift, and focus on developing capabilities around quality control, and embrace its interplay with the whole-of-organisation.

Quality transformation in the Indian economy will also result in quality and standards-related transformation in business organisations. While the government is ready and determined to move forward, businesses are at various stages of awareness and sensitivity to the issue. To integrate the quality control strategy with business operations, businesses need to develop both functional competencies and engage in board-level strategic discussions. I am confident that businesses will catch up and contribute adequately.

In this background, I am glad that Himanshu and his passionate team have taken on the task of contributing to the need for debate on the rising relevance of quality control and BIS standards in India. Through this book, Himanshu has moulded a simple narrative infused with the sharpness of a seasoned professional lens. I appreciate his sense of brevity and the arrangement of the book's chapters in such a way that it does not require much time to absorb and reflect.

I am sure readers will find this book beneficial in adding to the conversation about standards and quality control given the subject's growing relevance. The discussion over mandatory certification will only intensify and sharpen over time. I am confident that this book will be a valuable resource for professionals, businesses, and regulators alike. I wish Himanshu and his team the best in their endeavors.

Respectfully,
Rajeev Dimri
National Head of Tax
KPMG in India

PREFACE

This book was born out of a desire to engage readers, both generalists and professionals, in the realm of quality and standards. This book is neither a technical treatise on quality and standards nor the pinnacle of research on the subject of quality—this is a business book!

When we tried to explain the BIS licensing process to manufacturers in Japan, Korea, Vietnam, Indonesia, the United States, Italy, and other countries, the book spoke to us. We became more aware of the need for a modular, business-focused, simple-to-read, quick-reference, bite-size compilation of useful information as we attempted to organise our communication on BIS licensing. So, we contributed and helped put the compilation together.

The book connects the dots of practical advice to create an easy-to-follow picture while encouraging action and flow in the midst of analysis. It can provide as a roadmap for companies looking to engage with India's high-quality licensing framework. It can help technology students comprehend the foundations of business standards and quality. It can serve as a lens for businesses to transform, synchronize, and administer the governance responsibilities associated with quality and standards.

Abhinay Kapoor and Joseph K. Antony, two of my colleagues, deserve my highest praise for their incredible passion, dedication, and labour of love in putting the knowledge jigsaw involving many products, industries, and standards together. They used the keenness of a practitioner's eye to drive narrative succinctness and clarity, and they organised the chapters so that readers may quickly absorb and reflect. Chapters of this book are lucid, easy-to-read reflections on the regulatory framework, business imperatives, and experiences that we have gained from working on standards and licensing specific work. Especially, look out for the '*Trends in Trade*' section in each chapter, which highlights emerging perspectives on product quality and international trade.

I am truly grateful to Mr. Yezdi Nagporewalla, CEO, KPMG in India; Mr. Rajeev Dimri, Head of Tax, KPMG in India; and Mr. Ajay Mehra, non-executive Chairman, KPMG in India, for their constant encouragement and support throughout the course of writing this book. I am also grateful to Shreesh Chandra, Priyanka Srivastava, and Bhupendra Yadav at OakBridge Publications for considering our proposal and fast-tracking the publication.

I am grateful to Mr. Piyush Goyal, the hon'ble Union Minister for Commerce and Industry, for the inspiration he provides. I am deeply indebted to

Mr. Pramod Kumar Tiwari (IAS), Director General, BIS, for his support and guidance. I'm also extremely grateful to Mr. Rajeev Sharma and Mr. Sanjay Pant, both Scientist-F and Deputy Director General, BIS.

In writing and editing this book, I am grateful to all those who supported us during research and brainstorming. Last but not least, I thank my family for the constant support that they have shown for me.

Among the numerous possibilities associated with the content of the book and its relationship with the reader, the reader is the best person to discover its one-of-a-kind relationship with the content. I dedicate the book to the reader's curiosity and comfort!

If you have any feedback, suggestions, or questions, feel free to reach out to me at feedback@himanshutewari.com. I appreciate your time and look forward to hearing from you!

Himanshu Tewari

CONTENTS

Introduction

Quality standards and product conformity assessments serve fundamental economic goals in the global marketplace by stimulating commercial interactions while safeguarding societal objectives such as health, safety, and environmental protection. Product conformity infuses an **element of trust** into commercial relationships and demonstrates that a product, service, or system meets the requirements of a published standard. Undertaking conformity assessment has several benefits, including:

- *Added confidence to consumers and other stakeholders.*
- *Competitive edge to the business.*
- *Support regulators to ensure health, safety, or environmental objectives.*

As a compliance requirement, conformity assessment plays a critical role in the life cycle of a product, be it voluntary or mandatory. Increasingly, product testing and certification are becoming a boardroom discussion rather than the last step of R&D activity. It is now an integral dimension of brand reputation, customer satisfaction, supply-chain partnerships, business strategies, and eventually, the bottom line of trade operations.

As the National Standards Body of India, the Bureau of Indian Standards recently completed 76 glorious years of its existence on 6 January 2023. The Hon'ble Union Commerce Minister, Mr Piyush Goyal, emphasised on the Prime Minister's mantra of 'Zero effect Zero defect'. Zero defects will help India produce goods and services of high quality for its people. He also pointed out that unless our lifestyle has zero effect on climate change, we will not be able to survive. The Indian Government, hence, intends to make consumers more aware regarding quality and build confidence in it!

In this context, this treatise is timely and topical given the pace at which the quality ecosystem is evolving. This treatise aims to build a framework around India's increasing focus on quality control that requires businesses, including foreign companies, to undertake mandatory compliance with Indian quality standards.

Besides the encouraging **foreword** by **Shri Pramod Kumar Tiwari, IAS** that demonstrates a strong vision for the future of quality standards in India, we have a befitting **message** from **Mr Rajeev Dimri**, an authority on tax and regulatory affairs in India. Their take on the relevance of quality standards is captivating and captures thematic viewpoints that set the tone for this treatise.

This treatise has **six broad sections** with **sixteen chapters** that introduce the readers to the concept of quality and how it is redefining contemporary business engagement with the Indian economy. Each section houses insightful content that outlines the quality framework and its trade considerations. Particularly, look out for the *Trends in Trade* segment in each chapter, which emphasises emerging views around product quality and international trade.

The first section is the **Quality Conformity Framework**. It houses three chapters intended to familiarise the reader with the substantive principles and policies in the product conformity space.

Chapter 1: Product Conformity in India: An Overview focuses on the evolution of the Bureau of Indian Standards (BIS), which formulates an extensive range of Indian Standards (IS). We discuss the recent surge in mandatory licensing requirements and its impact on trade, especially cross-border businesses.

Chapter 2: Legal and Regulatory Framework: An Overview focuses on the fundamental principles of standardisation and product conformity flowing from the BIS Act, Rules, and Regulations. We discuss the framework of operational BIS schemes and procedures and its interplay with international standards such as ISO and IEC. Its role as the WTO-TBT Enquiry Point has a critical bearing on trade facilitation.

Chapter 3: Policy, Administration, and Interlinkages focuses on the policy and administration of quality standards in India. We trace the interaction of various product regulatory bodies, besides the BIS, and see how they are interlinked in the larger product conformity ecosystem in India. It is interesting to note that the majority of the defined standards converge into the BIS framework in some way or another. The efforts of the Customs administration to integrate the regulatory bodies into the Single Window Interface for Facilitating Trade (SWIFT) are also a progressive initiative with immense possibilities for enabling such interlinkages.

The second section is **Certification**. It houses four chapters intended to familiarise the reader with the organisational framework of the BIS along with the practice and procedures of the product conformity schemes, especially those relevant to foreign manufacturers. The insights gathered from several industry experiences relating to the practice and procedure are enlightening.

Chapter 4: BIS: Organisational Framework primarily focuses on the structure of BIS as a regulatory body. It has a traditional mix of functional and geographical organisational structure that allows for diverse representation of stakeholders. We comprehend the realities of the current organisational structure and address certain issues to achieve rekindled operational efficiency.

Chapter 5: Compulsory Product Conformity: An Overview is an interesting chapter that summarises the mandatory compliance under BIS product conformity schemes, which includes the ISI mark scheme, the CRS scheme, and the hallmarking schemes. The coverage of these schemes has grown over time and will continue to expand in future.

Chapter 6: Foreign Manufacturers Certification Scheme (FMCS) is an exclusive chapter discussing the nuances of the product conformity schemes for foreign manufacturers. With the surge in cross border trade and mandatory BIS compliances, the trade significance of FMCS has intensified over the past few years and is increasingly sought after by foreign businesses. Although an important trade feature, it is also seen as a trade policy tool for operationalising technical barriers to trade. We discuss how businesses will need to adapt to the evolving ecosystem around product conformity and its impact on market access/market share.

Chapter 7: Authorised Indian Representative under FMCS is a subset of the previous chapter and elaborates on the role of an Indian representative of foreign manufacturers under FMCS. An AIR is reckoned as a person having crucial control over the affairs of the foreign manufacturer in India. We have elaborately discussed how the functions of an AIR must be empowered and operationalised through the organisation's structure and adequately supported with all necessary tools and administrative support.

The third section is **Testing.** It houses a chapter intended to familiarise the reader with the system of conformance testing under the BIS framework and its significance to businesses, especially foreign manufacturers.

Chapter 8: Testing Laboratory Services: An Overview discusses BIS testing laboratory services and how the laboratory network has thrived over the period. It is a significant component of the quality conformity ecosystem in India, thanks to the well-knit architecture of BIS conformity assessment schemes and licensing processes.

Several aspects, such as accreditation, laboratories recognition, initiatives to improve laboratory operations, etc. indicate the government's resolve in achieving working efficiency and better access of these services to businesses.

Chapter 9: Samples and Testing Infrastructure further delves into the scheme of sampling and the nuances of testing laboratories under the BIS framework. We have highlighted touchpoints in the entire cycle of sampling and testing and how businesses should navigate various infrastructural requirements to ensure operational efficiency.

The fourth section is **Enforcement**. It houses a chapter intended to familiarise the reader with enforcement and surveillance provisions under the BIS and various efforts of the BIS to ensure operational efficacy.

Chapter 10: Consumer Awareness and Market Surveillance focuses on the market surveillance and enforcement practices of the BIS for protecting the larger public/consumer interests. Several measures are introduced to overcome abuse of the standards mark, including routine inspections and enforcement raids, which include search and seizure operations. We will see how the BIS has made significant efforts to establish a strong digital presence for easy access of consumers.

Chapter 11: Penalties, Prosecution, and Judicial Remedies discusses the system of consequences for violations under the BIS framework—a typical combination of civil and criminal penalties—for non-conformity and related offences.

The fifth section is **Global Perspectives.** It houses three chapters intended to familiarise the reader with the interplay of standards and innovation, international mutual recognition measures, and product conformity practices in select foreign jurisdictions, along with certain international trade policy initiatives that have the potential to bolster a global product conformity framework. The chapter on the interplay of standards and innovation is especially thought-provoking in the product conformity space.

Chapter 12: Standards, Innovation, and Global Trade is an interesting discussion about the interaction of product conformity regulations with innovation and global trade. Standards play an important role in the mainstreaming and commercialisation of innovative technologies and, hence, are critical for businesses to be more and more competitive. Given today's dynamic technological innovation, quality conformity delivers the objective of economic growth and strengthens the journey of a business as it progresses along the value chain.

Chapter 13: Effective Collaboration through Mutual Recognition is another interesting discussion about the principle of mutual recognition playing a pivotal role in facilitating mutual market access with respect to product conformity. Mutual recognition of quality certification signals economic cooperation, trade facilitation, and seamless interaction in the international value chain. While the BIS is actively engaged in such international cooperation, there is a need for a more forceful mechanism to achieve the true objectives of MRAs—easing technical barriers to trade.

Chapter 14: Product Conformity Framework in Key Jurisdictions discusses quality conformity practice in the international trade scenario. We have an insightful discussion on the broad frameworks and practices relating to product conformity in key jurisdictions like the US, the UK, Singapore, and Australia.

The sixth and final section of this treatise is **Business Consideration**. It houses two chapters that specifically address the renewed aspirations of the Indian economy and the relevance of business preparedness to comply with quality conformity regulations.

Chapter 15: Re-Aligning with India's Aspirations is the penultimate chapter of this treatise that discusses various dimensions of India's aspiration to be a US$ 5 trillion economy. Policies such as Production Linked Incentive Scheme, Phased Manufacturing Programme, mandatory quality conformity requirements, and the expanding footprint of bilateral FTAs are key to realising India's aspirations. Businesses feel the need to align with these aspirations and reorient their engagement with the Indian economy. It is an opportune time for foreign companies to enter, expand, and thrive in the Indian economy—to 'Make in India' and 'Make for the World'.

Chapter 16: Towards Discovering a New Symmetry concludes the treatise with a futuristic viewpoint on the need for business preparedness for the emerging play of quality. Several engagement opportunities could be explored by the industry to establish an enduring interaction with the government and other stakeholders. A reality check is pertinent for businesses to assess their internal capacity and capabilities to handle the increasing compliance requirements. This will help to achieve a desirable product conformity ecosystem with an emphasis on ease of doing business in India.

Quality conformity is indeed a global phenomenon—it is the currency of trust in trade. With the world linked as a global market, consistency in compliance is practically non-negotiable. The Indian quality conformity experience is a picturesque tale of progress. It has received due attention from policymakers. It is evolving as a deep-rooted, national commitment to attract investment, foster innovation, protect consumer and societal interests, enhance competitiveness, and promote ease of doing business in India.

List of Abbreviations

AIR	:	Authorised Indian Representative
AIS	:	Automotive Industry Standards
ANAB	:	ANSI National Accreditation Board
ANSI	:	American National Standards Institute
AS / NZS	:	Joint Australian / New Zealand Standards
ASSOCHAM	:	Associated Chambers of Commerce and Industry of India
BCA	:	Bilateral Cooperation Agreements
BIS	:	Bureau of Indian Standards
BSI	:	British Standards Institution
CAB	:	Certification Assessment Bodies
CBTF	:	Cluster Based Test Facility
CDSCO	:	Central Drugs Standard Control Organization
CEN	:	European Committee for Standardisation
CENELEC	:	European Committee for Electrotechnical Standardisation
CEPA	:	Comprehensive Economic Partnership Agreement
CII	:	Confederation of Indian Industry
CMED	:	Complaints Management and Enforcement Department
CPSC	:	Consumer Product Safety Commission
CRO	:	Compulsory Registration Order
CRS	:	Compulsory Registration Scheme
CSA	:	Canadian Standards Association
DoT	:	Department of Telecommunications
DGFT	:	Directorate General of Foreign Trade
DPIIT	:	Department for the Promotion of Industry and Internal Trade
ES	:	Enterprise Singapore
e-Sanchit	:	e-Storage and Computerised Handling of Indirect Tax Documents
ESMA	:	Emirates Authority for Standardization and Metrology
ESOs	:	European Standardisation Organisations

ETL	:	Electrical Testing Laboratories
ETSI	:	European Telecommunications Standards Institute
FDI	:	Foreign Direct Investment
FMCD	:	Foreign Manufacturers Certification Department
FMCS	:	Foreign Manufacturers Certification Scheme
FSSAI	:	Food Safety and Standards Authority of India
FTA	:	Foreign Trade Agreement
FTP	:	Foreign Trade Policy
GCC	:	Gulf Cooperation Council
GSO	:	Gulf Standardization Organization
IEC	:	International Electro-Technical Commission
INSS	:	Indian National Strategy for Standardisation
ISI	:	Indian Standards Institution
ISO	:	International Organization for Standardization
ICEGATE	:	Indian Customs Electronic Gateway
ICES	:	Indian Customs EDI System
IGCR	:	Import of Goods at Concessional Rate of Duty Rules
IPR	:	Intellectual Property Rights
LIMS	:	Laboratory Information Management System
LIS / LMS	:	Laboratory Information System / Laboratory Management System
LMA	:	Legal Metrology Act, 2009
LRS	:	Laboratory Recognition Scheme
MeitY	:	Ministry of Electronics and Information Technology
MoIAT	:	Ministry of Industry and Advanced Technology
MRA	:	Mutual Recognition Agreements
MSME	:	Small and Medium Manufacturers
MTCTE	:	Mandatory Testing and Certification of Telecommunication Equipment
NABL	:	National Accreditation Board for Testing and Calibration Laboratories
NBQP	:	National Board for Quality Promotion
NSB	:	National Standards Bodies

NABCB	:	National Accreditation Board for Certification Bodies
OSL	:	Outside Laboratories
PESO	:	Petroleum and Explosive Safety Organisation of India
PGAs	:	Participating Government Agencies
PLI	:	Production Lined Incentives
PMP	:	Phased Manufacturing Programmes
QCI	:	Quality Council of India
QCO	:	Quality Control Orders
SA	:	Standards Australia
SAARC	:	South Asian Association for Regional Cooperation
SAC	:	Singapore Accreditation Council
SARSO TMB	:	South Asian Regional Standards Organization Technical Management Board
SIT	:	Scheme of Inspection and Testing
SKD / CKD	:	Semi Knocked Down / Completely Knocked Down
SMB	:	Standardization Management Board
SNAP	:	Standards National Action Plan
STAMEQ	:	Directorate for Standards, Metrology, and Quality
SWIFT	:	Single Window Interface for Facilitation of Trade
TAC	:	Type Approval Certificate
TEC	:	Telecommunication Engineering Center
TFA	:	Trade Facilitation Agreement
TMB	:	Technical Management Board
TN&MD	:	Think, Nudge, and Move Department
UKCA	:	UK Conformity Assessment
UL	:	Underwriter Laboratories
WPC	:	Wireless Planning and Coordination
WTO-TBT	:	WTO Agreement on Technical Barriers to Trade

QUALITY CONFORMITY FRAMEWORK

CHAPTER 1

PRODUCT CONFORMITY IN INDIA: *An Overview*

'Quality means doing it right when no-one one is looking.'

Henry Ford

Standards play a fundamental role in the global marketplace. Standardisation[1] and product conformity serve economic goals, facilitate business interactions, and support societal goals such as health, safety, and environment. They ensure consistency in quality and establish an objective basis for the trade to conduct business. The presence of a Standard Mark on a product is an assurance of conformity to the specifications.

- *The Indian standards journey started with the establishment of the Indian Standards Institution (ISI) in 1947.[2] This was the beginning of standardisation activity in India. The ISI ensured quality control and competitive efficiency in the rapid industrialisation expected in the early decades of India's independence.*
- *To make standardisation benefits more accessible to common consumers, the ISI started operating the Certification Marks Scheme under the ISI (Certification Marks) Act, 1952.*
- *The ISI (Certification Marks) Act, 1952 regulated product certification. However, there was no law governing the formulation of standards.*

1 The practice is generally described as the process of developing, releasing, and applying standards.

2 In January 1947, the Indian Standards Institution, as the then National Standards Body of India, was registered as a Society under the Societies Registration Act, 1860.

- *It was with the introduction of Bureau of Indian Standards*[3] *('BIS' or 'Bureau') under the BIS Act, 1986 that formulation of standards and other related work became statutorily governed. The Bureau was introduced as a dedicated agency for the development and enforcement of Indian Standards.*

The Indian Standards certification has been voluntary in nature, except for specific product standards that are made mandatory by the Central Government. However, this trend has been fast undergoing a change since the past 5 years with the Government bringing over 370 products under compulsory BIS certification through the issuance of various Quality Control Orders (Technical Regulations).

The Ministry of Consumer Affairs, Food, and Public Distribution is the primary Government department responsible for BIS product standards. However, each Government ministry or department is responsible for developing and disseminating standards corresponding to the products administered by it. Several laws (both sector-specific and general) regulate such standard-setting processes. Below is an illustration of important laws that have influenced the product conformity space:

- *Bureau of Indian Standards Act, 2016.*
- *Drugs and Cosmetics Act, 1940.*
- *Prevention of Food Adulteration Act, 1954.*
- *Export (Quality Control and Inspection) Act, 1963.*
- *The Petroleum and Natural Gas Regulatory Board Act, 2006.*
- *The Food Safety and Standards Act, 2006.*
- *Explosives Act, 1984.*
- *Environment Protection Act, 1986.*
- *All the rules and regulations framed under these Acts, including the BIS Act.*

---

3 The Bureau is a Body Corporate consisting of 25 members representing both Central and State Governments, Members of Parliament, industry, scientific and research institutions, consumer organisations, and professional bodies.

This book focuses on capturing relevant aspects of BIS certification; the product conformity ecosystem is much larger and includes other certification systems like:

- *AIS/TAC: Type Approval Certificate*[4] *under the Automotive Industry Standards, the automotive technical standards for India.*
- *TEC: Certification issued by the Telecommunication Engineering Center (TEC) in India is a mandatory process for telecommunication products (MTCTE).*[5]
- *WPC: Wireless Planning & Coordination (WPC) certification is a mandatory product certification for wireless products in India.*[6]
- *PESO: Petroleum and Explosive Safety Organisation of India certification is a mandatory product certification for oil and gas processing machines or storage equipment in India.*[7]
- *FSSAI: Certification under Food Safety and Standards Authority of India*[8] *lays standards for food articles and regulates manufacturing, processing, distribution, sale, and import of food.*

In the global context, the of *International Organization for Standardization (ISO)* is the agency responsible for developing global standards, which was also established in 1947. India is one of the founding members of the ISO and has been involved in such international standards for a long time.

Revamped BIS Law, 2016

The scope of BIS Act, 1986 was limited to goods and merchandise alone. As the Indian economy grew and the services became an important contributor to the economy, there was felt a need that the scope of the BIS Act be expanded to cover services as well. Accordingly, the BIS Act, 2016 was introduced with an expanded scope to include goods, articles, processes, systems, and services.

---

4 AIS is issued by the Ministry of Road Transport and Highways, which is the ministry regulating the automotive sector in India. TAC is issued for products that meet the required standard and meet technical and safety requirements.

5 TEC functions under Department of Telecommunications (DoT), Ministry of Communications.

6 WPC functions under the Ministry of Communications; WPC registration is generally required for BIS approvals.

7 PESO functions under the Department for the Promotion of Industry and Internal Trade (DPIIT), Ministry of Commerce and Industry.

8 Established under the Food Safety and Standards Act, 2006.

The amendment also strengthened compliance and enforcement. The stated objectives of the BIS Act, 2016 are:

- *To establish the BIS as the* ***National Standards Body of India,*** *exclusively authorised to publish Indian Standards.*
- *To ensure the* ***harmonious development of standardisation activities,*** *conformity assessment, and quality assurance of goods, articles, processes, systems, and services.*
- *To enable the Government to bring under the* ***mandatory certification*** *regime such article, process, or service it considers necessary from the point of view of health, safety, environment, prevention of deceptive practices, national security, etc.*
- *To allow a variety of* ***simplified conformity assessment schemes*** *that offer manufacturers more options for adhering to standards.*
- *To* ***strengthen the surveillance, enforcement, and penal provisions*** *for better and effective compliance, and enable compounding of offences for violations.*

The 2016 law was introduced to align with the Central Government's broader set of nation-building initiatives, including the 'Make in India' and 'Ease of Doing Business' campaigns.

Certification Overview

The BIS has introduced several standards for goods, processes, systems, and services, although BIS certification is primarily intended for products. BIS product conformity schemes generally result in one of the three BIS certification marks (see below). The most common and well-known plan for domestic manufacturers is the **ISI mark scheme**, which grants the right to use the ISI mark.

ISI Standard Mark

The Standard Mark for Registration

The Hallmark

The certification scheme is voluntary in nature. However, the Government has notified mandatory certification on limited products considering public health and safety, besides other purposes. The BIS is authorised to conduct compliance assessments of products, facilities, procedures, and processes under the BIS Act, Rules, and Regulations. It issues licenses or certificates of conformity under the product approval schemes, according to the conformity testing systems outlined in the BIS (Conformity Assessment) Regulations, 2018 (Conformity Regulations). Some interesting facts and features are:

- *With over 38,000 licensees covering over 1,000 product standards, the BIS product certification scheme is one of the **largest in the world.***
- *During 2020–21, 992 (554 new and 438 revised) standards were formulated, 3,747 standards were reviewed, and 310 Indian Standards were harmonised with International Standards.*[9]
- *Scheme-I*[10] *(**ISI mark scheme**) and Scheme-II*[11] *(**Compulsory Registration Scheme**) are two crucial BIS conformity assessment schemes.*
- *Under Scheme-I, besides the normal procedure, domestic manufacturers are also offered a '**simplified procedure**' option for select products, which entails a relaxed licensing process and faster timelines.*
- *Under the **Foreign Manufacturers Certification Scheme** (FMCS)*[12]*, a foreign manufacturer can obtain a license under FMCS through an on-site audit.*[13] *Currently, over 1,000 licences have been issued in about 60 different countries.*
- *The Compulsory Registration Scheme (CRS) under Scheme-II relies on self-declaration of conformity backed by a third-party test report.*[14]

---

9 A total of 6,608 Indian Standards have so far been harmonised with International Standards of the ISO and the IEC. Data based on the statistics released by the Bureau/Government.

10 The ISI Mark Scheme covers product categories ranging from cement, electrical goods, food and related products, medical equipment, etc.

11 The Compulsory Registration Scheme (CRS) covers Electronics, IT Goods, and Renewable Energy (Solar Products).

12 FMCS is an extension of the domestic scheme that requires pre-evaluation of manufacturing capabilities and product conformance and post-certification surveillance inspections and testing.

13 Simplified procedure option is not available in FMCS. Also, FMCS does not apply to the products covered under the CRS.

14 The BIS does not conduct any factory or sample evaluation, but registers the manufacturers based on the legal documents submitted, thereby permitting them to apply the BIS Registration Mark.

- *Under the Hallmark[15] Scheme, gold as well as silver jewellery sold in India are certified to guarantee of purity or fineness of precious metal articles.*

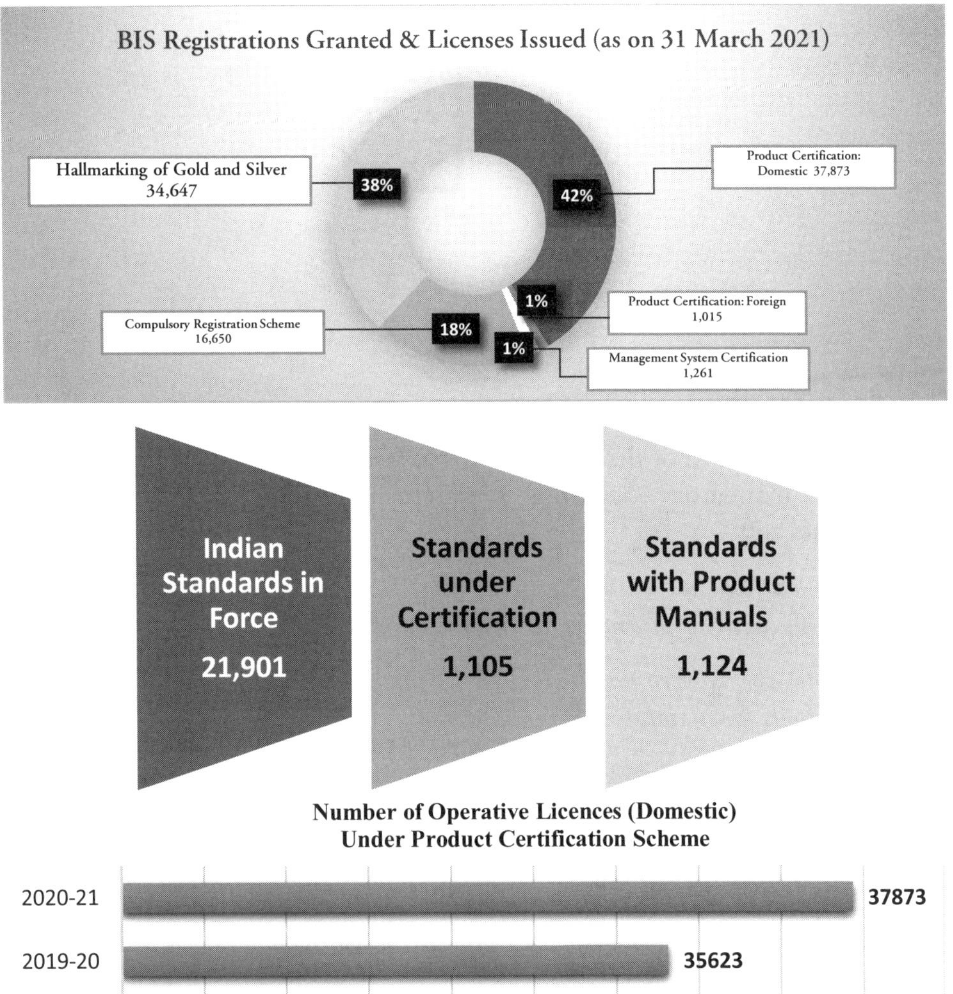

Number of Operative Licences (Domestic) Under Product Certification Scheme

15 Hallmarking is the accurate determination and official recording of the proportionate content of precious metal in the jewellery/artefacts or bullion/coins.

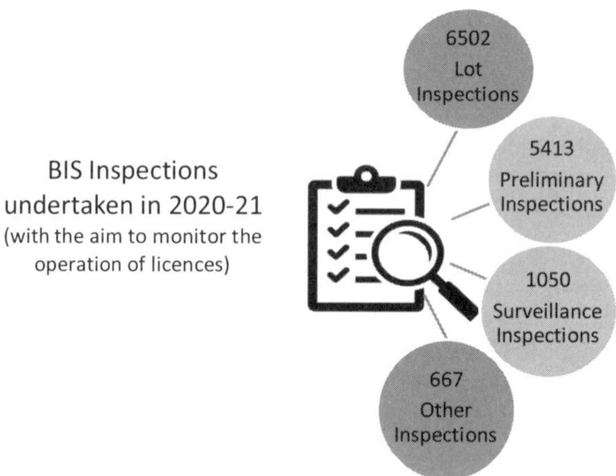

Trends in Trade

Since the introduction of the BIS Act, 2016, trade has witnessed a surge in the number of mandatory licensing requirements. Some recent interesting developments are:

- *The current data suggest that there are* ***over 370 products under mandatory compliance*** *with Indian standards.*
- *Lately, the Government expressed its intention to further* ***add about 600 products*** *for mandatory compliances.*
- *The Union Commerce Minister recently proposed to add '****Standard****' as a fourth dimension to the* ***Prime Minister's 3S mantra*** *for faster economic development and governance—Skill, Scale, and Speed.*
- *The Government has also proposed to embark on the '****One Nation One Standard****' mission and place India as the world pioneer in setting norms and benchmarks.*

The move echoes India's commitment to greater transparency, faster administering, and positioning Indian standards as per global benchmarks. The structural reforms are aimed at encouraging ***Ease of Doing Business in India*** and accelerating its economic growth.

Summing Up

India's standards ecosystem gradually developed since India's independence in 1947. India has witnessed three distinct phases in the evolution of the legal framework around product conformity and standards.

- *[1947 to 1986] Quality standards spread across industries with increased participation of the Government.*
- *[1986 to 2016] India witnessed streamlining of the quality conformity process under the headship of the Bureau of Indian Standards.*
- *[2016 onwards] Significant increase in the influence of product conformity and quality in the Indian economy.*

Hence, it becomes relevant for businesses to be aware of this change and integrate a quality-mindset as an essential part of business strategy.

The BIS is the National Standards Body of India exclusively authorised to publish Indian Standards. *It has one of the most extensive product conformity programmes globally; it has developed and published about 22,000 voluntary and mandatory standards in the interest of public health and safety.* The recent surge in mandatory licensing requirements and several other reforms such as the 'One Nation One Standard' mission mirror India's commitment to greater transparency, faster administering, and encouraging ease of doing business in India.

CHAPTER 2

Legal and Regulatory Framework: *An Overview*

'The golden rule is that there are no golden rules.'

George Bernard Shaw

Over the years, the Indian standardisation laws have substantially expanded their span and influence while deepening their roots in the Indian economy. Setting the benchmarks for standards and quality is a sovereign function and its mainstreaming is achieved through market forces. Recent developments in this space indicate the Government's intention to deepen the influence of quality in the Indian economy.

BIS product conformity administration is enabled by:

- *Bureau of India Standards Act, 2016 (**BIS Act**).*
- *Bureau of India Standards Rules, 2018 (**BIS Rules**).*
- *Bureau of India Standards (Conformity Assessment) Regulations, 2018 (**Conformity Regulations**).*

The Framework

The BIS operates under the aegis of the ***Ministry of Consumer Affairs, Food and Public Distribution, Government of India***. The **BIS Act** establishes standardisation and product conformity fundamentals, and the **BIS Rules** stipulate the procedural aspects.[16] Some of the unique features of the BIS Act are:

- *Provisions made for grant of license (GoL) or certification of conformity.*
- *The Government can* ***mandate*** *standard mark in public interest for the safety of the environment and national security or to prevent unfair trade practices.*
- *Restrictions have been placed on the* ***manufacture, import, distribution, sale, hire, lease, storage, or exhibition for sale*** *of such products that do not comply with prescribed standards.*
- *The Government has the power to appoint* ***any agency or authority*** *(besides the BIS) to verify the conformity of products and services and issue the conformity certificates.*
- *Provisions made for* ***recall or repair of products*** *that bear the Standard Mark but do not conform to the required Indian standard.*
- *The* ***penalty*** *for non-compliance will be a fine of up to ₹ 5 lakhs, besides* ***criminal prosecution****. However, the fine goes up to 10 times the value of goods in particular circumstances.*
- *Provisions made for* ***compensation*** *measures and* ***compounding*** *of offences.*
- *The* ***appeal process*** *against an order on licensing, certification, or imposition of restriction is also provided.*

The **Conformity Regulations** establish the procedures for:

- *Administration of various certification schemes.*
- *Application for the grant and conditions of the licence to use or apply a Standard Mark.*
- *Validity, renewal, suspension, or cancellation of licence to use or apply a Standard Mark.*
- *Application for the grant and conditions of certificate of conformity.*

16 These Rules are administrative in nature.

- *Validity, renewal, suspension, or cancellation of certificate of conformity.*

Some of the prominent certification schemes under the BIS are:

- *ISI Mark Scheme (Compulsory Licensing under Scheme-I)*[17]
    - o *It includes both normal procedure and simplified procedure.*
- *Registration Scheme (Compulsory Registration under Scheme-II)*[18]
- *Foreign Manufacturers Certification Scheme (FMCS)*
- *Grant of Certificate of Conformity (Certification under Scheme-IV)*

Figure 2.1 Hierarchy of CAP Activities of BIS

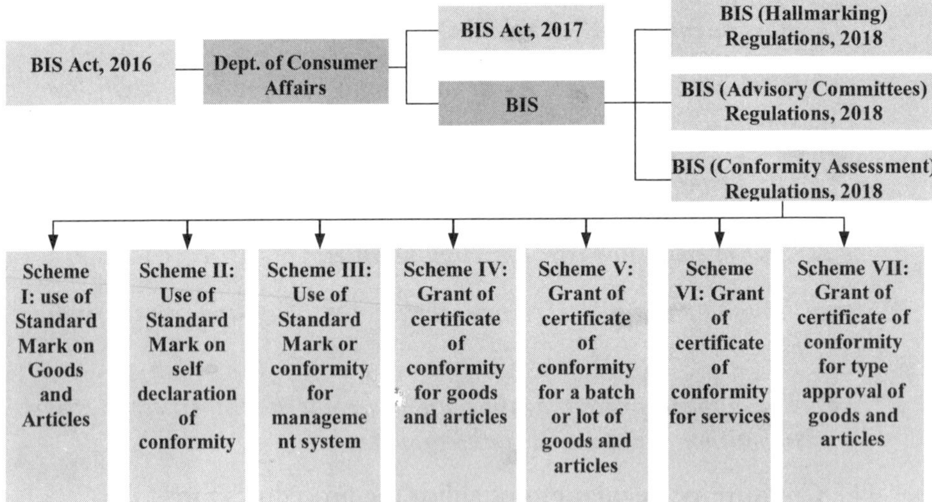

***Sources*: BIS Act, Rules & Regulations, BIS, https://bis.gov.in/index.php/the-bureau/bis-act-rules-and-regulations/.**

The orders for implementing mandatory licensing are framed by the concerned ministries/departments. Such orders are supplemented by departmental guidelines. In other words, the licensing framework is guided by

17 ISI Mark Scheme covers product categories ranging from cement, electrical goods, food and related products, medical equipment, etc.

18 Compulsory Registration Scheme (CRS) covers electronics, IT goods, and renewable energy (solar products).

subordinate legislation[19], and hence, is essentially an administrative function. These orders come in the form of:

- ***Quality Control Order (QCO)*** *under Scheme-I (ISI mark scheme).*
- ***Compulsory Registration Order (CRO)*** *under Scheme-II (Compulsory Registration Scheme).*

QCOs are issued by the ministry responsible for the respective sector. Over the years, the format of the QCOs has become standardised and they have referred to the BIS Product Certification or Registration Schemes as the mode of conformity assessment.

So far, over 450 products are under the ambit of mandatory certification.[20] For the purpose of facilitating the Indian Government for issuing QCOs, BIS regularly interacts with Line Ministries/Departments and provides technical inputs related to Indian Standards, appropriate Conformity Assessment Scheme etc. and also participates in stakeholder consultation meetings.

Product Manuals and Guidelines

The Bureau issues technical guidelines for products under the Product Certification Scheme as 'Product Manuals'. These include information on the scope of the technical standard, sampling, test equipment, scheme of inspection and testing, etc. The Bureau also issues certification guidelines which provide step-by-step guides for all prospective applicants.

Key Features of a Product Manual

- *Basic product description corresponding to IS.*
- *Sampling guidelines, including raw materials, grouping, and sample size.*
- *List of equipment required.*
- *Scheme of inspection and testing, including levels of controls.*
- *Scope of BIS license, product wise.*

---

19 Subordinate legislation is the legislation made by an authority subordinate to the legislature. Such legislation is to be made within the framework of the powers so delegated by the legislature and is, therefore, known as delegated or subordinate legislation.

20 As per the press release dated 2 August 2022 at https://pib.gov.in/PressReleaseIframePage.aspx?PRID=1847501 (last accessed on 31 August 2022).

Hierarchy of BIS-related documents in India is illustratively tabulated below:

BIS Act	Primary Legislation	Legal framework and general principles	Issued by the Indian Parliament
BIS Rules, Conformity Regulations, etc.	Secondary Legislation	Details related to an Act, operative schemes, and procedures	Issued by the Department of Consumer Affairs
QCOs and CROs	Delegated Legislation	Technical details related to the implementation of the Act, schemes	Issued by the relevant line ministry
Product Manuals	Administrativ e Guideline	Product-specific technical manuals, guidelines for prospective applicants	Issued by the BIS

Some of the recent orders are illustratively tabulated below:

Product Category	**QCO/CRO**	**Line Ministry/Department**
Footwear Products	Footwear (Quality Control) Order, 2020 (*multiple QCOs covering various footwear products*)	Ministry of Commerce and Industry (Department for Promotion of Industry and Internal Trade)
Steel and Steel Products	Steel and Steel Products (Quality Control) Order, 2020	Ministry of Steel
Electrical Equipment	Electrical Equipment (Quality Control) Order, 2020	Ministry of Heavy Industries and Public Enterprises (Department of Heavy Industry)
Chemical Products	Methanol (Quality Control) Order, 2019	Ministry of Chemicals and Fertilisers (Department of Chemicals and Petrochemicals)

Product Category	QCO/CRO	Line Ministry/Department
Non-Electric Toys	Toys (Quality Control) Order, 2020	Ministry of Commerce and Industry (Department for Promotion of Industry and Internal Trade)
Electronics and IT Products	Electronics and Information Technology Goods (Requirement of Compulsory Registration) Order, 2021	Ministry of Electronics and Information Technology

Applicability on Imports

BIS standards do not apply to products meant for export. However, the standards are inevitably applicable on imported products. The Foreign Trade Policy (FTP) mandates the compliance of imports with domestic laws.[21]

- *Unless specifically exempted, any Indian law or regulation applied to products produced domestically shall, mutatis mutandis, apply to imports.*
- *Exemption from Indian Standards may be provided for products to be used to manufacture export products as notified by DGFT.*[22]
- *In addition, the '**General Import Policy Notes**' suggest that imported products must comply with the Indian mandatory standards if they apply to domestically manufactured products. When a product produced in India complies with conformity standards, it should also be complied with if it is imported into India.*
- *A **Foreign Manufacturer** is granted a licence under FMCS and is administered by the Foreign Manufacturers Certification Department (FMCD) located at the BIS Headquarters, New Delhi.*

21 Paragraph 2.03 of FTP.

22 The Directorate General of Foreign Trade is the agency of the Ministry of Commerce and Industry of the Government of India responsible for administering laws regarding foreign trade and foreign investment in India.

Global Integrations

BIS and related aspects are domestic concerns for India. However, the product conformity framework is incomplete without discussing the BIS's harmonisation efforts and global integrations. The BIS uses International Standards, wherever they exist, as a basis for standards development.

- *The BIS is the founding member of the **International Organization for Standardization (ISO)**. It was elected to the Technical Management Board (TMB) of ISO for 2020–22.*
- *The BIS also represents India in **International Electro-Technical Commission (IEC)** and participates in the Standardization Management Board (SMB) of the IEC.*
- *The BIS chairs the **SARSO TMB**[23] under the South Asian Association for Regional Cooperation (SAARC).*
- *BIS has signed several **Memorandums of Understanding (MoU)** and **Bilateral Agreements** with different countries.*

World Trade Organisation (WTO): The WTO is the only international organisation dealing with the global rules of trade that ensures that trade flows as smoothly, predictably, and freely as possible. It significantly facilitates transaction cost reduction through the Trade Facilitation Agreement (TFA).[24]

India is a signatory to the WTO Agreement on Technical Barriers to Trade (TBT). Through the ***Ministry of Commerce***, the Government of India designated the BIS as the ***WTO-TBT***[25] ***Enquiry Point*** to respond to all reasonable inquiries from members and interested parties in other countries regarding standards, technical rules, and conformity assessment procedures (except for the Telecom Sector). Since 2015, some of India's technical regulations have been subject to specific trade concerns before the WTO Committee on TBT, as raised by other member countries. India has consistently been of the opinion that such regulations aim to protect health, safety, and the environment and to prevent deceptive practices. These

---

23 South Asian Regional Standards Organization (SARSO), Technical Management Board (TMB)

24 The TFA contains provisions for expediting the movement, release, and clearance of goods, including goods in transit. It also sets out measures for effective cooperation between customs and other appropriate authorities on trade facilitation and customs compliance issues.

25 WTO-TBT mandates member countries of the WTO to notify other member countries through the WTO Secretariat, of all proposed technical regulations that could affect trade.

discussions demonstrate an active engagement of member countries on a global level. Hence, product conformity is not only a business topic but one that attracts international traction.

Trends in Trade

The BIS plays a vital role in boosting India's trade based on differentiation around quality and standardisation. It caters to broader objectives of nation-building, including the '***Make in India***' and '***Ease of Doing Business***' initiatives. Given the development in the quality conformity ecosystem since 2016, there is a definite way in which the Government is progressing under a comprehensive legal framework. Key highpoints include:

- *Product conformity regulations may create resistance at a global level for both, businesses as well as Governments. This is resulting in deeper engagement amongst such stakeholders; one needs to wait and look out for the final outcome.*
- *The resistance could be especially true in the case of foreign manufacturers who find it challenging to enter the Indian market. They often consider it a non-tariff barrier to trade.*
- *It is seen that multilateral forums like WTO-TBT Committee may become effective platforms for an intense debate on such concerns, to iron out wrinkles in the implementation and administration of the regulations.*

Although the current product conformity framework has a definitive framework, there is still scope for further handholding in the spirit of **fairness**, **equity**, and **facilitation**:

- *Piloting advance consultations to gather comprehensive stakeholders' perspective.*
- *Prospect for advance ruling mechanism to determine applicability of product conformity regulations.*
- *Need for an effective dispute resolution process.*
- *Realising simplified licensing procedure.*
- *Enhanced guidance from the Bureau for stakeholder facilitation in the form of guidance documents, product manuals, etc.*
- *Enabling mutual recognition of quality conformity from a global perspective.*

- *Certification/recognition of foreign test labs for BIS licensing.*

Lately, the BIS has signed Memorandums of Understanding (MoU) with several institutes of eminence for collaboration to enhance participation of these institutes in standardisation activity. The MoUs also aim to undertake R&D activities, design and conduct academic programmes/seminars, and set up a Centre of Excellence in the field of standardisation, testing, and conformity assessment.

Summing Up

The BIS plays a critical role in boosting India's trade by focusing on quality differentiation and standardisation. *Its influence is expected to rise progressively and penetrate deep into the economy.* It addresses broader nation-building goals, such as the 'Make in India' and 'Ease of Doing Business' initiatives. *The Government is leading from the front, while the industry and other stakeholders are following and will suitably respond.*

The BIS has made efforts to match Indian Standards with international standards such as ISO and IEC. Its role as the WTO-TBT Enquiry Point has a critical bearing on trade facilitation. Discussions at the WTO platform show that member countries are actively engaged on a global scale. As a result, product conformity is not only a business topic, but also one that has international traction. *Countries participate in the quality agenda on a global level, and hence, it is not just a business topic alone. The quality debate is bound to intensify, and hence, it is a watch-out space for businesses.*

CHAPTER 3

Policy, Administration, and Interlinkages

'Growth is never by mere chance; it is the result of forces working together.'

James Cash Penney

Standards play a significant role in progressively shaping the quality infrastructure. Product certification activities in India would continue to increasingly influence trade and commerce over the next decade. The Government is making persistent efforts to provide a strategic policy framework for quality conformity and increase its operational responsiveness and efficiency.

Rolling out measures like the Indian National Strategy for Standardisation (INSS)[26], and Standards National Action Plan (SNAP)[27] are indicators of the Government's concerted efforts to establish an efficient process for standardisation and to harmonise the standards framework. The BIS, as part of the ***Ministry of Consumer Affairs, Food, and Public Distribution, Government of India***, is statutorily involved with product certification, quality system certifications, and testing. As the National Standards Body, the BIS is designed to be the focal point of the quality conformity ecosystem in India.

---

26 The INSS document was released in June 2018 during the Fifth National Standards Conclave by the Indian Ministry of Commerce and Industry.

27 The SNAP 2022-27 document was released in January 2023 by the Bureau of Indian Standards.

Indian National Strategy for Standardisation (INSS)

The INSS recognised standardisation as a critical component of the country's quality infrastructure. Additionally, the INSS emphasised the importance of standards being positioned as a critical facilitator of all economic operations. Moreover, the strategy recognises the critical nature of constructing a comprehensive ecosystem for standards development in India through the adoption of best practices and the establishment of a response mechanism to address standardisation difficulties.

The BIS has established a four-pronged plan to increase the sufficiency and openness of its operations and to accomplish the INSS's objectives:

- *Enhance the system through increased IT infusion and process reengineering.*
- *Assure proper manpower availability and capacity building.*
- *Assure appropriate surveillance and testing resources.*
- *Increased engagement with stakeholders, such as manufacturers and customers.*

Standards National Action Plan (SNAP)

To effectively discharge its responsibilities as India's National Standards Body, the BIS developed and released the SNAP following extensive stakeholder consultation with policymakers, academia, industry, industry associations, research and development institutions, and government bodies, among others.

The action plan suggests a series of activities that would enable the BIS to accomplish the defined objectives and to stimulate national standardised activity and international standards engagement. With INSS's strategic objectives in mind, the BIS created the SNAP with the following objectives:

- *Identifying standardisation requirements and increasing stakeholder involvement.*
- *Streamlining and expediting the standardisation process.*
- *Assuring the country's standardisation operations are conducted in an orderly fashion.*
- *Participation and engagement in international standardising activities increased.*

- *Increasing awareness of and compliance with standards.*

A wide range of activities including engineering, services, IoT, AI, etc., have found prominent place in this action plan.

> *'**Sustainability**', '**Smartness**', and '**Services**' would be the pillars of future standards.*

Administrative Interplay with Other Regulators

Besides its close interactions with the trade and consumers, the BIS actively interacts with other regulators with respect to standards formulation and implementation. Over the years, several governmental agencies have also been increasingly engaged with the BIS to collectively develop envisioned standards in their respective spaces. This interlinkage has strengthened over a period. Certain key features of these interlinkages emerge as:

- ***Improved participation**: Mutual participation of regulators to ensure quality of products.*
- ***Increased awareness and transparency**: Transparency in the quality conformity process, market access for products, and the resultant business certainty.*
- ***Collective capacity building**: Government agencies and businesses collaborating with the BIS, that has a long-standing expertise in formulating and administering standards, continues to be critical and relevant.*

Several agencies have adopted BIS standards for their respective regulatory compliance requirements. Illustratively, the following merit due attention given their rising significance:

- *Food Safety and Standards Authority of India (FSSAI)*[28]
- *Central Drugs Standard Control Organisation (CDSCO)*[29]
- *Department of Chemicals and Petro Chemicals*

28 FSSAI is a statutory body under the Ministry of Health and Family Welfare, Government of India. It is responsible for protecting and promoting public health through the regulation and supervision of food safety.

29 CDSCO is India's national regulatory body for pharmaceuticals and medical devices under the Ministry of Health and Family Welfare, Government of India.

The BIS compliments these agencies/regulators in providing an enabling environment to the businesses. The BIS has spearheaded several product standards as per the needs of agencies. Likewise, such agencies have also adopted Indian Standards as a mandatory requirement for seeking respective licenses and authorisations. Illustratively:

- *In April 2021, BIS license was made a pre-condition for issuing FSSAI license to manufacturers of packaged drinking water/mineral water.*
- *In 2019, the BIS published a new safety and quality standard (IS 23485)*[30] *for certification of medical devices in India.*
- *Over the period, quite a few BIS standards for chemical products have been brought under the mandatory conformity assessment schemes.*

Trade Facilitation Initiatives

Over the years, India has introduced several trade facilitation initiatives as part of its Ease of Doing Business initiative. Of the lot, one of the most promising initiatives was the introduction of Indian Customs Electronic Gateway (ICEGATE)[31] and its Single Window Interface for Facilitation of Trade (SWIFT) as a trade facilitation measure for goods' clearances at the country's points of entry and exit.

- ***ICEGATE*** *is internally linked with multiple partner agencies including banks (including the Reserve Bank of India), DGFT, and various other Participating Government Agencies (PGAs) involved in export-import trade, enabling faster Customs clearance.*[32] *Interestingly, the BIS is one such PGA under this framework.*
- ***SWIFT*** *would allow importers and exporters to submit their clearance documents online at a single point without the need to approach different governmental agencies separately. It would not only reduce interface with PGAs, but also reduce operational time and the cost of doing business.*

---

30 Medical Devices: Quality Management System requirements and Essential Principles of safety and performance for medical devices.

31 Indian Customs Electronic Gateway (ICEGATE) is the national portal of Indian Customs of Central Board of Indirect Taxes and Customs (CBIC) that provides e-filing services to the trade, cargo carriers, and other trading partners electronically.

32 All electronic documents/messages being handled by the ICEGATE are processed at the Customs' end by the Indian Customs EDI System (ICES), which is running at about 250 Customs locations in India.

- *Launch of **e-Sanchit (e-Storage and Computerised Handling of Indirect Tax Documents)** for paperless processing, uploading of supporting documents facilitates trading across borders.*

- *The objectives of SWIFT are in line with key programmes of the Government, namely, 'Make in India' and 'Digital India'.*

Interestingly, the Government recently announced the integration of ICEGATE of Customs with the Foreign Manufacturers module of the e-BIS portal (www.manakonline.in) for surveillance of imported goods. Though the BIS is yet to fully integrate with the ICEGATE-SWIFT, there is a huge potential for ensuring ease of compliance from an international trade perspective. Especially, it will benefit the foreign players in the trade network.

Trends in Trade

India sees quality as key for its transformation to a global manufacturing hub, promoted by the ***Make in India*** campaign. The emergence of the Indian quality ecosystem proves to be a significant impetus to the sustainable economic growth aspirations of the Government.

- *The Government's efforts in introducing the INSS with a 5-year implementation plan (2018–2023) is representative of a focussed approach in developing a comprehensive ecosystem for standards development considering diversity of interests and expertise.*

- *Interlinkages between the BIS and other product regulators/agencies compliments the development of a comprehensive quality ecosystem.*

- *As the National Standards Body of India, the BIS is increasingly publishing new standards/revising existing standards for the operational benefit of regulators like FSSAI, CDSCO, etc.*

Summing Up

India regards quality as a crucial building block in its journey of becoming the manufacturing hub of the world. *As the National Standards Body responsible for ensuring the harmonious development of standards in the country, the BIS* is clearly positioned to be the focal point of this quality conformance environment. The Government, in this respect, has built a strong systemic foundation aligned to meet the needs and aspirations in this space.

The BIS has been making coordinated efforts to efficiently address emerging standardisation issues. Synergies between the BIS and other governmental agencies are proving to be an effective trade facilitation measure. Such interlinkages enable:

- ***Improved participation*** *of regulators to ensure quality of products.*
- ***Increased awareness and transparency*** *for business certainty.*
- ***Collective capacity building*** *towards formulating and administering standards.*

The growth of the Indian quality ecosystem could be an impetus to the Government's objectives for long-term economic prosperity.

- *Government's efforts in introducing the INSS and SNAP are commendable.*
- *Systemic efforts to integrate BIS licensing with the Customs Single Window Interface (ICEGATE-SWIFT) to enforce trade facilitation is a welcome move.*

Overall, the collective development and administration of standardisation, marking, and quality certification provides a thrust to the quality ecosystem. It integrates the quality phenomenon with growth and the development of the economy.

CERTIFICATION

CHAPTER 4

BIS:
Organisational Framework

'Nature uses only the longest threads to weave her patterns, so that each small piece of her fabric reveals the organization of the entire tapestry.'

Richard P. Feynman

The establishing of the Bureau in 1986 was a turning point in the history of quality conformity standards in India. It not only consolidated several standardisation efforts, but also rationalised the administration to oversee the development and implementation of the Bureau's objectives and goals.[33] The Bureau's two-pronged objective defines the direction of its endeavours:

- *Harmonious development of activities of standardisation, conformity assessment, and quality assurance of goods and services.*
- *Thrust to standardisation and quality control for growth and development of industry and meeting consumer needs.*

Structurally, the Bureau is a Body Corporate overseen by a ***Governing Council.***[34] It consists of 27 members including representations from:

- *Central and State Government(s)*
- *Members of the Indian Parliament*

33 The BIS has developed a citizen's charter encompassing vision, mission, and objectives of the BIS with a declaration of commitment towards achievement of excellence in diverse activities of the BIS. Citizen charter prepared in consultation with stakeholders has been implemented in the BIS.

34 As per the BIS Act, 2016.

- *Director General of the Bureau*
- *Industry and scientific and research institutions*
- *Consumer organisations, professional bodies, regulatory bodies, and national accreditation bodies*

The BIS is involved in a wide range of operations, all of which consider the needs of both consumers and industry:

- *Standards Formulation*
- *Product Certification Scheme*
- *Compulsory Registration Scheme*
- *Foreign Manufacturers Certification Scheme*
- *Hall Marking Scheme*
- *Laboratory Services*
- *Laboratory Recognition Scheme*
- *Sale of Indian Standards*
- *Consumer Affairs Activities*
- *Promotional Activities*
- *Training Services, National, and International Levels*
- *Information Services*

The administrative control of the Bureau rests with the ***Ministry of Consumer Affairs, Food, and Public Distribution, Government of India*** (Ministry), with the Union Minister[35] as its *ex officio* **President** and the Minister of State[36] as its *ex officio* **Vice-President**.

The Governing Council constitutes an ***Executive Committee***, chaired by the Director General (*ex officio*), which performs, exercises, and discharges such functions, powers, and duties of the Bureau as delegated by the Governing Council. The Governing Council and the Executive Committee together provide policy directives and strategic directions, and ensure overall

35 Cabinet Minister.
36 'Minister of State' is a junior minister who is assigned to assist a specific cabinet minister.

supervision of the Bureau. The Executive Committee further constitutes various ***Advisory Committees*** for the effective discharge of the functions of the Bureau.

The following illustration summarises the overall organisational structure of BIS:

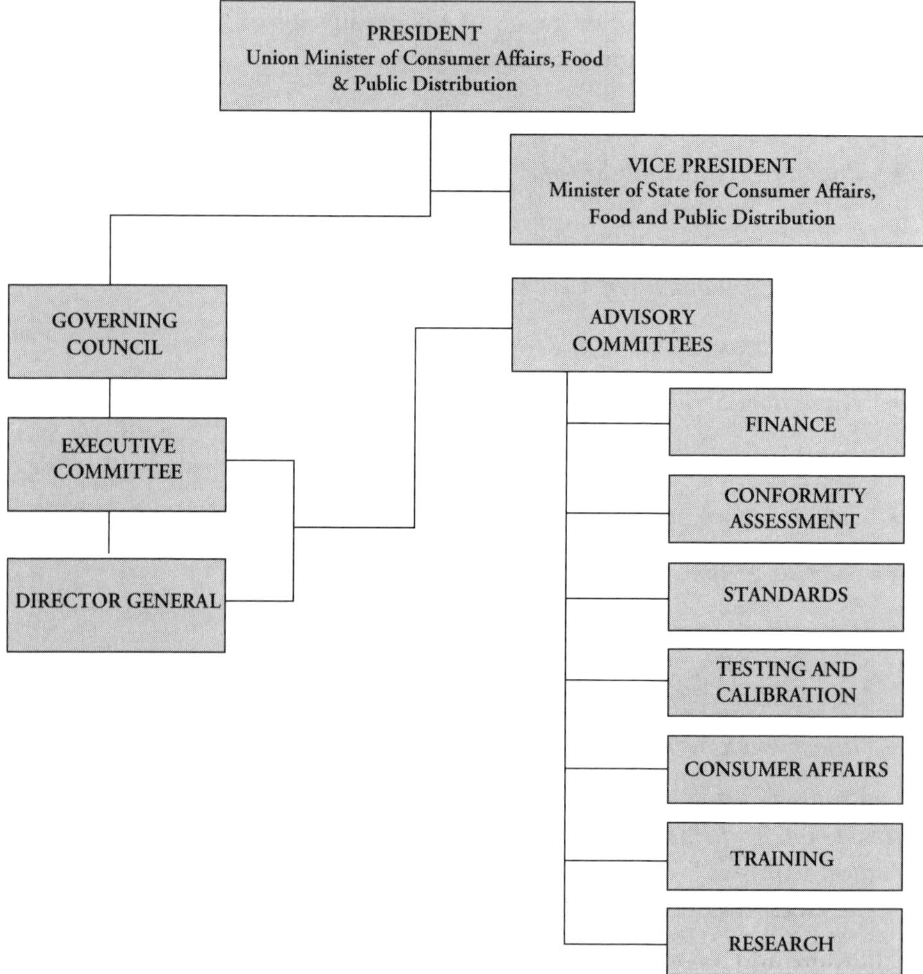

Organisational Network

The BIS follows a 3-tier functional structure with a Head Office in New Delhi (as its policy and developmental unit), Regional Offices and Branch Offices along with Inspection Offices at select locations. Presently, it operates through a network of five Regional Offices and 32 Branch Offices (BOs)[37] across the country:

- *New Delhi (Central Region Office)*
- *Chandigarh (Northern Region Office)*
- *Mumbai (Western Region Office)*
- *Kolkata (Eastern Region Office)*
- *Chennai (Southern Region Office)*

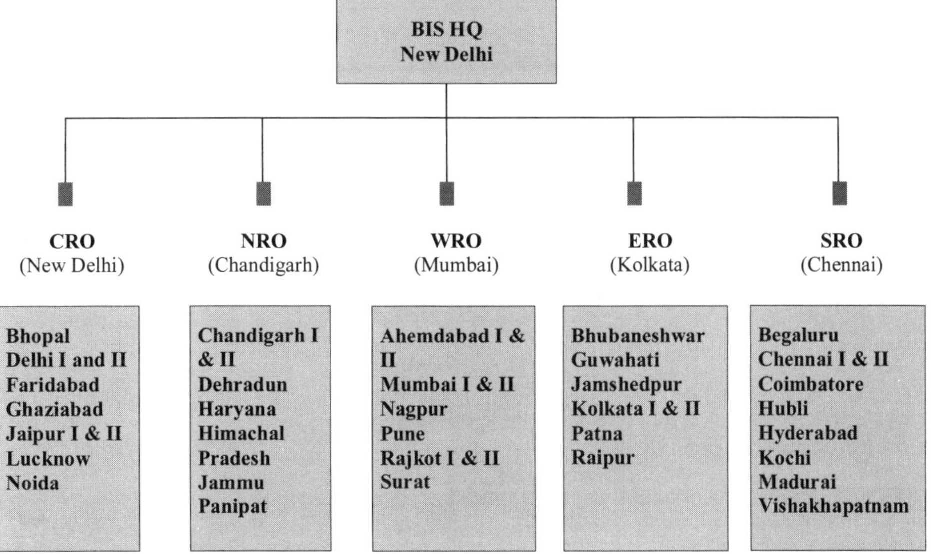

Divisions under the BIS

After receiving a proposal to develop a standard, the BIS employs its organisational structure of Technical Departments, Division Councils, Technical Committees, Working Groups, and so on. Several rounds of consultation and cooperation take place among all stakeholders, including government authorities, business entities, industry associations, consumer organisations, and specialists.

37 The BOs serve as an effective link between State Governments, industries, technical institutions, consumer organisations, etc., of the region.

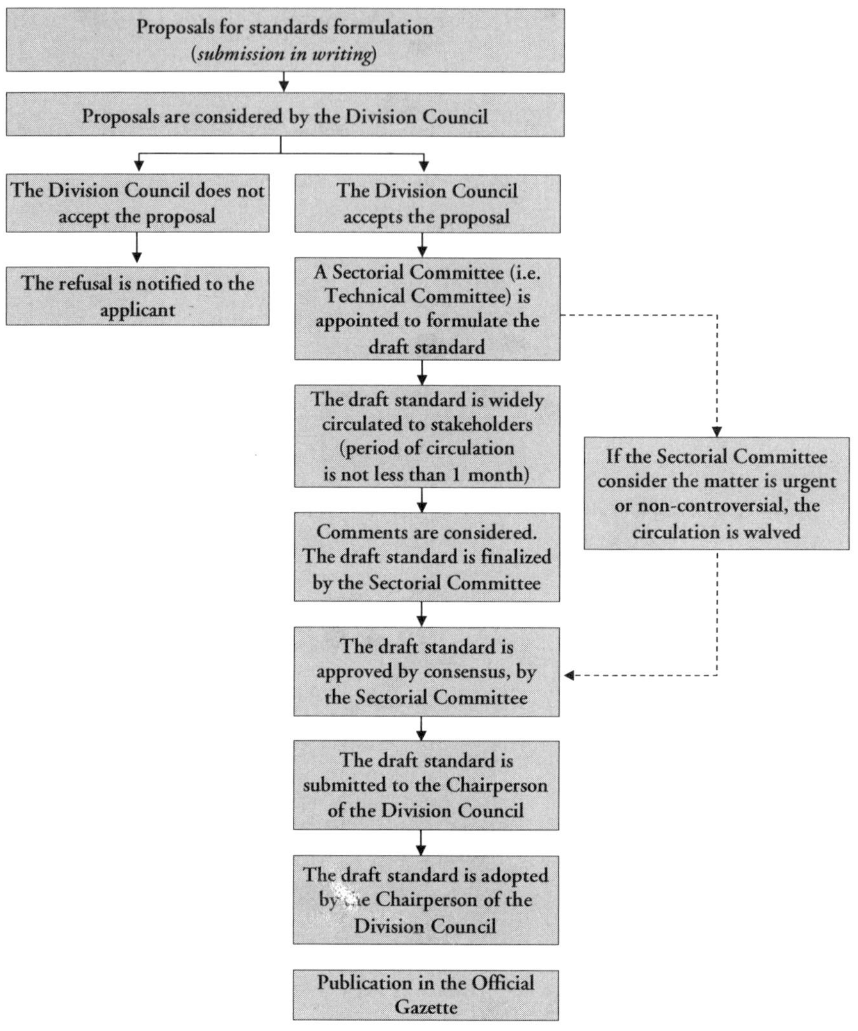

Source: WTO India Trade Policy Review Report

The BIS is involved in the development of Indian Standards in the following areas:

- *Chemicals*
- *Civil Engineering*
- *Electronics and Information Technology*
- *Electrotechnical*
- *Food and Agriculture*
- *Mechanical Engineering*
- *Management and Systems*

- *Medical Equipment and Hospital Planning*
- *Metallurgical Engineering*
- *Petroleum, Coal, and Related Products*
- *Production and General Engineering*
- *Services Sector Department*
- *Transport Engineering*
- *Textile*
- *Water Resources*

Each of the sectors outlined above has its own Technical Department and Division Council. Additionally, each Technical Department has Technical Committees that work within the Technical Department's authority. Currently, the BIS is comprised of about 400 Technical Committees.[38] Over a thousand specialists from government agencies, regulatory agencies, companies, consumer boards, scientists, technicians, and testing agencies comprise this group. These committees strive to develop voluntary national standards based on stakeholder consultation.

Development of Technical Regulations by DPIIT

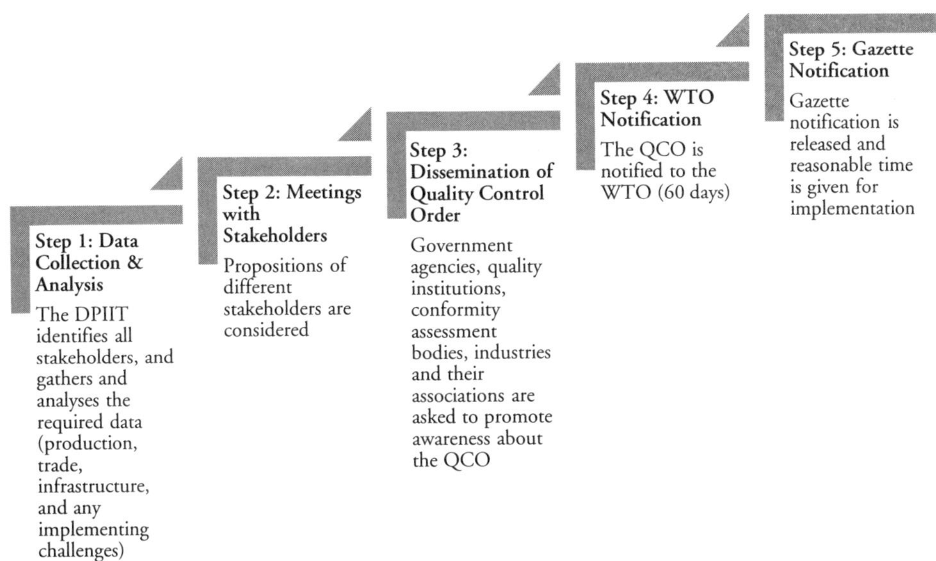

Source: DPIIT, Technical Regulations, accessed on https://dipp.gov.in/technical-regulations

38 As per the information available at https://www.services.bis.gov.in:8071/php/BIS_2.0/bisconnect/dgdashboard/committee_sso/ (last accessed on 17 May 2021).

Trends in Trade

The evolving globalisation scenario has required new standards to be formulated and implemented effectively and efficiently. While the BIS works in that direction, it is imperative for it to consider multiple stakeholders having different needs and expectations adequately.

- *In the wake of the 3rd Governing Council meeting*[39]*, several changes were proposed that impact the BIS' operational efficiency and stakeholder participation. Some interesting proposals:*
    - *Streamlining of the Technical Committees.*
    - *Modernisation of testing labs; widening labs network.*
    - *Introduction of a Consumer Engagement Portal on the e-BIS portal.*[40]
- *The BIS launched*[41] *an online consumer community and an online industry community for standards consultation.*
- *Numerous initiatives have been taken to alleviate the compliance burden on stakeholders, including automation of the entire certification process, including licence issuance and renewal via the Manak Online Portal of e-BIS, rigorous timelines for application processing, and real-time compliance monitoring.*
- *Despite a vast network, the ease of convenience for the businesses is felt lacking*—and *this is especially true for foreign manufacturers, where testing is often a pain point.*
    - *India was called upon by nations such as the US and Canada and the European Union to establish a more comprehensive network of overseas laboratories.*[42]
- *The BIS is increasingly utilising its* ***Training Institute***[43] *which organises training programmes for various stakeholders.*

---

39 1 March 2021.
40 *www.manakonline.in* (last accessed on 31 May 2022).
41 The BIS, Press Note No: PRD/Press Note/25/2018-19, 11 February 2019.
42 Statements made to the WTO-TBT Committee.
43 National Institute of Training for Standardisation, Noida, Uttar Pradesh.

Summing Up

The BIS has a traditional mix of functional and geographical organisational structure. Its structural construct allows diverse representation of stakeholders, which is encouraging. While under the overall administrative control of the Ministry, the Bureau's interlinkages with several Indian and international organisations have a critical bearing on the development of the Bureau.

A rekindled operational efficiency has been a pressing priority for the Bureau. It is encouraging to see the Government's renewed focus on ensuring ease of compliance and a robust supporting network. Recent digital transformation efforts of the Bureau are steps in the right direction and significant operational efficiency for business will be welcomed.

CHAPTER 5

COMPULSORY PRODUCT CONFORMITY: *An Overview*

'Anything worth doing is worth doing right the first time.'

Unknown

Product certification is mandatory by exception for reasons of public health, safety, etc. Even for products under voluntary certification, manufacturers may opt for the Product Certification Scheme due to consumer expectations or public procurement requirements. In the case of public procurements, BIS standards could be made mandatory by the issuing authority for qualifying the tender—while the Line Ministry may not have made it mandatory.

The BIS operates several schemes for certification of goods and articles, which are briefly discussed below. It issues the licence after a thorough examination of the manufacturer's manufacturing infrastructure, process controls, quality control, and testing capabilities. This is accomplished through a visit to the company's manufacturing facilities, and conformity of the product to the relevant standard(s) is also established through third-party laboratory testing, testing on-site, or a combination of the two.

ISI Mark Scheme (Scheme-I) 

Scheme-I can be broadly described as below:

Option 1: Normal Procedure for Domestic Manufacturers

- *Apply for BIS license with necessary documentation and requisite fees through the e-BIS portal (www.manakonline.com).*

- *On such application, the BIS officer shall carry out a preliminary assessment of the plant—review the license application, highlight any deficiency through the communication window on the e-BIS portal, and reply to the deficiency.*
- *The BIS to intimate date of factory visit—BIS officer/scientist to assess manufacturing infrastructure, review production process, testing facilities, factory capabilities, and control techniques.*
- *Sample(s) will be drawn for testing in third party laboratory(s).*
- *On receipt of test report, if the product qualifies, the applicant is granted a licence.*
- *License can be expected within 3–6 months of submission of the application.*

ISI Mark Scheme: Normal Procedure for Domestic Manufacturers

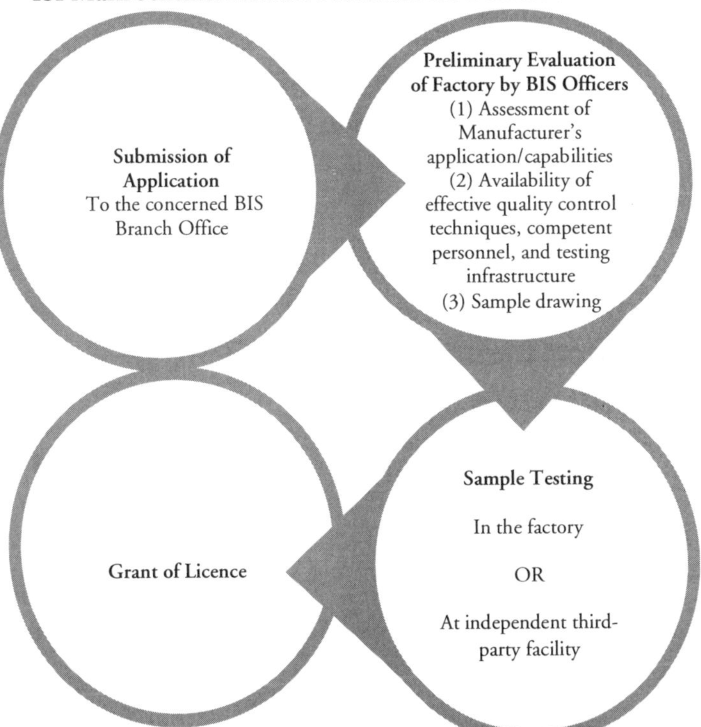

Option 2: Simplified Procedure for Domestic Manufacturers

- *Applicant must generate test request on the e-BIS portal for receiving third party laboratory test report of samples.*

- *The applicant should fill the application for BIS license and submit the test report of samples through the e-BIS portal (www.manakonline.com).*
  - *Limited products as prescribed the Bureau are covered under Option 2.*
- *If the test report is satisfactory, then a verification of the factory premises is carried out by a BIS officer.*
- *A 'verification sample' shall be drawn during the visit and the licence will be reviewed after receipt of the verification sample test report.*
- *License is granted if the verification of BIS Officer is satisfactory—license is issued first and testing is done later.*
  - *License is reviewed when the test report is received. In case of non-conformity of samples, the license is suspended immediately.*
- *Expected timeline: License may be issued within 30 days of submission of application.*

ISI Mark Scheme: Simplified Procedure for Domestic Manufacturers
(Voluntary Certification Only & Not Available to Foreign Manufacturers)

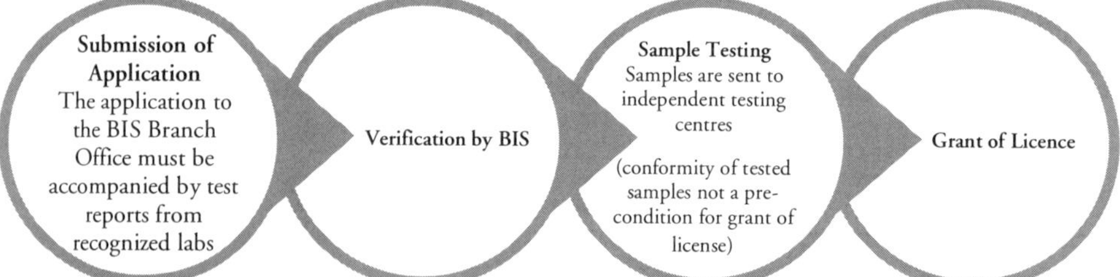

Foreign Manufacturers Certification Scheme (FMCS)

FMCS is an extension of the domestic scheme that requires pre-evaluation of manufacturing capabilities and product conformance and post-certification surveillance inspections and testing.

- *Overseas manufacturers are required to comply with FMCS in order to use the ISI Mark and sell their products in India.*
- *It extends to licensing of all products except for those notified under the Compulsory Registration Scheme.*
- *License can be expected within 6 months of submission of application.*
- *Option 2 is not available under FMCS.*

Note: The practice and procedure under FMCS is discussed in the next chapter.

Compulsory Registration Scheme (Scheme-II) 

CRS was introduced in 2012 as a simpler certification scheme for both domestic and overseas manufacturers. It is an alternative mechanism to the Compulsory Certification to facilitate growth of fast-growing sectors like IT[44] and protect consumers from illegitimate and inferior products manufactured in India or abroad.

- *For grant of registration, applicants need to submit a test report from a 3rd party testing laboratory recognised by the BIS.*
    - *Unlike in Scheme I, licensing under Scheme-II often does not require a BIS official to visit the factory—registration is based on self-declaration of conformity.*
- *All foreign applicants without liaison or branch office in India have to appoint an authorised Indian representative.*
- *After approval of the application by the BIS, registration is granted for two years and needs to be renewed subsequently.*
- *The Scheme includes random surveillance testing of products placed in the market by the responsible regulatory body.*
- *The BIS grants licence to the manufacturers to use or apply Standard Mark.*

CRS is based on self-declaration of conformity and is backed by a BIS-certified third-party lab report that is largely limited to laboratories located in India. Foreign manufactures with products that fall under this scheme often need to have their products re-tested and certified in India.

44 Through Ministry of Electronics and Information Technology (MeitY) notification of 'Electronics and Information Technology Goods (Requirement for Compulsory Registration) Order, 2012'.

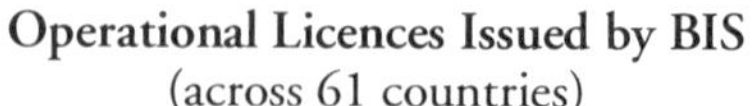

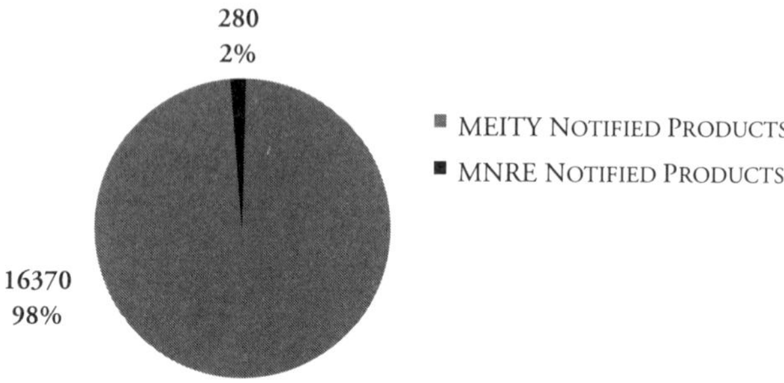

Hallmarking Scheme[45] 

The BIS Hallmarking Scheme was launched in 2000 as a mark of purity on gold jewellery and artefacts. Until June 2021, it was a voluntary compliance.[46]

- *Hallmarking scheme requires the testing of each batch of gold jewellery in BIS-approved assaying centres which are authorised to laser engrave the jewellery with the Hallmark logo and other essential details, if the purity is found conforming to the mark.*
- *As on date, mandatory hallmarking has initially commenced with 256 Indian districts which have assaying and hallmarking centres.*
- *It is aligned with international criteria on hallmarking according to the Vienna Convention, 1972. Assaying and hallmarking centres are recognised based on international criteria in line with the marking and control of precious metals.*

Compulsory Use of Standard Mark

Quality Control Orders (QCOs) or Compulsory Registration Orders (CROs) are framed by the concerned regulators or ministries/departments under the provisions of the BIS Act. They empower the Central Government to make compliance to an Indian Standard and its essential requirements mandatory in India.

---

45 Under the Bureau of Indian Standards (Hallmarking) Regulations, 2018.

46 Hallmarking of Gold Jewellery and Gold Artefacts Order, 2020 came into force from 16 June 2021.

Being a statutory mandate, there are certain ***restrictions*** imposed on the persons dealing with such products requiring compulsory licensing or certification:

- *No person can* ***manufacture, import, distribute, sell, hire, lease, store, or exhibit for sale*** *any product that is covered under mandatory BIS compliance.*
- *There must be a valid BIS license and the goods must conform to relevant standards.*
- *Incorrect and confusing claims cannot be made in public advertisements, in relation to product conformity.*

Furthermore, certain ***obligations*** are also imposed on the licence holders:

- *The licence holder shall always remain responsible for conformance of the goods and articles bearing the Standard Mark.*
- *The license holder will be required to provide such information and with such samples of any material or substance used in relation to any products as the Bureau may require for monitoring its quality.*
- *In case of non-conformity of products, the Bureau may direct the licence holder to stop the supply and sale of such products and recall those that have already been supplied or offered for sale and bear such Standard Mark from the market.*
    - *The licence holder or his representative may also be directed to repair or replace or reprocess the standard marked products or pay compensation to the consumers.*

QCOs/CROs are framed with the objective of protecting human or animal life, health, and safety, protection of the environment, prevention of deceptive trade practices, and/or for national security. Further, issues of safeguarding consumer interests, manufacturing or import of sub-standard products, protection of the domestic industry from cheap imports and unfair trade practices, and cross-border tensions, are essential considerations.

Trends in Trade

The policy shift in product conformity for wider coverage of products and industries will continue to influence businesses and their operating models. Illustratively:

- *Brand owners may need to add a Product Conformity function in their organisational structure.*
- *Foreign manufacturers to set up testing facilities as per requirements under Indian Standards for their specific products.*
- *Import-sale models may consider shifting manufacturing to India, in a phased manner.*
- *Engagement with the Government for inclusion of products under the Phased Manufacturing Programmes (PMP) and consequent duty exemptions linked to increased value addition in India.*
- *Contract manufacturing may require adding management bandwidth to be able to deliver on additional responsibilities.*

Product conformity becomes a critical requirement in accessing the Indian consumer. It will also become a fulcrum for competitiveness of Indian products in the international market. Product conformity could also get mainstreamed as a qualifier for public procurements in India.

Summing Up

Standards play an essential role in the design and manufacture of products. When such standards are mandated under law, manufacturers are obligated to ensure testing of products and assess their conformity to established requirements. At the same time, mandatory certification adds to operational cost and strategic realignment for businesses. If the standards do not keep pace with the dynamic environment, it also does not encourage adoption of new technologies.

Mandatory compliance is defined under various schemes, which includes ISI mark Scheme, CRS Scheme, and Hallmarking Scheme. *The coverage of these schemes has gathered momentum over the period and will only expand in future.* Nonetheless, conformity assessment is essential to ensuring *competitiveness anchored in quality*—a critical dimension of strategic performance of businesses.

CHAPTER 6

Foreign Manufacturers Certification Scheme (FMCS)

'Play by the rules, but be ferocious.'

Phil Knight

With the liberalisation of the Indian economy, the number of foreign market actors has increased dramatically. Global firms have had a strong presence in India for the past three decades. Business supply chains are ever more influenced by the progressive increase in regulatory compliances around product conformity. These compliances impact the depth of supply chain from the raw material stage to the finished goods stage. They also impact business relationship amongst the manufacturers, vendors, and the distribution network—requiring an enhanced level of transparency, engagement, and regular monitoring. It necessitates re-calibrating the existing relationships.

The Foreign Manufacturers Certification Scheme (FMCS) was established by the Indian Government in 2000 to ensure that Indian consumers get products of consistent quality from foreign markets. The BIS licence is granted in accordance with Scheme-I of Schedule II of the BIS (Conformity Assessment) Regulations, 2018. The initiative makes it easier to import products into India that meet applicable Indian standards.

The Scheme and Procedure

Foreign Manufacturers Certification Scheme (FMCS) is an extension of the domestic scheme and is largely comparable to the normal procedure (Option 1).

FMCS should also be considered as a trade policy tool for operationalising technical barriers to trade.

- *The BIS has established* ***Foreign Manufacturers Certification Department (FMCD)****—a separate department to exclusively cater to the licensing requirements of foreign applicants.*
- *The Line Ministry/Agency is the enquiry point for communicating with the WTO regarding mandatory quality control orders proposed to be implemented.*
- *The FMCD grants a licence based on successful assessment of the manufacturing infrastructure, production process, quality control, and testing capabilities of a foreign manufacturer.*
- *The assessment is made over a formal visit to the foreign manufacturing premises.*

Who can Apply?

Manufacturers who have their factories located outside India can apply for the BIS licence under FMCS. They shall:

- *Ensure conformity of their product(s) to applicable Indian Standards (IS).*
- *Have requisite manufacturing machineries/facilities at their factory premises.*
- *Have all arrangements/equipment in their factory premises for testing of the product(s) as per applicable IS.*
- *Have competent personnel in their labs for testing responsibilities.*
- *Accept the Scheme of Inspection and Testing (SIT)*[47] *and Marking Fee.*
- *Accept the Terms and Conditions of BIS licence.*

How to Apply?

- *Fill-up the prescribed Application Form along with necessary documentation.*

---

47 Scheme of Inspection and Testing (SIT) is a document which specifies the control over production process, which the manufacturer is required to exercise while operating the certification marks scheme. This document is included in the Product Manual issued by the BIS for any product.

- *Nominate an Authorised Indian Representative (AIR) using prescribed Nomination Form.*
- *Submit duly filled-in and complete application along with requisite fees; documentation (in duplicate) and AIR Nomination Form with FMCD located at the BIS Headquarters, New Delhi.*
- *Separate application is required to be submitted for each product/Indian Standard and for each factory location/manufacturing premise(s).*

Grant of Licence

- *On receipt of the **application** along with the requisite **application fee**, the Bureau will scrutinise the application and **queries**, if any, will be communicated by email.*
- *Once queries are satisfactorily met and the application is complete, it will be **recorded.***
- ***Factory premises will be visited** by BIS scientists for verification of manufacturing and testing infrastructure and drawing of samples for independent testing.*
- *Responsibility for **safe depositing of sample(s)** and remittance of **testing charges** shall lie with the applicant.*
- *Application will be processed for grant of licence after receipt of **satisfactory inspection report and independent test report(s)** conforming to applicable IS.*
- *Applicant will be required to pay **licence fee**, advance **minimum marking fee,** and any other outstanding dues before grant of licence.*
- ***Agreement** bearing conditions of licence, **indemnity bond** will be signed **and Performance Bank Guarantee** of US$ 10,000 would be required to be furnished immediately on grant of licence.*
- *Licence will be initially granted for not less than one year and up to two years, which will be renewable for up to five years.*

***Note:** Average time taken for grant of licence is generally 6 months from the date of recording after receipt of complete application. It may vary for reasons like delay in response to queries, organising physical inspection(s), testing of samples, etc.*

Operation of Licence

After grant of licence, surveillance is carried out by the BIS through visits of the market during which the BIS certification officer:

- *verifies operation of licence as per duly accepted STI.*
- *carries out testing in the factory.*
- *collects production and dispatch details of the standard marked products.*
- *draws sample(s) for independent testing in BIS/BIS-recognised labs.*

Samples are also collected by the BIS from the market for testing as part of market surveillance.

Typical process flow for Grant of Licence under FMCS (Foreign Manufacturers Certification Scheme)

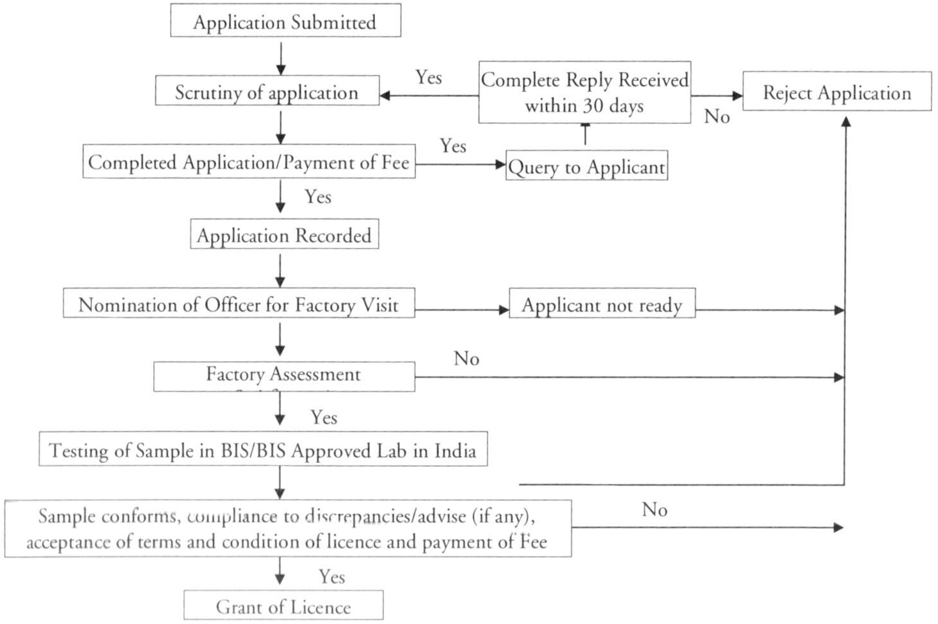

Note: The normal time period for Grant of Licence under FMCS is 6 months. The time period will be counted from date of recording of application. Under FMCS scheme, the actual time taken may exceed if some actions are pending on the part of the applicant. Arranging visa and other clearances may also take additional time. The licence is granted. Initially up to 2 years and subsequently can be renewed up to 5 year based on performance

Source: BIS FMCS webpage[48]

48 https://www.bis.gov.in/index.php/fmcs/fmcs-overview/ (Last accessed on 21 June 2022).

Trends in Trade

Although FMCS has been in operation for over two decades, its trade significance intensified over the past few years with more and more products being mandated for quality certification amidst rising cross-border trade.

A major challenge that businesses face is the mounting cost of compliance (in relation to IS) despite having certified under other internationally-recognised standards. Since testing of products required BIS-recognised labs, availability of foreign-recognised laboratories is also challenging. Some of the other noticeable challenges are summarised below:

- ***Ease of applying:*** *Contrary to other certification schemes which are managed through the e-BIS portal, FMCS applications are still manually managed through the FMCD office. Although queries and other communications are made through emails, there is no digitalised system of application and follow-up available for foreign manufacturers.*
    - ***Stringent documentation:*** *The process of data and document compilation is often time consuming and prolonged—and this is especially true in case of foreign manufacturers coordinating from multiple countries.*
    - ***Simplifying the implementation process:*** *The issuance of product-specific manuals and guidelines is helpful without doubts; however, business expectations for simplified guidelines and guidance documents for all products under product conformity schemes cannot be emphasised enough. These documents act as a bridge between legal requirements and technical requirements for all stakeholders.*
- ***Factory awareness:*** *Foreign manufacturers must ensure their manufacturing infrastructure and production process comply with IS requirements. They will need to assess the factory conditions and make requisite adaptations, even before making a licence application. Besides, adequate understanding must be gathered to ensure an efficient compliance.*
- ***In-house test equipment:*** *Product Manuals issued by the Bureau elaborately list out major test equipment as per IS requirements—though not exhaustively. Majority of these test equipment are required to be installed in the factory premises; only few tests can be sub-contracted to third party BIS-recognised labs.*

- ***Testing labs in other countries:*** *Due to the limited availability of BIS/BIS-recognised labs in other countries, products often require local testing in India for licensing requirements. Absence of option to carry out tests in foreign accredited labs attesting such compliance to BIS standards is a pain point for several businesses.*
- ***Keeping pace with technology:*** *BIS standards need constant enhancement to keep pace with growing trends in consumer expectations, innovations, technological advancements, and related on-ground realities. Businesses need to make additional efforts for IS enhancement if they face such a technical impasse.*
- ***Scientist visit:*** *Physical inspection of factory premises entails time-consuming logistical arrangements for BIS scientists, including arranging travel documents. The recent pandemic-induced disruption has nearly frozen this process, and hence, caused operational hurdles for relevant stakeholders.*
- ***AIR obligations:*** *Locating a suitable local Indian representative as AIR is a challenging exercise for foreign manufacturers, especially when they have no operations/presence in India.*

  Note: *AIR practice and procedure is exclusively discussed in the next chapter.*

Development of BIS Consignment Portal on Manakonline (e-BIS portal)

The BIS has developed an online consignment portal using which foreign companies (licensees) are required to share information of their ISI-marked shipments before entering India. Market samples are accordingly drawn to evaluate their adherence to applicable Indian Standards. This provides consumers with access to high-quality goods.

Provisions for Speedier Processing of Applications

The BIS website now allows various Government Ministries to check the status of foreign manufacturer applications and licences against the QCOs issued.

Online Licensing Process: Coming Soon…

Foreign Manufacturers will soon be able to submit applications, check their progress, and renew their licences online through the Manakonline portal, which is currently under development.

Summing Up

With the surge in cross-border trade and mandatory BIS compliances, the trade significance of FMCS has intensified over the past few years and is increasingly sought after by foreign businesses. *Although an important trade feature, it is also seen as trade policy tool for operationalising technical barriers to trade. Hence, businesses will have to engage with the Government at different levels, including on policy and administrative affairs.*

Businesses will have to learn the play of quality and adapt to the evolving ecosystem around product conformity and its impact on market access/market share. Proactive, cross-functional collaboration within the organisation structure will facilitate capacity building. *Investing in establishing an efficient compliance system will certainly help in mitigating risks from the rising regulatory obligations down the line.*

CHAPTER 7

AUTHORISED INDIAN REPRESENTATIVE UNDER FMCS

'Accountability breeds response-ability.'

Stephen Covey

BIS Conformity Regulations mandate the role of an Authorised Indian Representative (AIR) for foreign manufacturers who do not have their own operations or subsidiaries in India. The nomination and appointment of an AIR is critical to the registration process and the ongoing compliances under FMCS[49]. Indeed, the AIR role envisages a two-way relationship:

- ***Towards the Foreign Manufacturer**: An AIR is someone who has received and accepted a written mandate from a foreign manufacturer to act on the manufacturer's behalf as the person-in-charge for ensuring compliance under the BIS Law.*
- ***Towards the Bureau**: An AIR is required to agree to the terms and conditions of the agreement as a pre-requisite for the grant of licence. Thus, an AIR also is duty-bound towards the Bureau to ensure all compliance under the BIS Law.*

49 Foreign Manufacturers Certification Scheme (FMCS) is essentially Scheme-I (ISI mark scheme) under the BIS conformity assessment schemes.

An AIR plays a pivotal role as a person having crucial control over the affairs of the foreign manufacturer in India[50] because:

- *FMCS application process cannot be initiated without nominating and appointing an AIR.*
- *Ensure that the AIR is adequately qualified by education[51] and reasonably familiar with the rules and compliances under the BIS law.*
- *'AIR' role should not remain un-represented at any time during the operation of the license.*
- *Any violation in agreed conditions, especially in the case of AIR, could lead to cancellation of BIS license.*

The salient features of an AIR under FMCS are:

- *AIR must be a natural person.[52]*
- *AIR must be based in India.*
- *An AIR can represent only one foreign manufacturer.*
    - *The restriction will not apply if the AIR is an importer and related to such multiple foreign manufacturers as part of the same group of companies.*
    - ***Illustration:** For an Indian subsidiary of a foreign group company that has multiple manufacturing locations, if the Indian subsidiary acts as the importer, then an employee of the Indian subsidiary can be appointed as the AIR for all related foreign manufacturing units.*

Roles and Responsibilities

An AIR is meant to act on behalf of the foreign manufacturer, among other things, to assume communication with competent authorities. Some prominent roles and responsibilities of an AIR are:

---

50 Based on the standard Agreement between BIS and the licensee/manufacturer which includes provision for fees, nomination, rights, and responsibilities of licensee, determination/termination, indemnity, performance bank guarantee, non-renewal, cancellation of licence, etc.

51 At least graduate by qualification.

52 In jurisprudence, a natural person is a person that is an individual human being, as opposed to a legal person, which may be a private or public organisation.

- *Responsibility towards the Bureau that the foreign manufacturer fulfils the requirements of the conformity regulations, license agreement, and any undertaking(s) connected with the grant and operation of license.*
- *Ensure a responsible conduct to avoid any conflict of interest (as an AIR) with testing of sample(s) in third party laboratories.*
- *Be a facilitator for inspections and make logistical arrangement for their execution.*
- *Ensure prompt redressal of queries from the BIS officials regarding application and licence.*
- *Responsible and liable for all the acts and omissions and violations of BIS law in their personal capacity.*

Trends in Trade

The requirement of a local representative for a foreign entity aligns with several other certifications and international practices. It is both a ***legal/ regulatory requirement and an administrative precaution*** for instituting a system of obligatory compliance. Interestingly, while other certifications such as TEC and PESO demand technical competence for such representatives, the requirement is limited to minimum educational qualification under the BIS framework.

Implementation Paradox

- *Foreign manufacturers may find it a challenge to locate suitable candidates unless they have a local branch/liaison office to assume such responsibility.*
    - ***Illustration:*** *This paradox gets more enhanced for brand owners who deal with multiple contract manufacturers and fall short of options—since an AIR can represent only one foreign manufacturer.*
- *Absence of definite skills, formal training, certification, etc. for the AIR appointees is also a challenge, especially when the AIR is obligated to know it all.*
- *Corporate entity still not allowed as AIR.*
- *Persuading an 'unrelated' individual to accept the terms and conditions of BIS license—given the stringent measures and consequences in case the foreign manufacturer fails to comply.*

Interestingly, the restriction on legal/corporate entity is unique for product conformity under Scheme-I (ISI mark scheme/FMCS)—a corporate entity is permitted to represent a foreign applicant under the Compulsory Registration Scheme (under Scheme-II[53]). Such an option is also present in other certification frameworks like TEC and CDSCO. Even in foreign jurisdictions, like in the European Union, authorised local representatives can be a 'person' or 'entity'.

Need for a Business Enabler to Support AIR Function

While the BIS regulations envisage an individual person to be appointed as AIR, a reliable compliance cannot be ensured by one person alone. It requires constant monitoring, adequate infrastructure, and workforce support and must be backed by a support system for sourcing of information and effective performance of requisite responsibilities.

Furthermore, adhering to the terms and conditions of the licence also requires meticulous planning and periodical appraisal. Hence, the absence of a support system within the business organisation could become counterproductive and may even cause business disruptions.

Thus, there is a need for integrating a dynamic role for product stewardship and regulatory affairs within business organisations to take control of such complexities. Clearly, while a 'Product Manager' is mainly responsible for the product planning and execution throughout the product lifecycle, the role of AIR goes above and beyond, involving several intricacies.

Summing Up

BIS law mandates the role of an Indian representative of foreign manufacturers under FMCS. It is a crucial pre-requite for the BIS license application. *The role of AIR is not only limited to the application period but remains a critical characteristic throughout the operation of the BIS license.*

Under FMCS, an AIR can represent only one foreign manufacturer unless the AIR is related to such multiple foreign manufacturers that are part of the same group of companies. Considering this, coupled with their varied roles and

53 Compulsory Registration Scheme (CRS) covers electronics, IT goods, and renewable energy (solar products).

responsibilities, an *AIR is reckoned as a person having crucial control over the affairs of the foreign manufacturer in India.*

Although it is a legal and regulatory requirement aligning with domestic and international best practices, this local representation requirement often causes operational hurdles for foreign manufactures. *Functions of AIR must be empowered and operationalised through the organisation structure, adequately supported with all necessary tools and administrative support.*

Considering that the role of AIR may often overlap that of a 'Product Manager', businesses should consider realigning such role and responsibilities to facilitate the functions of an AIR. Since it is an ongoing effort, the AIR role could also emerge as a standalone strategic role within the organisation structure when it comes to dealing with multiple foreign manufacturers of the same group of companies.

TESTING

CHAPTER 8

TESTING LABORATORY SERVICES: *An Overview*

'Quality is not an act; it is a habit.'

Aristotle

Product testing is grounded on the notion that, with the advent of mass production, manufacturers should be able to back up their marketing claims with technical standards. In today's world, businesses understand the value of testing to obtain unbiased, third-party professional feedback on their products. Quality and conformance testing, as well as safety and calibration testing, are all examples of such testing. Because of the well-knit architecture of BIS conformity assessment schemes and the licencing process, testing laboratory service is an important component of the quality conformity ecosystem in India.

BIS Laboratories

For supporting its product certification service, the BIS has 8 laboratories of its own:

- *Central Laboratory (CL), Ghaziabad, Uttar Pradesh*
- *Northern Regional Office Laboratory (NROL), Mohali, Punjab*
- *Southern Regional Office Laboratory (SROL), Chennai, Tamil Nadu*
- *Eastern Regional Office Laboratory (EROL), Kolkata, West Bengal*
- *Western Regional Office Laboratory (WROL), Mumbai, Maharashtra*

- *Bengaluru Branch Office Laboratory (BNBOL), Bengaluru, Karnataka*
- *Guwahati Branch Office Laboratory (GBOL), Guwahati, Assam*
- *Patna Branch Office Laboratory (PBOL), Patna, Bihar*

Besides, the BIS uses the test facilities available in over 250 private BIS-recognised Outside Laboratories (OSLs).[54] In addition to this, there are several government laboratories empanelled by the Bureau for testing services.[55] These laboratories supplement BIS certification schemes by testing surveillance samples sent by the BIS or for pre-testing product samples submitted by applicants under the Registration Scheme or the simplified procedure of product certification.

Laboratory Recognition Scheme

The BIS operates a Laboratory Recognition Scheme (LRS)[56] for recognition of OSLs with the objective of having enough labs in India and abroad to cater to the needs of product conformity schemes.

- *The statutory provisions empower the BIS to recognise any laboratory in India or abroad for the purpose of testing samples in connection with the use of the Standard Mark and performing other essential functions.*
- *This Scheme establishes the criteria for laboratory recognition and de-recognition.*
- *Additionally, BIS maintains a list of laboratories that it recognises for conducting tests on samples of items or processes in accordance with applicable Indian Standards.*

Recognition of Foreign Laboratories

The BIS also grants recognition to laboratories outside India, with a dedicated set of rules and conditions under the LRS. Although the criteria set forth for the recognition of foreign laboratories is same as for Indian laboratories, additional conditions and safeguards are imposed on the recognition process:

---

54 Lab recognition is Indian Standards (IS) specific labs need to apply separately for multiple ISs. For more information, visit https://lims.bis.gov.in (last accessed on 15 March 2022).

55 Data gathered from https://lims.bis.gov.in/home/bis_labs/ (last accessed on 25 March 2022).

56 LRS is governed by the provisions under Section 13(4), BIS Act, 2016 and Rule 32, BIS Rules, 2018.

- *Such foreign laboratories must set up a branch/liaison office in India to coordinate the process and ensure the statutory mandates are complied with.*
- *Branch/liaison office not required if:*
  - *the concerned Foreign Government enters a MoU for implementation of BIS regulations in such jurisdiction, or*
  - *an AIR is appointed to ensure compliance of BIS rules and regulations on behalf of the Foreign Laboratory.*
- *Decisions relating to recognition of Foreign Laboratories may be influenced by existing Mutual Recognition Agreements with the concerned Foreign Government.*

NABL Accreditation for BIS Laboratories

LRS requires laboratories to be accredited to Laboratory Quality Management System as per IS/ISO/IEC 17025[57]. It is now a recognised hallmark for quality in laboratory management. Commonly known as '*NABL Accreditation*'[58] in India, ISO/IEC 17025 has been embraced by majority of laboratories.

Brief overview of Accreditation framework in India:

In India, accreditation is administered by the Quality Council of India (QCI), an organisation established by the Government of India in collaboration with industry associations.[59] QCI administers independent certification programmes and supervises the operation of the five constituent bodies charged with issuing accreditation.[60] The QCI operates accreditation programmes through its five executive boards.

57 ISO/IEC 17025 is an international standard which sets outs the general requirements for the competence of testing and calibration laboratories.

58 National Accreditation Board for Testing and Calibration Laboratories (NABL) is a constituent accreditation body of the Quality Council of India.

59 The Quality Council of India (QCI) was established as a National Body for Accreditation in the 1990s. It was set up through a PPP model as an independent autonomous organisation with the support of the Government of India and the Indian Industry represented by the three premier industry associations, (i) Associated Chambers of Commerce and Industry of India (ASSOCHAM), (ii) Confederation of Indian Industry (CII), and (iii) Federation of Indian Chambers of Commerce and Industry (FICCI).

60 These accreditation schemes span multiple industries and encompass the universe of Certification Assessment Bodies (CABs) and are open to both public and private actors.

Constituent Boards of QCI

- QCI
  - Accredition Board
    - NABL
    - NABH
    - NABCB
    - NABET
  - Quality Promotion
    - NBQP

NABL was an independent accreditation organisation until it was absorbed by the QCI in 2017. It was founded to provide a framework for third-party assessment of the quality and technical competence of testing and calibration laboratories to the government, industry associations, and industry in general. It promotes quality standards in a range of sectors, including infrastructure, environmental protection, healthcare, education, and government.

Laboratory Information Management System (LIMS)[61]

An integrated and unified workflow management system has been made operational for managing the workings of BIS Laboratories, BIS-recognised OSLs, and empanelled Laboratories. With the design of LIMS software, the BIS has automated the entire process of laboratory operation and enabled real-time monitoring of lab operations. It allows for real-time tracking of each sample's testing progress. For more information, visit https://lims.bis.gov.in

61 A laboratory information management system (LIMS), sometimes referred to as a laboratory information system (LIS) or laboratory management system (LMS), is a software-based solution with features that support a modern laboratory's operations.

Trends in Trade

The BIS has taken appreciable efforts to support the activities of conformity assessment schemes. Although laboratory services remain a crucial and integral layer of the quality conformity ecosystem, its trade significance has intensified with a rise in certification requirements. Some sharp takeaways from market interactions are summarised below:

- ***Extent of recognised laboratories***: *There could be an uneven spread of recognised labs with respect to the number/variety of Indian Standards. Lab recognition is even expected to be in proportion to BIS licenses issues.*
- ***Recognition process***: *LRS needs to establish a set process workflow for lab recognition while adhering to standard timelines. This will ensure operational efficiency and trade facilitation.*
- ***Foreign Laboratories***: *Need for recognising laboratories in foreign jurisdictions is often felt due to the logistical hurdles. Despite prescribed criteria and conditions under the LRS, there is limited accessibility to recognised labs in other jurisdictions. The inability to conduct tests in foreign accredited labs that certify to compliance with BIS requirements is a pain point.*
- ***LIMS software***: *It has reduced the need of human intervention in the testing process while boosting transparency and monitoring at all levels using IT resources. It is expected to alleviate issues with test report delays and any corruption that occurs during the process.*
- ***Training and development***: *Third-party laboratories feel the need for BIS to offer training to meet competency and regulatory requirements for those working in labs. For this, existing infrastructure such as the National Institute of Training for Standardisation, Noida may be utilised as a service offering from BIS.*

Summing Up

Since testing is the foundation of standardisation activities, it is critical for the BIS to ensure adequate testing facilities, both domestically and internationally. *For business stakeholders, the resulting cost increase, lack of skilled manpower and the overall inadequacy in setting up a testing infrastructure is often a pain point.*

The BIS has developed a wide laboratory network across the country (and even overseas) to support the activities of conformity assessment schemes and to respond to the testing needs of samples generated from various BIS conformity assessment schemes. The Laboratory Recognition Scheme for the recognition of Outside Laboratories and Foreign Laboratories strengthens the BIS testing framework.

The BIS has made significant efforts to promote conformity assessment scheme activities. Testing services are fundamental to the quality compliance ecosystem, and hence, their commercial importance has grown with increasing cross-border trade and stricter certification regulations.

CHAPTER 9
SAMPLES AND TESTING INFRASTRUCTURE

'Quality is the best business plan!'

Steve Jobs

Building and incorporating a robust quality infrastructure is critical for every manufacturing facility. Manufacturers can serve the market aspirations for quality through various stages of product commercialisation—testing and benchmarking against quality parameters being critical factors in meeting those aspirations.

Sample collection, conformance testing, and calibration of test equipment are central to BIS conformity assessment schemes and the licencing process. The BIS issues a licence only after successful assessment of a manufacturer's infrastructure, production process, quality control, and testing capabilities at its manufacturing facility.

- *Each Indian Standard prescribes its own testing requirements that apply to the product at various stages of manufacturing—the methods of sampling and test vary from product to product.*
- *Sampling and testing requirements are also prescribed by the BIS under respective Product Manuals—a comprehensive guidance document on sampling, testing equipment, scheme of inspection and testing, the scope of licence, etc.*

Navigating through Sampling Touchpoints

While dealing with the certification marks scheme, manufacturers steer through multiple touchpoints with respect to drawing of samples. These are critical for the grant of license. Generally, the BIS framework visualises drawing of samples and their testing at multiple junctures to ensure efficient decision-making in licensing. This is especially true in the case of foreign manufacturers.

Sample Testing Touchpoints

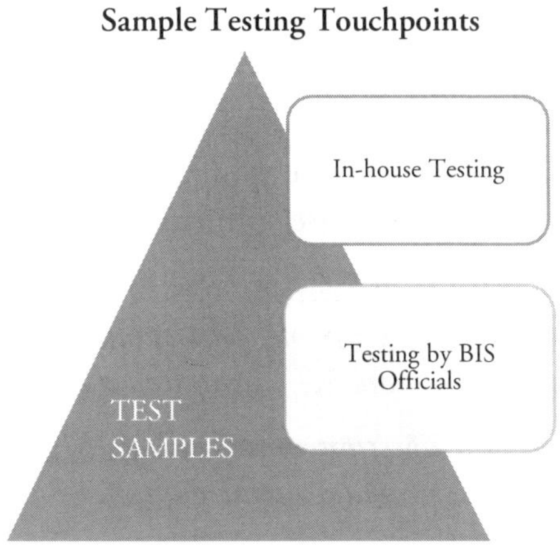

- ***In-house testing**: This is generally the first touchpoint in the BIS application process wherein in-house test reports are submitted along with application.*
- ***Testing by BIS official**: At the time of making factory visit for assessment of the manufacturing facility and quality control and testing capabilities, the BIS official would generally draw samples for testing in-house labs. This often acts as a validation of the originally submitted in-house test reports.*
- ***Third party testing**: Part of the samples drawn during the factory visit may also be sealed and sent for testing at designated BIS/third party laboratories.*

Testing Equipment and Calibration Requirements

- The in-house testing laboratories are expected to be suitably equipped with recommended equipment and trained personnel by following respective Indian Standards. It ensures that the scheme of testing and inspection is carried out in accordance with the prescribed testing methods.
- Indian Standards, read with the respective product manuals, comprehensively list the test equipment required at the manufacturing facility.

- Additionally, manufacturers are also required to follow a calibration plan for their test equipment—although the parameters of it are not readily prescribed under the Indian Standards or product manuals.

Trends in Trade

Given the wide-ranging requirements for the grant and maintenance of BIS licences, businesses are beginning to set up in-house testing facilities that will allow them to test their products as per applicable Indian Standards. Some key takeaways from market interactions are summarised below:

- *Generally, when QCOs are issued, the BIS also issues a corresponding product manual. This document particularly proves to be handy for businesses to ensure operational efficiency and a quicker licensing process.*
    - *The Scheme of Inspection and Testing (SIT), often housed in such product manuals, provides useful guidance on quality control during production process.*
- *The BIS allows for utilisation of common test facilities for the purpose of in-house testing by Indian small and medium manufacturers (MSMEs). One such provision is the* ***cluster-based test facility (CBTF)*** *as an alternative to in-house testing facility. This is beneficial for manufacturers operating in a cluster industrial area having geographical proximity to common testing infrastructure.*
- *Similarly,* ***laboratory sharing*** *is also allowed for other Indian and foreign businesses. With the permission of BIS authorities, manufacturers may share:*
    - *Laboratories of other manufacturers who hold a BIS license.*
    - *Third party laboratories recognised by the BIS.*
    - *Other independent NABL accredited laboratories in India.*
    - *Laboratories of same group company as that of the manufacturer.*
    - *Laboratories of other manufacturers who do not hold a BIS license (not available for foreign manufacturers, under FMCS).*
- *In the case of foreign manufacturers, such sharing is possible only with BIS-recognised laboratories or test facilities of another existing BIS license holder—no outsourcing is possible to unrecognised laboratories.*

- *Accessibility to Indian laboratories become useful for domestic manufacturers. However, it is often a pain point for foreign manufacturers to find BIS-approved labs for the licensing process.*

Summing Up

Every manufacturing facility must develop and implement a robust product testing infrastructure. BIS conformity assessment schemes and the licencing process rely heavily on sample collection, conformance testing, and test equipment calibration. *Only after a successful assessment of a manufacturer's quality control process and testing infrastructure and capabilities does the BIS issue a licence.*

A critical factor for the grant of license: manufacturers navigate through multiple touchpoints when dealing with BIS licensing, including sample drawing. These samples undergo examination at multiple instances, which makes the BIS licensing process vigorous and exhaustive. *A product's conformity to the relevant Indian Standard is confirmed through factory testing as well as comprehensive testing in BIS/independent third-party laboratory.*

ENFORCEMENT

CHAPTER 10

Consumer Awareness and Market Surveillance

'Trust, but verify'

Ronald Reagan

Product conformity standards is a critical business requirement in an increasingly customer-centric economic environment. At the same time, promoting consumer awareness for wider and deeper adoption of product conformity laws in business, and for improving enforcement, is of crucial importance for the Government.

Government outreach to regulators, academia, professionals, and industry forums helps to build increased awareness. Enforcement requires better intelligence network, routine investigations, detecting violations, imposing legal sanctions on such violators, and creating a formidable deterrence against violation of quality conformity laws. Likewise, the BIS framework also attempts to enforce accountability through a set of practices to safeguard consumer interests.

Consumer Awareness

The BIS is committed to providing standardisation and conformity assessment services to all stakeholders. For wider adoption of these services offered by the BIS, there has to be awareness in the consumer of these services, i.e., businesses and public at large. To deliver awareness, the BIS has a designated department for consumer-related activities called the Think, Nudge, and Move Department (TN&MD) at the BIS Headquarters.

- *TN&MD serves as a bridge between the BIS and consumers.*
- *Its key goal is to educate and safeguard BIS consumers' interests.*
- *Awareness programmes, such as Consumer Group registrations, aim to promote consumer quality consciousness and create customer awareness about the benefits of purchasing BIS-certified products.*
- *The emphasis is also on advising consumers about the dangers/ill-effects of using things that have not been BIS-certified.*

While the TN&MD takes the agenda of consumer awareness forward, lots can be done with increased engagement with academia, professionals, industry forums, etc. to improve the quality of engagement between the Bureau and consumer of its services.

Market Surveillance

Market surveillance[62] provides a feedback loop which then becomes the input for increasing/calibrating the awareness in the marker and becomes the trigger point for enforcement actions. Awareness and enforcement together ensure a better compliance.

Market surveillance is mainly a part of conformity assessment for regulated products. Through its surveillance operations, the BIS maintains a close vigil on the quality of certified products. The BIS carries out both pro-active surveillance and reactive surveillance under the product certification scheme, which aims to check conformance to standards on a continuous basis.

- ***Pro-active surveillance** includes:*
  - *Pre-market surveillance activities (like surprise factory inspections).*
  - *Post-market surveillance activities (like market sample drawing and testing, obtaining feedback from organised buyers) and follow up activities.*
- ***Re-active surveillance** will involve attending to consumer complaints, its investigation and follow up activities.*

***Counterfeiting**:* Another crucial element of the market surveillance process could be to keep a check on counterfeit products that use bogus BIS marks. Counterfeit goods are typically manufactured with lower-quality materials and

62 India does not have a centrally-coordinated market surveillance system.

are designed to look like the goods produced by a particular brand. Delinquents have been detected contaminating the market by selling counterfeit and substandard goods, which threatens customer safety.

- *Since the BIS is only concerned with granting quality standards licenses and keeping a check on the quality of such products, it is not technically authorised to control unauthorised commercial units.*
- *Yet, the BIS is cautious about counterfeit brands and violators will be penalised.*
- *Brand owners need to assume a joint responsibility with the regulatory/law and order authorities to track instances of counterfeiting and instantly report for appropriate actions.*

Counterfeiting of goods is not expressly addressed by Indian law. There are, however, some legal elements (like the Indian trademark laws) that may help brand owners to initiate a legal action against counterfeiting under their brand name. Interestingly, the Indian Customs law lays the groundwork for identifying instances of counterfeiting in imported goods through the IPR Enforcement Rules[63]. It enables an expedient IPR border enforcement mechanism and prevents such goods from entering the domestic market.

Enforcement Activities

The BIS Standard Mark is a distinct mark of quality and has established its brand identity amongst cognizant consumers for over six decades. The mounting popularity and value perception around 'quality' attracts players who wish to make quick money by leveraging the brand positioning of BIS/ISI marks. To mitigate this challenge, the BIS carries out such enforcement activities that ultimately keep consumers from being misled about the quality of products.

Violations under the BIS framework could include use of ISI mark without obtaining a license or sale of products without mandatory ISI marks. On receipt of intelligence of such violations or non-compliance, the BIS conducts search and seize operations. Successful search and seizure would logically lead to prosecution and/or penalty consequences. These actions create a deterrence in the market against violations of the product conformity laws.

63 Intellectual Property Rights (Imported Goods) Enforcement Rules, 2007.

- *Complaints Management and Enforcement Department (CMED) has been set up at the BIS headquarters at New Delhi to oversee the complaint-redressal mechanism.*
- *CMED synergises with Public Grievances Officers at Regional and Branch offices to provide consumers with prompt attention and quick redressal of their complaints.*
- *Routine inspections and enforcement raids, which include search and seize operations, are carried out based on gathered intelligence.*

Trends in Trade

- *Efforts are made to ensure greater consumer confidence through online grievance redressal channels:*
    - *BIS online* ***Consumer Engagement Portal***

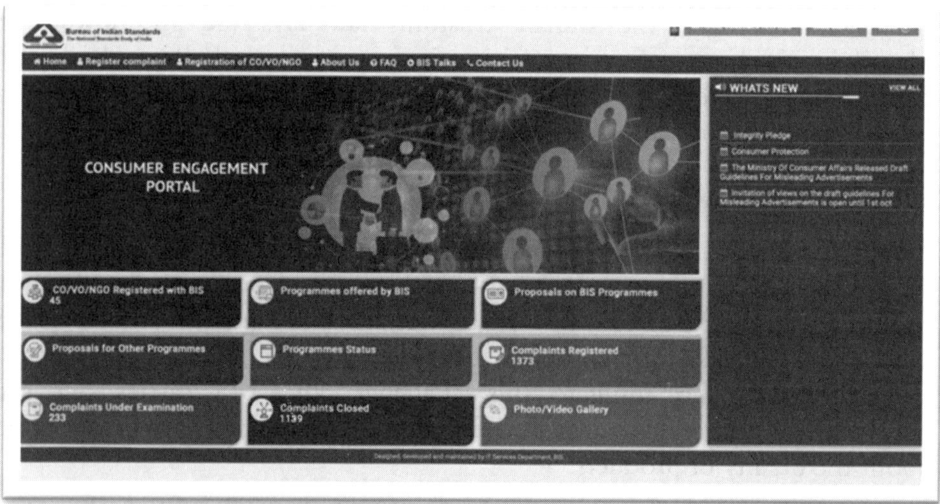

Source: https://www.services.bis.gov.in/php/BIS_2.0/consumer/publicdashboard

- ***BIS CARE mobile application:*** *Allows consumers to verify authenticity of an ISI mark or the Registration mark on any item or a product. It also allows users to verify licenses and manufacturers by license/registration number, firm name, or product name.*

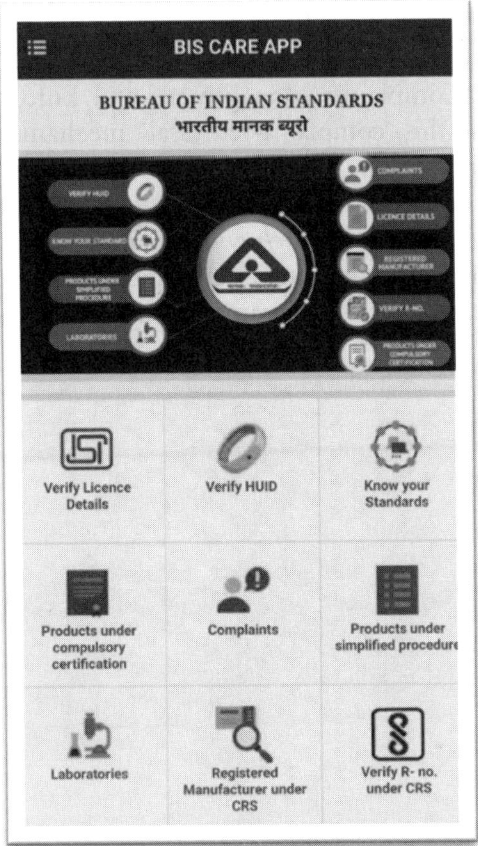

Source: BIS Care App

- *Such online/digital grievance redressal channels keep a close check on:*
  - *Quality of BIS-certified products*
  - *Misuse of BIS Standard Mark*
  - *Violation of QCOs*
  - *Misleading claims of product conformity*

Summing Up

The BIS framework envisages a set of surveillance and enforcement practices for protecting the larger public/consumer interest. The Bureau keeps a close watch on the market movement to capture instances of violations/non-conformity. Though India is yet to have a centrally coordinated market surveillance system, the BIS keeps a check on product conformance in the market through its **pro-active and re-active surveillance measures.**

The BIS' dedicated Complaints Management and Enforcement Department ('CMED') oversees the complaint-redressal mechanism under the BIS framework. *To overcome the challenge of violations/non-compliance, the BIS carries out continuous enforcement activities in the form of routine inspections and enforcement raids, which include search and seize operations.* It is encouraging to see the Bureau's efforts in laying down a strong digital presence to facilitate the process and ensure easy access of the same to the consumers.

CHAPTER 11

Penalties, Prosecution, and Judicial Remedies

'In nature there are neither rewards nor punishments; there are consequences.'

Robert Green Ingersoll

Punishment of delinquents is considered a just and an effective means to prevent wrongdoings in the society. Jurisprudence[64] generally suggests that the severity of the punishment should reflect the seriousness of the violation. The BIS framework establishes a system of punitive consequences for violation and misuse of law. It envisages a combination of civil and criminal penalties, besides such administrative measures (suspension and cancellation of license) that are imposed on the offender.

Consequences of Non-Compliance

The BIS Act prohibits use of the Standard Mark deceivingly. It prohibits manufacturing, importing, distributing, selling, hiring, leasing, storing, or exhibiting for sale any product that does not conform to mandatory BIS standards.

- *In case of* ***offence by a Company*** *(including a firm or other association of individuals), the persons responsible for the conduct of business*[65]*, including the authorised representative, are jointly liable for any consequence along with the company.*

---

64 The word jurisprudence derives from the Latin term *juris prudentia*, which means 'the study, knowledge, or science of law'.

65 Including a director or partner, manager, secretary, or other officer of the company.

- *In the context of FMCS, an AIR is also jointly liable for any penal consequences along with the foreign entity.*

Civil Penalty: In the event of violation of compulsory licensing, generally, a complaint is filed by the concerned BIS officer of CMED[66] for initiating prosecution before a Criminal Court[67]. The following are the broad civil consequences:

- *Fine of minimum ₹ 2,00,000 for a first-time offender or up to ₹ 5,00,000 for a repeat offender.*
- *Upper-limit of fine is up to 10 times the value of goods in question. (If such value is not ascertainable, then the turnover of the entire financial year is considered as such value).*

Interestingly, the BIS Act also provides for a **compensation mechanism** where a license holder, who sells such products the bear the Standard Mark but do not conform to BIS standards, shall be liable to compensate the consumer for any injury caused.

Criminal Penalty: In the same prosecution, the Court may even impose imprisonment of up to 2 years. In other words, offences (attracting penalties) under the BIS law will be tried based on a formal compliant before a Metropolitan Magistrate Court (Criminal Court):

- *Regular appeal process as per the Code of Criminal Procedure, 1973 will be followed in all such instances.*
- *Determination of the quantum of penalty or decision on imprisonment varies on a case-to-case basis, as may be decided by the competent Court.*
- *Option for compounding of offence is available. However, it is limited to first-time offences punishable only with fine and is not offence-specific. Compounding is a settlement mechanism by which the offender is given an option to pay money in lieu of prosecution, thereby avoiding a long and lengthy litigation proceeding.*

---

66 The court can also take cognizance of a compliant from other specified parties such as police officers, any consumer, etc. [Section 32(2), BIS Act, 2016].

67 No court inferior to that of a Metropolitan Magistrate or a Judicial Magistrate of the first class, specially empowered in this behalf, shall try any offence punishable under the BIS law [Section 32(1), BIS Act, 2016].

Trends in Trade

It is widely agreed that the severity of the punishment should correspond to the gravity of the violation—following the general principle of proportionality between penalties and offences. Under the BIS law, penalty for violations include both civil and criminal penalties.

- *Based on available information, it is seen that courts do not resort to imposing stringent penalties on violators.*
  - *In several cases, courts have only imposed nominal monetary fines in case of violations; imprisonment is occasional.*
- *Even in the case of compounding, BIS officials tend to impose nominal compounding amounts (fines) as sufficient deterrent for not repeating the violations.*

Criminalisation of minor omissions or commissions during the course of business often hurts business sentiments, sometimes irreparably. Besides, it also results in an avoidable burden on the criminal justice system. Some critical market sentiments in this context are:

- *Businesses may feel threatened about disruptions in business operations when it comes to criminal consequences of minor procedural or technical violations.*
  - *Minor or technical violations can be objectively identified as where no fraud is present nor is there any severe harm to public interest.*
- *The stringency of law and imposition of criminal liability has a somewhat deterrent effect on the ease of doing business and could be discouraging.*

(De)-Criminalisation Rationale: In this context, in the past, we have witnessed Government endeavours in relation to other regulatory laws in which non-substantive, minor and/or procedural omissions and commissions were de-criminalised to improve the ease of doing business and unclog courts of law. A befitting example is the recent reform proposal to the Legal Metrology Act, 2009 (LMA)[68], a law similar to BIS as regards the underlying

68 The Department of Consumer Affairs (Ministry of Consumer Affairs, Food, and Public Distribution, Government of India) had, in July 2020, sought feedback regarding a proposal to decriminalise minor offences under the Legal Metrology Act, 2009. The LMA is the law which prescribes and enforces the standards for weights and measures, as well as regulates trade and commerce in weights, measures, and pre-packaged commodities that are meant to be sold to consumers.

objective of consumer expediency. To effectively deter offenders, it was proposed that criminal liability be replaced with stiff civil compoundable monetary penalties, as well as the cancellation of licences if the offence has not been compounded with the department.

Summing Up

The BIS law has established a comprehensive punitive framework to check violations of law and any non-compliance with the Indian standards. Penalty for violations—a typical combination of civil and criminal penalties—establishes a system of punishment for non-conformity and related offences.

Although a standard punitive measure under the BIS law, *businesses often feel vulnerable to business disruptions in business operations in view of criminal consequences of procedural or technical violation*. With reference to the recent reform proposal to LMA, it is felt that a similar reform could be introduced to the BIS law with an objective of adopting alternative mechanisms for speedy resolution of disputes. It will not only improve the ease of doing business in India but also protect businesses from disproportionate duress and avoidable disruptions.

GLOBAL PERSPECTIVES

CHAPTER 12

STANDARDS, INNOVATION, AND GLOBAL TRADE

'Quality is never an accident; it is always the result of intelligent efforts.'

John Ruskin

Standards have become an essential part of global trade. They facilitate trade between countries and reduce transaction costs by providing common reference points. Interaction between product conformity regulations and innovation is indispensable. Regulations that are intended to improve the efficiency of markets in delivering quality products have a strong interplay with product innovation.

- *New technology and products may require a separate category of regulations to be introduced that are suitable for the intended functionality and usage.*
- *Quality regulations create an enabling environment for mainstreaming of new technologies and inspire customers trust in new products and technologies.*

Regulations play a positive role in encouraging innovation—there is a positive interaction between compliance, quality, and innovation.

Mapping the Interactions

Innovation is the practical application of ideas that result in the introduction of new products or services or improvement in product or service offerings.[69] Innovation drives efficiency and progress. Businesses dealing with product innovation are impacted by quality regulations in the following manner:

- ***Disclosure:*** *Product-related information to the regulator and, through that, to the end consumer. This ensures transparency and reinforces public trust in the system.*
- ***Accountability:*** *Regulations serve the cause of improving public trust and business accountability.*

However, with the fast-paced changes in technology and business models, the governing regulations are also under tremendous pressure to keep pace with these changes. This is a systemic cycle where different factors of the economy drive change towards increasing awareness and appreciation of the role of quality in the economic development.

Systemic Loop of Economic Growth

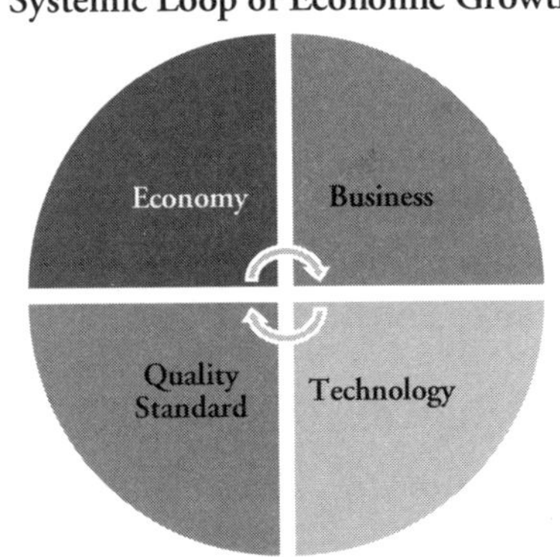

Each element seen above drives the other, thus forming a systemic loop of economic growth.

Review of Indian Standards (Confirmation, Revision, and Withdrawal)

According to the BIS Rules, 2018, all established standards must be reviewed periodically, at least once in five years, to determine the need for revision or withdrawal. If there is no need for revision or withdrawal, the standards need to be re-affirmed. This is aligned with the established norms of the ISO where

69 Schumpeter, Joseph A., The theory of economic development: an inquiry into profits, capital, credit, interest, and the business cycle. ISBN 0-87855-698-2.

International Standards are reviewed at least once every five years by all the ISO member bodies. Standards have been widely recognised as the catalyst for technical development, industrial growth, well-being of the society, and convergence of emerging technologies.

- *Standards formulation activity of the BIS is carried out through various Technical Committees comprising stakeholders as technical committee members drawn from government, technical institutions, academia, consumer organisations, industries, etc.*
- *Various Indian standards are formulated/revised/amended based on the technical inputs provided by these members or other stakeholders as per their knowledge, experience and research/analysis done on subject.*

The standards, being dynamic in nature, need to be reviewed periodically for their continued relevance and revision/amendment from time to time.

Global Trade Perspective

Quality standards-related trade measures, as part of technical barriers to trade (TBT) under the WTO, are an important policy tool to control and regulate market access. The WTO's idea of standards[70] was developed in a pre-liberalisation era for India and a pre-digital era for the global economy. However, it does not appear to consider:

- *India's aspiration of playing an important role in the global value chain.*
- *Rapid change in business models, driven by technological disruptions.*

Quality regulations are stereotypically influenced by political economy forces—especially in the context of TBT. They may even reflect protectionist motivations of Governments. However, the need for aligning product conformity regulations with innovation and technological advancements is non-negotiable. Consequently, there is a need for the WTO to update its conceptions of quality standards as well as its underlying processes to reflect current realities. It should drive further inclusion and openness towards innovation.

---

70 As embodied in the TBT Agreement.

Scope of Technical Barriers to Trade: The WTO vs. India Perspective

Comparison	WTO Framework	India Level	Nature
Technical Regulations	Lays down product characteristics or related process/production methods	Quality Control Orders (QCOs) issued by the concerned Line Ministry	Mandatory
Standards	Approved and published by a recognised body	Indian Standards published by the BIS (voluntary)	Voluntary
Conformity Assessment Procedure	Lays down relevant requirements for fulfilment of technical regulations or standards—including testing, inspection, evaluation, etc.	The BIS Conformity Regulations, Product Manuals, etc.—statutory framework	Applicable to both on technical regulations well as standards

Trends in Trade

Evolution of economy and increased play of quality triggers the need for increased role of product conformity and quality standards. We can see this in the Indian context as more and more quality standards are being mandated. An integral part of this increased play of quality is the lockstep march of product innovation with the relevant standards, especially the mandatory standards. However, there needs to be certain checks and balances for businesses to embrace it in the right spirit. Some issues currently being faced by businesses include:

- ***Outdated Indian Standards:*** *There is a need for updating existing standards and introducing new ones based on technological advancements and innovation.*
- ***Transitional provisions:*** *Compliance with product conformity regulations often require financial commitment and additional resources, specialisation, and training.*

  - *It could be part of Government's responsibility to provide structural support for migrating businesses into the mandatory framework of conformity.*
  - *Such structural support could include incentives, subsidies, subvention, common infrastructure support, and an expanded and easily accessible testing network.*
  - *Diversity of economic activity may require a calibrated intervention to support each business segment.*

- ***Exemptions linked to de-minimus principles:*** *Drive the quality agenda to focus on specific/relevant segments of economy. It will have a positive impetus without burdening the larger population.*
  - *Involvement of academia and institutions for bringing a diverse perspective to the quality agenda.*
- ***Sunset provisions:*** *Enable automatic grandfathering of regulations or standards that have lost relevance on account of evolution of products, technology, change in societal contexts, change in business models, etc.*

The Government needs to take ownership of this entire sequence of quality agenda to ensure seamlessness. As this happens, the technical standards will instinctively evolve to keep in pace with innovations and technological advancements.

Summing Up

The ongoing interaction between technical regulations and innovation is critical for businesses to be more and more competitive. As a technical barrier to trade, these technical regulations often take cover under political motivations, although established in the larger interest of public. *Given today's dynamic technological innovation, mandatory technical standards may become outdated just within a short period.*

The increased play of quality delivers the objective of economic growth and strengthens businesses in progressing the value chain of product categories. Although the BIS norms mandate the updating of Indian Standards at regular intervals, it is pertinent for the Bureau to keep a close watch on the changes surrounding the standards and act appropriately in the interest of businesses efficiency.

CHAPTER 13

Effective Collaboration Through Mutual Recognition

'Coming together is a beginning. Keeping together is progress. Working together is success.'

Henry Ford

Countries frequently employ the tools of harmonisation, equivalence, and mutual recognition to facilitate trade and, in particular, to reduce barriers created by regulations and product quality standards. Recognition as a tool for trade facilitation is represented in the form of Mutual Recognition Agreements (MRAs). Countries utilise them as a method to acknowledge each other's NSBs and CABs with partner countries. MRAs enable countries to formally recognise one another's accreditations with mutual confidence.

Understanding MRAs

MRAs are trade agreements that attempt to improve market access and promote greater international harmonisation of product conformity requirements while maintaining consumer safety. It boosts confidence in conformity assessment between countries by formally recognising the outcomes of each other's testing, inspection, certification, or accreditation, reducing conformity assessment duplication.

MRAs have a limited scope. Their main goal is to prevent duplicative testing in international trade. The regulatory objectives, technical criteria, and conformity assessment procedures are not the same or 'similar'. MRAs are one of the methods for addressing TBTs caused by differences in national technical regulations. What is mutually recognised is:

- *the technical competency of specific conformity assessment bodies in the export country to perform conformity assessment at the expected level of the import country; and*
- *the knowledge of these bodies about the technical requirements and conformity assessment procedures in the import country.*

MRAs thus recognise the competency of designated CABs in the export country to test and issue certificates based on the import country's technical requirements and procedures, and *vice versa*, allowing such imports to enter the destination country without further barriers or delays. Benefits of mutual recognition include:

- *Manufacturing to meet a single standard to ensure lower costs to business and improved competitiveness.*
- *Greater product availability and choice for consumers.*
- *Reduced importer risks and approval time delays.*

The Indian Perspective

The BIS is actively involved in bilateral cooperation with other countries' National Standards Bodies and other Standards Developing Organisations for standardisation, testing, certification, and training, among other things. We have already seen in earlier chapters how the BIS assumes authority to recognise/accredit testing institutions, both within and outside of India. The BIS is delegated with the duty to promote, monitor, and manage the quality of goods.[71] Altogether, these provisions evidence the authority of the BIS to enter MRAs.

The BIS has signed several Memorandums of Understanding (MoU) in the fields of standardisation and conformity assessment and is in the process of having such arrangements with several other countries. In addition, the BIS has also signed Bilateral Cooperation Agreements (BCA) with the National Standards Bodies of several countries.[72]

---

71 As reflected under Section 9 of the BIS Act, 2016.

72 Details of agreements found at https://www.services.bis.gov.in:8071/php/BIS_2.0/bisconnect/agreement_mou (last accessed on 13 July 2022).

Trends in Trade

So far, the BIS has signed MoU/MRA with national standards bodies of over 30 countries.[73] Unfortunately, the MoUs have a soft law flavour to them and hence lack binding effect. In the case of BCAs, for example, signatory countries would be compelled to recognise each other's results. The MoUs, on the other hand, merely compel signatory countries to exchange information on standardisation and certification standards, methods, and technical information, as well as to provide training programmes. *In other words, the MoU imposes no duty on the acceptance of the results.*

- *Although MOUs and BCAs are both used to manage cross-border issues by facilitating international cooperation, India's current limited number of BCAs may not help to ensure lower costs and increased competitiveness for enterprises.*
- *The soft law nature of MOUs, as well as their lack of legal force, may make it difficult for countries to achieve successful partnership through mutual recognition in the long run.*

The FTA Perspective

Another interesting characteristic of MRAs is their tight relationship with Free Trade Agreements (FTAs). Despite being negotiated as stand-alone accords, modern FTAs include trade facilitation measures due to their expanding coverage of non-tariff obstacles. As a result, in some circumstances, MRAs are also included in FTA negotiations.

Illustration: India–UAE CEPA

For example, on 18 February 2022, India and the United Arab Emirates signed the Comprehensive Economic Partnership Agreement (CEPA), which includes a Chapter 5 on Technical Barriers to Trade. It aims to ensure cooperation in the areas of standards, technical regulations, and conformity assessment procedures with the goal of facilitating trade in accordance with the WTO.

FTAs are growing as a vehicle for trade rule integration in the sense that they are increasingly covering regulation of sectors that are not directly addressed by the larger multilateral framework.

73 See Note 72.

Summing Up

Mutual recognition is a thoroughly studied notion of international law that has made a significant contribution to the situation of international regulatory cooperation. It is critical in promoting reciprocal market access in terms of product quality compliance. *It not only lowers technical trade barriers, but also signifies economic progress, trade facilitation, and unrestricted interactions among transnational value chains.*

MRAs can be a useful tool for decreasing regulatory barriers and increasing trade, depending on the issues that exporters confront on a case-by-case basis. From the standpoint of an importing country, mutual recognition makes regulatory expenses more visible and diminishes the cost advantage enjoyed by a foreign producer due to a lower degree of regulation. On the other hand, domestic authorities will tend to shy away from protectionist measures to safeguard their own industry.

CHAPTER 14

PRODUCT CONFORMITY FRAMEWORK IN KEY JURISDICTIONS

'If you look the right way, you can see that the whole world is a garden.'

Frances Hodgson Burnett

Standardisation is a joint effort of businesses and governments. It drives product innovation, impacts development of quality infrastructure, and ensures health and safety of the consumer. Deep rooting the play of quality in the economy brings profound change in consumer expectations and inspires confidence in domestic products entering the global market.

Quality standards serve three-pronged objective:

- *Inspire confidence in the buyers and stakeholders of the product or service.*
- *Provide a competitive edge in the domestic and international markets.*
- *Facilitate regulators to ensure the product quality, health, and safety for the consumers.*

Standards and their compliance have become crucial for all market players in an increasingly global marketplace. Thus, countries are considering developing a global consensus on standards to eliminate trade barriers, foster innovation, and stimulate business and economic growth.

- *Countries have technical regulations in relation to imported goods to ensure safety, quality, and conformity. These regulations are generally aligned to domestic quality conformity standards.*

- ***National Standards Bodies (NSB)*** *enforce quality standards (voluntary and mandatory) and notify products that should mandatorily comply. E.g., the BIS in India.*
- ***Conformity Assessment Bodies (CAB)*** *(or certification bodies) include testing and calibration laboratories, certification bodies, as well as inspection bodies that provide conformity assessment services. E.g., the NABCB[74] and the NABL[75] in India.*

While the focus of this book is the BIS and product conformity in India, it is relevant to briefly discuss quality conformity regimes in other jurisdictions, namely, ***the United States of America, the European Union, Singapore, the United Kingdom, Australia, the United Arab Emirates, and Vietnam.***

The United States of America (the US)

In this market-driven and diversified economy, the quality standards system provides greater authority to consumers and stakeholders to facilitate trade, improve quality, promote interoperability, and protect health, safety, and the environment.

Voluntary Standards: *Efforts of US voluntary standards organisations are coordinated by the American National Standards Institute (ANSI) and the ANSI National Accreditation Board (ANAB), which are private, non-profit organisations. Additionally, the ANSI coordinates US standards with international standards to ensure that American products are compatible worldwide.*

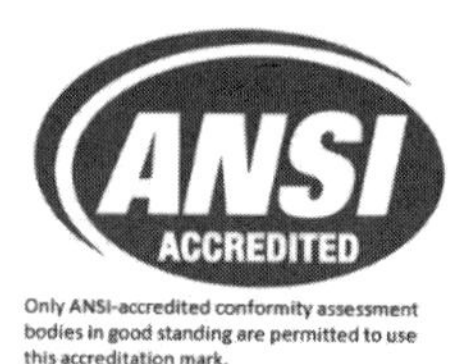

Mandatory Standards: Mandatory standards are those that have been incorporated into a federal law and are subject to compliance by legislation, regulation, government policy, or contractual agreement. In most cases, non-compliance with a statutory requirement results in civil or criminal punishment.

74 The National Accreditation Board for Certification Bodies (NABCB) undertakes assessment of Certification and Inspection Bodies applying for accreditation as per the Board's criteria, in line with international standards and guidelines.

75 The NABL is a Constituent Board of Quality Council of India.

- The US Consumer Product Safety Commission (CPSC) staff participates in the development of voluntary standards.
- The CPSC may only adopt required rules in the absence of voluntary standards for a particular issue.
- Voluntary standards may be 'integrated by reference' into the US law, thereby making them mandatory.
- Federal agencies may enforce voluntary standards in the same manner as they enforce mandatory standards, even if the voluntary standard is not incorporated by reference into a federal statute.

In many countries including India, the standardisation system is top down, where a single standards body—often a government agency (like the BIS)—drives all national standardisation activities. The US system is bottom up, allowing standards users to drive standardisation activities.

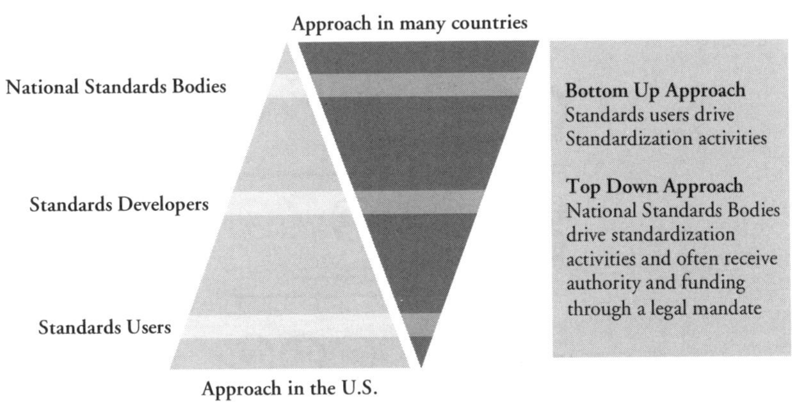

Source: ANSI Website

Key illustrations of the often-used quality marks in the US are shown below. Except for the body that issues the certificate, there is no difference between UL or ETL or CSA listings.

≅

≅

The United Kingdom (The UK)

The British Standards Institution (BSI), the *world's first national standards body* established in 1901, is the regulatory NSB operational under the Crown in the UK. The BSI helps improve the quality and safety of products, services, and systems by enabling the establishment of standards and encouraging their usage.

- *The BSI represents the UK's economic and social interests in all European and international standards organisations and in the development of business information solutions for all sizes and sectors of British businesses.*
- *In the wake of Brexit, UK CABs are issuing a new UKCA mark (UK Conformity Assessed), where applicable.*[76]

The UKCA (UK Conformity Assessment) mark is a new UK product marking requirement for certain products placed on the market in the United Kingdom (England, Wales, and Scotland). It applies to the majority of products that previously required an EU CE mark.

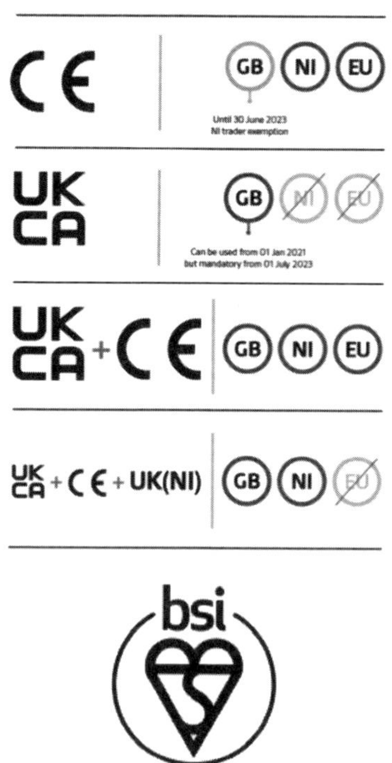

76 From 1 January 2023, CE Marking will no longer be accepted on most new products placed on the market in Great Britain and UKCA will be required.

UKCA is also not the only option for conformity within the UK. Where a product falls outside of the designated standards under the technical regulations, businesses consider a global voluntary mark like Kitemark™. The BSI Kitemark™ is a popularly recognised mark of its kind in the UK that inspires consumer confidence and trust.

The European Union (the EU)

In general, harmonisation of EU standards has resulted in significant simplification of technical requirements amongst Member States. Prior to harmonisation, each European Union country produced its own standards through its national standards organisation, resulting in inconsistent and contradictory standards, laws, and conformity assessment methods. European standards ('harmonised EN [European Norm] standards) are adopted by one of the 3 European Standardisation Organisations (ESOs):

- *European Committee for Standardisation (CEN)*
- *European Committee for Electrotechnical Standardisation (CENELEC)*
- *European Telecommunications Standards Institute (ETSI)*

Standardisation is managed at the national level by NSBs, which adopt and publish national standards. Additionally, the NSBs transpose all European standards into identical national standards and eliminate any national standards that conflict.

- *EU-wide standards and technical specifications exist for several product categories. Businesses must ensure their products comply with any relevant EU rules before they can be traded freely in the EU.*
- *There are over 19,000 European standards.*

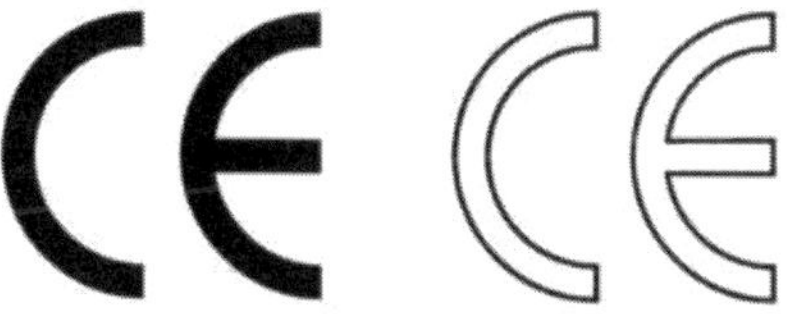

The CE mark, which has been in use since 1985, indicates that a manufacturer has evaluated a product and determined that it complies with EU safety, health, and environmental protection requirements. It is mandatory only for products that meet EU specifications and require CE marking.

Australia

Australia's standards and conformance infrastructure instil confidence in businesses and consumers in the products and services they develop or use. This infrastructure is based on trade measurement, standards, and certification and inspection accrediting bodies.

Standards Australia, founded in 1922, is an independent standards organisation recognised by the Australian Government as the apex NAB in Australia. Standards are voluntary on their own. The public is not required to adhere to standards. However, state and federal governments frequently make legislative reference to Australian Standards® (AS) or joint Australian/New Zealand Standards (AS/NZS). When this occurs, these standards have the potential to become mandatory.

Singapore

As the national standards body, Enterprise Singapore (ES)[77], under Singapore's Ministry of Trade and Industry, administers the Singapore Standardization Program through an industry-led Singapore Standards Council. The Singapore Accreditation Council (SAC) is the national independent accreditation CAB for the country and operates under Enterprise Singapore.

The SAFETY Mark helps consumers and suppliers identify registered Controlled Goods.

77 Under Singapore's Ministry of Trade and Industry.

Product conformity in Singapore is voluntary in nature but becomes mandatory when used by government bodies in regulations or administrative requirements. Currently, there are more than 1,600 standards partners and volunteers who are involved in the development and promotion of standards.

The UAE

In 2001, the UAE established the Emirates Authority for Standardization and Metrology (ESMA) as its sole national standards body. In June 2020, the ESMA was merged into the newly formed Ministry of Industry and Advanced Technology (MoIAT), which assumed responsibility for all standards and metrology-related activities.

- *The MoIAT, as the UAE's sole standardisation body, issues (and monitors the implementation of) standards in the fields of safety, health, and environment.*
- *The UAE is a member of the GCC*[78] *Standardization Organization (GSO), which coordinates the development and approval of GCC standards and technical regulations aimed at protecting consumers and the environment and facilitating trade and economic integration.*
- *The MoIAT actively participates in the GSO's standards-setting committee.*

Vietnam

Vietnam's national standards body is the Directorate for Standards, Metrology, and Quality (STAMEQ) of the Ministry of Science and Technology. Following Vietnam's entrance to the WTO, the Directorate for Standards, Metrology, and Quality (STAMEQ) became the WTO Agreement

78 The Cooperation Council for the Arab States of the Gulf, also known as the Gulf Cooperation Council, is a regional, intergovernmental, political, and economic union that consists of Bahrain, Kuwait, Oman, Qatar, Saudi Arabia, and the United Arab Emirates.

on Technical Barriers to Trade's central inquiry and notification point. Vietnam's national standards system is theoretically transparent, based on the ISO/IEC Guides for standard development.

Over 47 per cent of Vietnamese national standards are currently compliant with international and regional standards. Vietnam does not appear to deploy technological barriers as non-tariff barriers in general. Exceptions include certain goods regulated by specific ministries, such as chemicals, toxic chemicals, and intermediate materials used in their manufacture, wild animals, pesticides, and materials used in their manufacture, pharmaceuticals, substances that may cause addiction, cosmetics that may have a negative effect on human health, and medical equipment. Vietnam's national standards system encompasses about 9,500 criteria (TCVN, in the Vietnamese language).

Trends in Trade

Adapting exported products to domestic technical regulations and standards is now an integral part of global trade. Furthermore, businesses must demonstrate compliance with domestic product regulations through conformity assessment procedures such as testing, inspection, or certification.

- *Member nations have regulatory autonomy under the WTO Agreements to adopt the measures that best meet their national policy issues, such as public health and safety, environmental protection, and consumer information, among others.*
- *In the same vein, they are allowed to choose the approach that will provide them with the best assurance that products offered on their market will meet their policy goals.*
- *As a result, a wide range of methodologies coexist in different countries, further complicating the already complex regulatory policy environment.*

When we look at FTA partner countries like the UAE and Australia, the relevant FTAs try to achieve the harmonisation of product standards and/or mutual recognition of each other's standards. In the case of non-FTA partner countries, the points of collaboration include public, private, and business-driven initiatives to achieve the harmonisation of product standards.

Interestingly, while India and several other countries have a government-driven quality regime, countries like the US and Australia make use of private or non-governmental organisations to carry out standardisation activities. It is also important to size the quality conformity activities to understand the depth of the play of quality in these jurisdictions. Due to limited information available for comparison, this continues to be developed as part of our focus of research.

Summing Up

Standardisation is a joint effort of businesses and governments. Standards that are international, transparent, and consensus-based become solutions rather than hurdles in international trade.

As we discuss quality conformity regimes in other jurisdictions, namely, the United States of America, the European Union, Singapore, the United Kingdom, Australia, the United Arab Emirates, and Vietnam—all these jurisdictions aim to promote product innovation, influence the development of quality infrastructure, and ensure customer health and safety. Most countries have prescribed a combination of voluntary and mandatory conformity standards and regulations—which is largely akin to the Indian quality ecosystem.

While India and several other nations have a government-driven quality system, some countries like the United States and Australia rely on private or non-governmental organisations to carry out standardisation operations. Due to the insufficiency of comparable data, this is still being worked on as part of our research agenda.

BUSINESS CONSIDERATION

CHAPTER 15

RE-ALIGNING WITH INDIA'S ASPIRATIONS

'To improve is to change; to be perfect is to change often.'

Winston Churchill

India is the world's largest democracy, with a population of over 1.4 billion people. The country's integration into the global economy has been accompanied by significant economic growth during the last decade. As transnational businesses look to invest and establish themselves in India, it is important that they understand India's aspirations and changing economic landscape.

Alignment with India's Aspirations

- India's export-led growth story has displayed an outstanding export performance in 2021–22, with merchandise exports of over US$ 400 billion.[79]
- Besides the global economic recovery, a key reason for this growth may be attributed to structural changes, thanks to the Make in India campaign—to transform India into a global manufacturing hub.
    - o This shift could assist India in achieving its 'China+1' goal, in which multinational firms shift their inputs away from China and towards India.
- India now aspires to:

79 Indian Government Press Release dated 23 March 2022 available at https://pib.gov.in/PressReleaseIframePage.aspx?PRID=1808831 (last accessed on 23 April 2022).

- Capture greater supply chain value addition in India.
- Spur job creation through manufacturing localisation.
- Greater market access, enhanced trade, and investment opportunities with developed economies through FTAs.
- Secure foreign exchange benefits in relation to the increased value addition.

Policy Solution to Realise India's Aspirations

- **Production Linked Incentives (PLI):** India has introduced several PLI schemes to enhance manufacturing capabilities, increase domestic value addition, and augment exports.
  - Recent announcement of PLI schemes for the 5G telecom, IT hardware, and solar energy sectors will be an impetus to foreign investors.
- **Ease of doing business:** Additionally, the government is also working on reducing compliance burden, improving the ease of doing business, creating multi-modal infrastructure to reduce logistics costs, digitisation, and so on.
- **Phased Manufacturing Program (PMP): Benefits of Customs duty exemption linked to increased value addition in India**
  - Under this scheme, there is a progressive reduction in basic Customs duty on import of inputs and raw material with deeper value addition in India. India implemented PMP in 2015 with the aim of increasing domestic production of mobile phone handsets.
  - Since then, mobile manufacturing sector in India has experienced exponential growth. *India eventually becoming the second largest manufacturer of mobile handsets is a resounding validation of the success of the PMP programme.*
  - The Ministry of Electronics and Information Technology has been a frontrunner in adopting PMP for various product categories.
  - Recently, PMP was introduced for products like smart watches, smart electricity meters, headphones, smartphones, etc.
  - PMP seems to be addressing 3 issues that are critical to the Indian economy:

        - *Addressing significant foreign exchange loss.*
        - *Providing domestic market access to products.*
        - *Substantial job creation within the country.*
    - Now, other industries are also considering representations to their Line Ministries for inclusion of their products under PMP.
    - Operations of PMP have been brought under the ambit of Import of Goods at Concessional Rate of Duty Rules, 2017 (IGCR).
- **Quality Conformity Regulations**
    - Surge in mandatory certification, combined with progressively higher duty rates on import of finished goods, nudges companies to increase manufacturing in India.
    - Use of this policy tool changes the profile of products imported into India-from finished goods to raw material and inputs—and increases value addition in India.
- **Free Trade Agreements**
    - India's renewed focus on bilateral FTAs and recent developments with the signing of CEPA with the UAE are a bedrock for potential future negotiations with other jurisdictions, including the US—a strong trade partner for India
        - *Especially under the CEPA, the UAE is set to remove duties on over 80 per cent of its tariff lines which account for nearly 90 per cent of India's exports to the UAE by value.*
    - The new CEPA contains several indicators regarding India's approach to future free trade agreements. Besides reduced tariffs, businesses can expect significant benefits in terms of ease of regulatory barriers with enhanced market access.
    - The pace of ongoing negotiations with UK, the European Union, Australia, Canada, and Israel will also be an impetus to long delayed negotiations between India and US.
- **Tax exemption policy**
    - India has undertaken a comprehensive review of Customs duty exemptions, resulting in withdrawal, or phasing out, of several exemptions.

- Exemptions are now being rolled out with appropriate sunset clauses.

Re-Orient Engagement with Indian Economy

Manufacturing has emerged as one of India's high growth sectors. India is unwaveringly moving ahead with the idea of *'Make in India, Make for World.'* The business environment is improving in India, and the *'Atmanirbhar Bharat'* (Self-reliant India) campaign offers superior opportunity for economic engagement with other countries.

A successful and dynamic business environment requires an active and open dialogue between businesses and the Government. Businesses may engage with the Indian economy considering the following factors:

- **'Make in India, Make for World'**
  - Achieve economies of scale in manufacturing.
  - Explore brand manufacturing as well as providing *'manufacturing as a service.'*
  - Scale can also be achieved by manufacturing in India for multiple brands simultaneously.
- **India competing to be the preferred manufacturing location**
  - India is competing with other emerging economies like Vietnam and Indonesia who have a better FTA network as compared to India —hence, better access to the global market.
  - However, these other countries do not have their own significant consumer base.
  - Hence, businesses are gradually looking at India as one of the most sought-after manufacturing destinations; they want to manufacture for the world as well as for the domestic market.
    - *This is indicated by the growing interest shown by foreign manufacturers in India as a preferred global manufacturing hub.*
- **Capacity and capability building**: India can offer both scale and large resource capacity for deeper value addition. Especially, capability building may remain a high strategic priority with adequate resource mobilisation, training, and development initiatives. At the same time, raw materials/input supply ecosystem and sufficient trained/skilled manpower is a work in progress.

- **Advocacy efforts of businesses:** Businesses may actively engage with the Government and regulators for cost and operational efficiency.

Re-orienting Indian Economy:
The Four-Pronged Approach

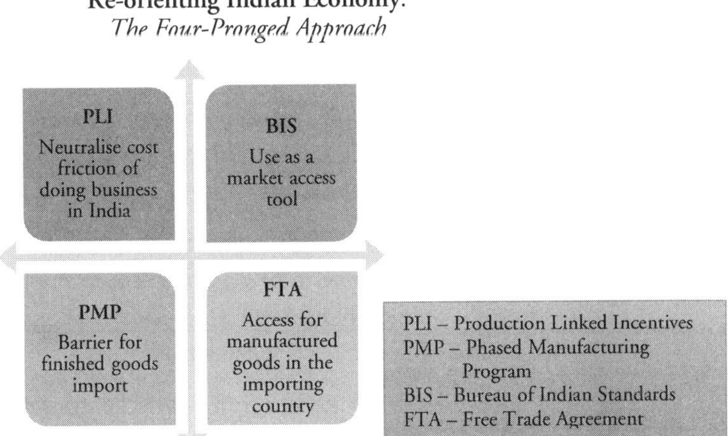

Trends in Trade

India is progressing on being a trustworthy global supply chain hub. Initiatives under the ***Atmanirbhar Bharat*** campaign are promptly encouraging indigenous manufacturing and ease of doing business. This will attract investments including FDI and strengthen the policies for the ***Make in India*** initiatives.

- *Supply chain models in India are undergoing a seismic shift to focusing on domestically manufactured finished goods to increase value addition in India.*
    - *Supply chain models are gradually undergoing a seismic shift from SKD/CKD to domestic manufacturing—business focus is shifting from imports to domestic manufacturing.*
    - *Manufacturing by the brand and manufacturing as a service should both become relevant.*
- *With more comprehensive FTAs, there is scope for change in the dynamics of Standards application with partner countries—with simplification and relaxations in the licensing and approval process.*
    - *While the thought process and the enabling provisions are present, the implementation of the same is still a work-in-progress.*

  - *Active engagement between the regulators of the partner countries is required to streamline and simplify the standardisation process.*
  - *FTAs/CEPAs with some of the developed jurisdictions such as Australia, the UK, the US, and Canada will have a greater leverage on India to influence the implementation dynamics around trade facilitation and customs cooperation.*

- *Customs duty structure on several products is being calibrated to provide a graded duty rate structure to facilitate domestic manufacturing under the Government's PMP, following the IGCR.*
  - *Such changes in the import regime are poised to increase manufacturing footprint in India. Hence, it is an opportune time for foreign businesses to re-align their business model from 'import and sale' to 'manufacture, sell, and export.'*
  - *The Government is encouraging this dynamism through PMP/IGCR compliances that are now being expanded across multiple products/sectors involving multiple Government Ministries.*

Going forward, we will see more and more businesses evaluating India as a serious manufacturing destination. However, other fast-growing economies such as Vietnam and Indonesia will continue to pose tough competition for India due to their existing FTAs that allow duty free access to manufactured goods in those countries.

Summing Up

India's integration into the global economy has been accompanied by tremendous economic growth. It is critical for transnational businesses looking to invest and establish themselves in India to comprehend the country's aspirations and changing economic landscape.

Numerous multinational corporations are exploring opportunities in India. With pragmatic investor-friendly initiatives of the Government like the '*Make in India*' and '*Ease of Doing Business*' campaigns, the Indian economic landscape is being consistently eased to support both Indian and foreign businesses.

Manufacturing is one of India's fastest-growing sectors. India is steadily moving forward with the idea of *'Make in India, Make for World'*. An improved business environment under the *Atmanirbhar Bharat* campaign offers greater opportunities for economic engagement with other countries.

Businesses need to align with India's aspirations. For a successful and dynamic business environment, it is critical to maintain an active and open conversation between businesses and the Government.

CHAPTER 16

TOWARDS DISCOVERING A NEW SYMMETRY

'Ideally a book would have no order to it, and the reader would have to discover his own.'

Jon D Harrison

India offers enormous market opportunities to both domestic and foreign businesses; however, it is a large and complex market that needs careful navigation to achieve success. Given today's fast-paced technological changes, a quality ecosystem continues to be dynamic and is still evolving. Businesses must therefore be able to recognise the business imperative of the play of quality to ensure efficiency and consistency.

The Stakeholder Ecosystem

Quality conformity assessment activities form a vital link between standards and products, services, processes, systems, personnel qualifications, and organisations. Product (and process) conformity regulations call for greater transparency across the supply chain to effectively mitigate risks and ensure compliance. In a typical business environment, there will be multiple relationships catering to procurement, manufacturing, and distribution needs. These relationships can be internal or external as illustrated below:

Internal Relationships	*External Relationships*
• *Product Stewardship Personnel* • *Regulatory Affairs and*	• *Contract Manufacturers* • *Toll Manufacturers*

Internal Relationships	*External Relationships*
Compliance Advisors • *Quality Control Managers* • *Trade and Customs Managers* • *Product Managers* • *Product Design/Technical Teams* • *Nodal Personnel at Headquarters of MNCs* • *Related-Party Vendors*	• *Raw Material Suppliers* • *Testing Equipment Suppliers* • *Testing Laboratories* • *Regulatory Authorities* • *Product Licensing Authorities* • *Intergovernmental Agencies Such as the WTO (Technical Barrier to Trade Committee)* • *International Standards Setting Organisations such as the ISO and the IEC* • *Premier Industry Associations Such as FICCI and CII*

The Business Imperative

For businesses to successfully operate in the context of product conformity, it is essential that the spirit of compliance resonates across the supply chain network. The ever-increasing product quality monitoring requires them to continuously keep track of their products (including raw materials) and evaluate them against the relevant regulations. A four-pronged approach may be relevant to efficiently deal with the product conformity requirements:

(1) *Evaluate regulations against existing business operations.*

(2) *Evaluate existing commercial arrangement.*

(3) *Mainstream supply chain network awareness and capacity development.*

(4) *Make the compliance process transparent, systemic, and repeatable.*

1. Evaluate regulations in relation to business operations

Product conformity is not merely a business check-list compliance, but a strategy to be adopted for gaining competitive advantage and market access.

- *Different business models may need to approach product conformity differently. Hence, it is required to incorporate product conformity into the decision-making strategy and develop an absorptive capacity*[80] *through the standardisation process.*
- *Businesses may want to revisit the definitions as to what constitutes 'business sensitive' or 'business proprietary' information versus what needs to be disclosed to the regulators through their business partners. This may entail revisiting the existing commercial arrangements, which is discussed in the next strategy point.*
- *Businesses also need to evaluate the intricacies of product conformity regulations and identify the impact points in the supply chain for an informed decision-making.*

2. Evaluate existing commercial arrangement

Re-aligning business strategy involves revisiting existing business transactions and examining them against the product conformity requirements.

- *There is an inherent need to have in place a product conformity governance structure across the supply chain.*
- *Contractual obligations may need to be revisited to align with (re)arrangements pursuant product conformity compliances.*
  - *It may entail change in definitions, responsibility, accountability, milestones to overcome aberrations, and variances.*
  - *It may also entail provisions for situation-based escalations and defining consequences.*

3. Mainstream supply chain network awareness and capacity development

Once the impact points have been identified in the supply chain, it the essential to attend to each impact point and establish a system of compliance.

- *Perhaps, the most important factor in compliance is understanding the depth of supply chain, including all suppliers, sub-suppliers, raw materials, factories, as well their interdependencies.*

---

80 In business administration, absorptive capacity has been defined as 'a firm's ability to recognize the value of new information, assimilate it, and apply it to commercial ends'.

- *By mapping these supply chain elements in a centralised system, businesses gain more awareness of their product and supply chain and can identify and mitigate compliance risks quickly.*
- *Businesses will need to ensure capacity development activities to strengthen, adapt, and maintain compliance capacity over time.*
- *There may be a need for re-alignment or overhaul of the supply chain and revisiting the existing control mechanism to ensure product conformity compliance efficiency.*

4. Make the compliance process transparent, systemic, and repeatable

Product conformity compliance is not a one-time activity. Being an ongoing process, it needs to be done in the right way to ensure efficiency.

- *Product conformity strategy and process should be defined in a way that is repeatable for all internal and external stakeholders.*
- *Brands/Principals engaged in contract and/or toll manufacturing may need to extend adequate handholding support to the suppliers in fixing up a proper infrastructure:*
    - *Ensure education, collaboration, and corrective-action agendas for business suppliers.*
    - *Extend financial support for unhindered operations, monitor changes in cost of manufacturing based on product compliance requirements.*
    - *Enable governance management.*
    - *Encourage sound investment decisions.*
- *Businesses should have a dedicated function within the organisation to have a 360-degree control over the compliance process and regular monitoring. This could mean convergence of different roles and a cross-functional collaboration within the organisational structure.*

Play of Quality: Relationships Re-Defined

The product conformity network has three key participants. With the emerging significance of the product conformity framework, the relationship between these three players gets redefined:

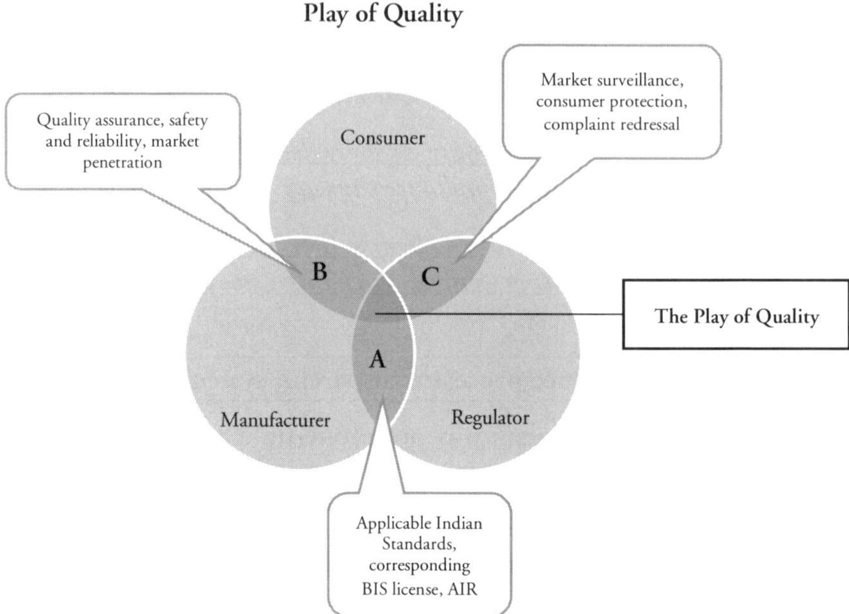

This relationship matrix defines the play of quality as an overlapping relationship between the Manufacturer, Consumer, and the Regulators. Product quality, safety, reliability, interoperability, efficiency, and environmental sustainability are all important to businesses, consumers, and the regulators. Conformity assessment ensures that products meet these requirements in accordance with applicable standards, rules, and other specifications. It fosters trust by ensuring that products are safe to consume.

Striking a New Balance

In terms of the business imperative of the play of quality, the discussion will be anchored on the premise that each business supplier relation has its own nuances that requires a detailed analysis to understand the dynamics. Finding the right balance with suppliers will be an invaluable tool in the quest for efficient compliance.

- *Businesses may need to revisit business models and efficiency of operating with delegated manufacturing.*
- *Cost–benefit analysis could reveal the strengths and weaknesses of having one's own manufacturing facility in place of delegated manufacturing.*

Product conformity compliance is an intricate fact-driven exercise and could mean an overhaul of business operations. *In fact, a business can only be as compliant as are the suppliers with whom it works.* Consumer sensitivity can be driven by utilising BIS compliance—if a product has high sensitivity for quality, it is prudent enough to think of embracing BIS standards, even if they are voluntary. As businesses indulge in this layered compliance processes—cost and supply chain efficiency can only be ensured if planned appropriately.

Trends in Trade

The depth of supply chain networks is increasingly being impacted by product conformity compliances. In a global factory model, while business–supplier relationships are significant for an effective business operation, introduction of the Regulator as a key participant in the play of quality is changing the dynamics of business relationship.

- *Businesses are already realising that product conformity may require rebalancing of their existing relationships with supplier networks.*
- *Being a fact-driven exercise, need for seamless visibility of information relevant to product conformity compliance requirements is felt across the supply chain.*
- *At the same time, regulations are also evolving.*
- *While trying to achieve its intended objectives, the Bureau is seen to carry an inherent responsibility of ensuring that the businesses are not overburdened with compliances.*

Summing Up

Both domestic and foreign businesses have significant market prospects in India; nevertheless, it is a large and complex market that requires careful navigation to succeed. Businesses must therefore be able to recognise the business imperative of the play of quality to ensure efficiency and consistency.

Businesses need to understand the dynamics involved in the play of quality and create competitive differentiators and develop better systems to adapt to the dynamic compliance requirements. This is an opportunity for businesses to redefine their competitive strategies and expand their market presence while developing efficient measures to meet regulatory requirements. *Supplier networks will need to align their operations, policies, and practices to demonstrate due compliance—a business can only be as compliant as are the suppliers with whom it works.*

SUPPLEMENTALS

FREQUENTLY ASKED QUESTIONS

(As adapted from various BIS FAQs, and industry feedback)

Product Certification

1. **What is a Standard?**

   A standard is a regulatory document that provides criteria against which the recurring problems in relation to the performance of a category of product, service, or system can be evaluated. Standards would include specifications, procedures, and guidelines to ensure that products, services, and systems are safe, consistent, and reliable.

2. **How are standards made?**

   Technical committees for Standards Developing Organizations develop standards, which include stakeholders such as manufacturers, consumers, R&D and scientific institutions, academia, government departments/ministries, regulators, and testing laboratories. Such organizations' nominated experts develop standards based on proposals received from stakeholders, following the process and practices of good standardisation through a consensus-building process aimed at reaching a common standpoint.

3. **Are there any other bodies in India that develop standards besides BIS?**

   Other dedicated standards bodies in India that develop standards in their respective domains include:

   i. Telecom Engineering Centre (TEC) in the telecommunications sector.

   ii. Indian Road Congress (IRC) in the area of roads and bridges.

   iii. Directorate of Standardization, Ministry of Defence, for defence standards.

   iv. Research, Design and Standards Organisation (RDSO) for standardisation of railway equipment and applications.

v. Automobile Research Association of India (ARAI) for automotive industry standards.

vi. Telecommunications Standards Development Society, India (TSDSI) for standards on telecom/ICT products and services.

Other ministries/departments and regulators create standards for their respective statutory/regulatory provisions/purposes. These are some examples:

i. Food Safety and Standards Authority of India (FSSAI) for standards on food safety.

ii. Indian Road Congress (IRC) in the area of roads and bridges.

iii. Central Pollution Control Board (CPCB) for standards on emission or discharge of environmental pollution.

iv. Atomic Energy Regulatory Board (AERB) for safety requirements and guidance for utilities and users of atomic energy.

v. Directorate of Marketing Inspection (DMI) for grading standards of agricultural commodities.

vi. Central Drugs Standards Control Organization (CDSCO) the standards for drugs and medical devices.

4. **How can I get involved in the development of standards?**

Anyone interested in participating in BIS standards development processes is welcome to do so. Any individual or organisation interested in participating has several options. They are as follows:

i. *By providing feedback on BIS published and/or draft standards:* All published/draft standards are available on the BIS website, along with the option to comment on such documents.

ii. *By proposing a subject for standardization:* On the BIS website, any individual or organisation can propose a subject for the development of a new standard to BIS.

iii. *By becoming a member of a technical committee:* Any organisation can express their desire to participate actively in standards development by becoming a member of a technical committee. The request is then considered for co-option by the technical committee, subject to limitations on maintaining a balanced representation of all interested groups and a workable committee size.

5. **How do I obtain/access a standard? Is it necessary for me to pay to access a standard?**

   Except for Indian Standards that are adoptions of international standards, all Indian standards are accessible and freely downloadable from the BIS website.

6. **What is a licence?**

   A licence is a permit granted under Section 13 of the BIS Act 2016 to use a specific Standard Mark in relation to any goods or articles that meet a standard.

7. **For which products is a BIS licence required? Is it necessary for me to obtain a BIS licence if I manufacture a product?**

   The Central Government requires mandatory certification of products under the provisions of the BIS Act, 2016 or other Acts. The BIS website contains information about the products that are subject to mandatory BIS certification. If your product is on this list, you must obtain a BIS licence for it.

8. **What are the essential requirements for a manufacturer to have in order to apply to BIS for a licence?**

   To obtain a BIS licence, the manufacturer must have the necessary manufacturing infrastructure, process controls, quality control, and testing capabilities for the product in accordance with the relevant Indian Standard Specification (ISS). The product must also meet all of the requirements outlined in the ISS.

9. **Are there any technical guidelines available for the products covered by the BIS Product Certification Scheme?**

   Yes, technical guidelines are available as 'Product Manuals' for all products covered by the Product Certification Scheme. Product manuals include sampling guidelines, a list of test equipment, the Scheme of Inspection and Testing (SIT), a scope description, and other information.

10. **Will I be able to obtain a BIS licence if product specific guidelines, such as the Product Manual, SIT, grouping guidelines, and/or marking fee rate, are not defined for my product?**

If your product's product-specific guidelines and/or marking fee are not defined, you may be the first manufacturer to apply for a BIS licence for a new product. You will, however, be able to obtain a BIS licence under Scheme I of the BIS (Conformity Assessment) Regulation, 2018. In such a case, the basic principles and procedure for granting a licence will remain the same, with specific relaxation as provided in the Guidelines for Granting a License. BIS will work with you to define the product-specific guidelines and marking fee rate throughout the certification process. This will be known as the 'All India First Licence.'

11. **Can I submit a single application for multiple products and Indian Standards (ISS) manufactured at the same factory?**

    No, even for the same factory location, a separate application for each product and ISS is required.

12. **Can I submit a single application for the same product manufactured at different factory locations?**

    No, separate applications must be submitted for each factory location, even if the product and ISS are the same.

13. **How long is the BIS product certification licence valid?**

    The licence to use the Standard Mark shall be granted initially for not less than one year and up to two years under Scheme-I of the BIS (Conformity Assessment) Regulations, 2018. The licence may be renewed for a period of no less than one year and no more than five years.

14. **What are the duties and responsibilities of the owner of a BIS-licensed manufacturing unit in terms of factory surveillance?**

    BIS licence holders are required to cooperate with BIS certification officers or agents appointed by BIS to conduct surveillance inspections. The licence holder must also share relevant records and requested information. He would also facilitate factory testing and sample collection for independent testing in a third-party lab. According to the officer's advice, the licence holder must deposit samples at the designated laboratory.

15. **I already have a BIS licence for the IS product in my factory. Can I use this licence on all variations of the product produced in the factory?**

    No, BIS grants a single licence for a single product category/Indian Standard. The 'scope of licence' granted to you specifies the products and varieties on which the Standard Mark may be used. It cannot be used for any other product varieties that are not included in the scope. However, the scope of the licence can be changed (inclusion or deletion of varieties) with reference to the standard against which the licence was granted and in accordance with applicable relevant guidelines.

16. **I manufacture a product that is subject to mandatory certification. Is it necessary to obtain a licence even if I manufacture them for export?**

    In general, products intended for export are exempt from the scope of Quality Control Orders (QCOs). However, before deciding, you should seek confirmation from the relevant QCO, which can be found on the BIS website as well as the websites of the respective line ministries/organizations. You can also contact the relevant line ministries about this.

17. **I intend to import a product listed in the mandatory certification section. Is it necessary for importers to obtain a BIS licence?**

    A BIS licence is granted to the factory that manufactures the product, not to the importer. If your product is subject to mandatory certification, the manufacturing factory in a foreign country must obtain a BIS licence under the Foreign Manufacturers Certification Scheme (FMCS).

18. **I intend to import parts of such product that is listed in the mandatory certification section. Is it necessary to obtain a BIS licence for such parts?**

    If a product is subject to mandatory certification, not only the finished products but also their parts, whether completely knocked down (CKD) or semi-knocked down (SKD), are likely to be covered if the said parts retain the essential character of the product listed in the QCO. Hence, the import of parts of a listed product may also require BIS certification.

19. **I am manufacturing a variant of a product that is covered by Indian Standards and requires BIS certification. Is it possible for BIS to exempt me from the mandatory BIS certification requirement?**

    Quality Control Orders are issued by Central Government ministries/departments such as the Ministry of Steel, DPIIT, and others to bring products under mandatory BIS certification. Requests for such an exemption or technical clarification regarding the applicability of

Quality Control Orders to your product should be directed to the relevant ministry/department rather than BIS.

Others

20. **In what manner should the BIS Standard Mark be affixed to products?**

    The licensee shall prominently display the 'Standard Mark' on the article or packaging, as applicable, in a visible location. According to the BIS Conformity Regulations, the Standard Mark must be legible, indelible, and non-removable, and its durability must meet the requirements of the relevant Indian Standard, wherever applicable.

21. **Is it possible for the applicant to appoint a new Authorized Signatory if the current Authorized Signatory is transferred to another location or department or resigns?**

    Yes. The applicant can submit an Authorization letter in the name of the new Authorized Signatory and request that BIS accept and record the change.

22. **What steps must licensees take when the BIS amends or revises the Indian Standard?**

    BIS issues guidelines to implement amendments/revisions made to the Indian Standards in the form of circulars. The circular provides information on amendments/revisions made to the Indian Standard as well as the date of implementation. As a result, the licensee must make the necessary changes to the licence. Any difficulties in implementation must be brought to the attention of the BIS as soon as possible.

23. **What steps must the applicant take if the BIS amends or revises the Indian Standard?**

    Existing applications in which a sample was submitted to the laboratory and a test report was issued by the laboratory may be processed without regard for the revised IS. However, if the applicant wishes to consider the revised IS, a declaration to that effect may be obtained from the applicant, and the application may be processed accordingly. An undertaking shall also be obtained from such applicants that if the sample fails while considering the provisions of the revised IS, the licence will not be granted in accordance with the previous version.

FMCS

24. What is FMCS?

Under the BIS Act, 2016 and Rules, BIS has been operating a "Foreign Manufacturers Certification Scheme" (FMCS) since the year 2000. This is a certification scheme for foreign manufacturers seeking a BIS licence. The scheme is for the certification of products other than electronic and information technology products.

25. **Is a BIS Licence required to import products into India?**

In general, the BIS certification scheme is voluntary; however, certain products, as notified by the Government of India under Quality Control Orders, can only be imported into India with a valid BIS licence.

26. **How to apply for BIS Licence?**

The application can be made in the FMCS forms and formats, with all relevant documents listed in the application. BIS is planning to make it possible to apply online in the future.

27. **Whether nomination of AIR is mandatory?**

Yes, when submitting the application, the foreign applicant must name an Indian Resident as an Authorized Indian Representative (AIR).

28. **What is the role of an AIR?**

The foreign manufacturer appoints an AIR to ensure compliance with the terms and conditions of the agreement with BIS for licence grant, as well as the provisions of the BIS Act, 2016 and the rules and regulations framed thereunder. For the purposes of the Agreement, AIR is deemed to be a person with ultimate control over the manufacturer's affairs.

29. **Who quality as an AIR?**

The AIR shall be an Indian resident and shall declare his consent to be responsible for compliance with the provisions of the BIS Act, rules, regulations, and terms and conditions laid down in the BIS Licence, Agreement, Undertaking, etc. executed by or on behalf of the foreign manufacturer, by a senior person of the branch/office in India. In the absence of such a branch or office in India, or until such a branch or office is established in India, the foreign manufacturer shall nominate an AIR in the prescribed format on firm letterhead.

30. **Has the AIR to be an Indian resident only?**

The AIR must be an Indian national who resides in India. He can, however, be a foreign national if he works in any office/branch of the manufacturer in India and resides in India.

31. **What documents must be submitted to the BIS for a foreign applicant to nominate an employee of an Indian group company as an AIR?**

    In addition to Form VI and the Service agreement between the AIR and the foreign applicant, the following additional documents have to be submitted:

    i. a letter from the Indian employer of the employee stating that the employer has no objection to nominating him/her as an AIR of the applicant company, and

    ii. employee's ID card.

32. **What is the foreign manufacturer's obligation if AIR decides not to represent the manufacturer?**

    The foreign manufacturer must ensure that its AIR is not left unrepresented for any reason at any time during the licence period. The foreign manufacturer must also ensure that a new AIR is nominated (updated) in BIS records well before the incumbent AIR's obligations or liabilities are released.

33. **Can I submit a single application for multiple products manufactured at the same factory location?**

    No, each factory location requires a separate application for each product category.

34. **Can I submit a single application for a product manufactured in multiple locations?**

    No, each factory location requires a separate application for each product category.

35. **Is it necessary to file a separate application for each brand of a product manufactured at the same location?**

    No, the licence application is for a product at a manufacturing facility. The company must submit an undertaking for the brand name along with supporting documentation.

36. **As an importer, may I apply for a licence on behalf of the manufacturer?**

    No, the FMCS scheme requires only the foreign manufacturer to apply for license.

37. **What is the validity of BIS Licence?**

After paying the advance minimum marking fee, BIS certification under Scheme I may be granted for up to two years. The licence is only valid for the varieties specified in the licence. To extend the validity and varieties covered by the licence, an application with the required fee and documents must be submitted under the existing licence. Licenses can be renewed for up to five years from the expiration date.

38. **Is it possible to appoint the same AIR for multiple foreign manufacturers?**

Under the BIS conformity assessment schemes, AIR represents only one manufacturing firm and does not represent any other foreign manufacturer(s). However, the restriction shall not apply to foreign manufacturers belonging to one group of companies and importers (related to the foreign manufacturer) nominated as AIR.

Factory visit by BIS scientist

39. **How long does it take for the BIS Scientist to complete the visit?**

Generally, the BIS Scientist spends 2-3 days in the factory location to complete the verification process.

40. **Who all should be present for the BIS Scientist visit at the factory location?**

The foreign manufacturer should ensure that besides the operational level personnel of the factor, the Authorized Signatory (as stated in the application form), the quality control personnel and test lab staff are present and available for the Scientist visit at the factory location.

41. **What are the important tasks that the BIS scientist will perform during the factory visit?**

Factory visit by BIS scientist is done for verification of production process and drawing of verification sample for third party laboratory testing. Typically, a factory visit would consist of the following:

i. Review of the application and verification of documents submitted.

ii. Review of manufacturing facility, plant, and machinery, etc.

iii. Review of the quality control process, test lab, and verification of test equipment.

iv. Random interviews with quality control personnel.

v. Drawing of samples to be sent for testing and validation.

42. **Can one scientist be appointed for multiple factories (applications) located in the same Country?**

    The appointment of a scientist for a factory visit is made by the Foreign Manufacturers Certification Department (FMCD). There is currently no formal process in place to consolidate scientist visits at the request of an application for multiple factory locations because each factory location requires a separate application for each product/ISS.

43. **Will BIS scientist also visit my sub-contractor's facility/location?**

    Generally, if the final testing, labelling and removal of goods for supply happens in the applicant's factory location (for which BIS license is sought), then the BIS scientist may not require to visit the applicant's sub-contractor's factory location.

44. **Whether BIS will arrange for a visa, air fare, and lodging for a factory visit, or if the applicant must make such arrangements?**

    BIS makes such arrangements, but the applicant is responsible for the costs. To obtain a visa from the respective consulate, the applicant must send an invitation letter in the name of the BIS scientist assigned to the factory visit.

45. **Does BIS refund factory visit charges paid by the applicant prior to the factory visit if the actual expenses incurred are less than the amount paid in advance?**

    Additional payments made to the BIS are settled/adjusted against future payments of the marking fee or statutory fee.

Payment of Statutory Fee/Charges

46. **Does BIS issue an invoice for the application fee, visiting charges fee, and any other statutory payments that the foreign manufacturer applicant must make?**

    BIS does not issue invoices for statutory fee payments. In their official communication to the applicant via email following the submission of the application, BIS raises the demand for payment of the statutory fee. Upon receiving a specific request from the applicant, the BIS scientist-in-charge of the application may issue a letter for payment of the statutory fee in lieu of an invoice to the applicant.

47. **Whether statutory fee can be paid by a third party/person?**

Payment can be made by a third party/person by exercising the following precautions:

a. Third party/person:
   i. complete name of the applicant factory (entity that is making an application for the BIS licence)
   ii. application reference number provided by the BIS, and
   iii. particulars of the fee, for example, the amount of the fee towards a BIS licence application or the amount of the fee towards factory visit charges, etc.

b. Applicant:
   i. obtain payment advice/payment acknowledgment document issued by the bank, from the third party/person.
   ii. submit proof of payment to the BIS.
   iii. indicate transaction ID in the email/letter, while submitting proof of payment to the BIS for reconciliation purpose.

Performance Bank Guarantee

48. Whether Performance Bank Guarantee (PBG) can be executed by an applicant's group company or third party on behalf of an applicant?

According to BIS specifications,

i. PBG must be executed through a bank with a Reserve Bank of India (RBI) approved branch in India, in the format prescribed in the BIS Regulations;

ii. Original PBG must be endorsed and routed through the Indian branch of the issuing bank.

The BIS has provided no guidance in this regard. Because the matter involves local banking and exchange control regulations, a specific request for accepting PBG executed by a group company, or third party may be made to the BIS officer-in-charge if the PBG issuing bank (of the group company or third party) can provide written confirmation that they can issue PBG in accordance with BIS regulations. If allowed, the applicant may exercise this option.

49. Can the BIS accept a stand-by letter of credit in place of a PBG?

No, unless the Head BIS-FMCD allows it in exceptional circumstances.

50. **Is it necessary for the applicant to execute separate PBG for each product manufactured by him?**

    Yes, a separate PBG is required for each licence if an application for a BIS licence is made under different Indian Standards for different products.

Scheme of Inspection and Testing (SIT) and test equipment

51. **Where to get my product tested for the purpose of applying for the various conformity assessment schemes of BIS?**

    The Indian Standard-wise list of Laboratories recognized by BIS, and which can be used for the purpose of testing for conformity assessment schemes of BIS is available on the BIS website.

52. **Does BIS use outside laboratories for testing purposes and what is the scheme for same?**

    Yes. BIS uses the test facilities available in BIS' own eight laboratories, BIS recognised labs which have been recognised under the BIS Laboratory Recognition Scheme 2018, and test facilities available in government laboratories empanelled by the Bureau.

53. **Can a test report prepared in accordance with IEC or any other standard other than Indian Standard be accepted?**

    No, only the test report in accordance with the relevant Indian Standard identified in the Quality Control Order can be accepted.

54. **Can the product sample drawn during inspection be tested in any ILAC/APLAC approved lab or any government lab in the manufacturer's country?**

    No, samples drawn during inspection shall only be tested in BIS laboratories or those recognised by BIS. The applicant firm will send the BIS sample to a laboratory in India. The applicant firm is responsible for the actual testing costs.

55. **Is it possible for a foreign manufacturer to share testing facilities with another foreign manufacturer or a third-party testing lab?**

    Yes. Foreign manufacturers may share testing facilities for:

    i. A BIS licensee who has been granted a licence under the same Indian Standard.

ii. Group company, if the group company is a BIS licensee and has received a licence under the same Indian Standard as the group company.

iii. Third-party testing lab recognised by the BIS, provided that such third-party lab is recognised by the BIS in the country of manufacture and that the lab is equipped to conduct tests in accordance with Indian Standards.

(This option is typically available for conducting tests that can be subcontracted or for tests that cannot be conducted by the licensee under certain conditions. Because the licensee cannot use a third-party testing lab to meet all testing requirements, procuring test equipment and conducting tests in-house is the best practise for meeting the testing requirements under the BIS licence.)

iv. NABL-accredited third-party testing labs for conducting tests that can be subcontracted under the Inspection and Testing Scheme.

(The BIS, generally the Head-FMCD, permits the sharing of testing facilities of NABL accredited third party labs only if the product and situation are not normally addressed by other available options.)

Conditions and compliance requirement for sharing of testing facility are provided in Annexure-X of the Guidelines for Grant of Licence (GoL) as per the conformity assessment Scheme-I of Schedule-II of BIS (Conformity Assessment) Regulations, 2018.

56. **Can the foreign manufacturer subcontract the testing requirements to a third-party testing lab?**

Yes, if the lab is recognized by the BIS in the country of manufacture or an Indian lab is accredited by NABL, and the BIS allows the tests to be subcontracted either under the product manual or by granting specific permission.

57. **Does the BIS accept calibration certificates issued in accordance with national/international standards for the purposes of granting a licence to a foreign manufacturer under Scheme-I?**

Calibration certificates are expected to be provided in accordance with the calibration requirements specified in Indian Standards and the test method standard referred to in the respective standards.

Consumer perspective

58. **What are the major Consumer Engagement activities by BIS?**

    The Think Nudge & Move Department manages the BIS's consumer-facing activities (TN&MD). Within the realm of BIS activities, TN&MD serves as a bridge between BIS and consumers. The TN&MD's main goal is to educate and protect BIS consumers' interests. The TN&MD's main activities are as follows:

    i. Consumer awareness programmes

    ii. Industry awareness programmes

    iii. Educational Utilization of Standards programmes (EUS)

    iv. Consumer Protection

    v. World Standards Day

59. **Whether BIS has developed a Citizen's Charter?**

    BIS has developed a citizen's charter that includes BIS's vision, mission, and objectives, as well as a declaration of commitment to achieving excellence in BIS's various activities. BIS has implemented a citizen charter developed in consultation with stakeholders.

60. **What are the various Standard Marks of BIS?**

    i. For products covered under Scheme-I: ISI Mark and Eco Mark.

    ii. For products covered under Self Declaration of Conformity Scheme as per Scheme-II: Registration Mark.

    iii. For Hallmarked Articles: Hallmark.

61. **What are the categories under which complaints can be lodged with BIS?**

    Complaints may be lodged under the following categories:

    i. Quality of BIS Certified Products including products under Compulsory Registration Scheme and Hallmarking Scheme.

    ii. Misuse of BIS Standard Mark.

    iii. Violation of Quality Control Order.

    iv. Misleading Claims of Conformity to IS.

    v. Related to Services Rendered by BIS.

vi. Other Miscellaneous Complaints.

62. **How can a complaint can be lodged?**

Complaints can be submitted both offline and online, via postal mail, email, mobile app, or the BIS Consumer Engagement Portal. A complaint can also be filed in person at the nearest Branch Office.

63. **Can complaints regarding corruption in BIS be also made?**

For handling such complaints, BIS has a Vigilance Department. As a result, such complaints should be directed to the Vigilance Department (e-mail: vigilance@bis.gov.in).

64. **What is considered to be misuse of BIS Standard Mark?**

BIS grants a licence to use or apply a Standard Mark under the provisions of Section 13 of the BIS Act, 2016. Misuse of the BIS Standard Mark without a valid licence from BIS, or use of a colorable imitation thereof by a manufacturer, is a violation of Section 17 of the BIS Act, 2016.

65. **What is the basis for carrying out Raids (Search & Seizure Operations) by BIS and how it is carried out?**

Raids (Search and Seizure) are carried out following the receipt of information from informers via written complaints, e-mails, and the website, online portal, all of which are centrally recorded. The information obtained is verified through a covert investigation followed by a raid. Following the completion of a successful raid, a legal case is filed in a court of law under the BIS Act, 2016.

66. **How are consumers educated?**

BIS conducts Consumer Awareness Programs throughout India via its network of Regional and Branch offices. Furthermore, BIS is in the process of registering Consumer Groups in order to better reach out to consumers and raise awareness among them.

67. **What are the main issues addressed in consumer awareness programs?**

The awareness campaign focuses primarily on raising consumer quality consciousness by highlighting issues of standardization, hallmarking, or gold or silver, and educating them on the misuse of the BIS Standard Mark.

68. **How does BIS organize Consumer Awareness Programs?**

Through its various Regional Offices/Branch Offices, the BIS organizes regular Awareness Programs. Many of these public awareness campaigns are carried out in collaboration with consumer organizations. These programs aim to raise consumers' quality consciousness by highlighting issues of standardization, promoting the BIS Standard Mark, hallmarking gold and silver, and educating them on the misuse of the BIS Standard Mark and the Complaint Redressal System for products bearing the BIS Standard Mark. The importance of standardization is explained to industries in BIS awareness programs for industries/ licensees, and the difficulties encountered in the operation of licenses are also discussed.

Fees and charges

69. What are the charges/statutory fees for applying under FMCS for a BIS license?

Illustrative list of statutory fee/charges for Applicant/Licensee under FMCS			
Sl. No.	Description of Fee/Charges	Amount in INR	Estimated Amount in USD
I.	Statutory fees to be paid by BIS licence applicant:		
A.	**Application fee:**		
1	Application fee (Non-refundable)	1,000	13
2	Approximate testing charges (per sample)	15,000 to 26,000	199 - 325
B.	**Fee/Charges for appointment of a Scientist for factory visit:**		
3	Visit Charges, **per man-day**	7,000	88
4	**Per-diem charges** of Scientist appointed for factory visit *(as per BIS Regulations, charges vary depending upon level of scientist and country where inspection has to be carried. Charges provided are as applicable for the countries other than USA, Europe, SAARC member countries)*	19,000 to 28,000	238 - 350

5	Estimated Airfare (to-fro), Visa etc., per person *(These are estimated charges and subject to change depending on Country where factory visit to be carried out by the BIS Scientist)*	2,00,000	2,500
6	Contingency Funds	10,000	125
II.	**Statutory fees to be paid by BIS Licensee upon receiving BIS licence**		
C.	**Post-issuance of licence**		
7	Estimated Marking fee based on Minimum Marking Fee, per year	Per unit charges as prescribed under the relevant IS	
8	Amount of Performance Bank Guarantee to be executed by the licensee with the BIS (as per BIS Regulations)	8,00,000	10,000
9	Annual licence fee	1,000	13
D.	**Renewal fee at the time of renewal of BIS Licence**		
10	Renewal application fee	1,000	13
11	Annual licence fee (at the time of renewal)	1,000	13
12	Estimated Marking fee based on Minimum Marking Fee	Per unit charges as prescribed under the relevant IS	
13	Previous dues/other fee (as per BIS notice) if any	At actuals, if any	At actuals, if any
14	Late fee (if the application for renewal is made after validity of the licence)	5,000	63
E.	**Inclusion of series**		
15	Inclusion of series in the same BIS licence, per series	5,000	63
16	Application fee (Non-Refundable)	1,000	13
17	Estimated Marking fee based on Minimum Marking Fee	Per unit charges as prescribed under the relevant IS	

Notes:
Disclaimer: All the statutory fee/application fee/licence fee/testing charges/visiting charges and other charges like accommodation, travel etc. provided above are based on details available in public domain and as per BIS's official website and on our best estimation basis only. All above mentioned charges/fees are subject change and will apply as applicable on the date of payment. Amount in USD are estimated based on an average exchange rate of USD 1 = Rs. 80. Actual USD amount may vary as per exchange rate prevailing on the day of the transaction. For accurate estimation, please contact your Bank.

CASE STUDIES
Consumer Goods

Business problem statement:

The government introduced mandatory implementation of a specific Indian Standard ('IS') for products in the consumer goods space. It has bearing on a business that is highly dependent on the distributed manufacturing footprint of foreign vendors. Factories never had experience dealing with BIS licensing, the Indian regulatory authorities, the intensity of practice and procedure—all of which were unexplored and had a steep learning curve. The diversity and dynamism of the product portfolio and its interplay with the IS added complexity, which could potentially lead to supply chain disruptions and adverse revenue implications.

SCENARIO 1: Foreign manufacturing location for multiple brands

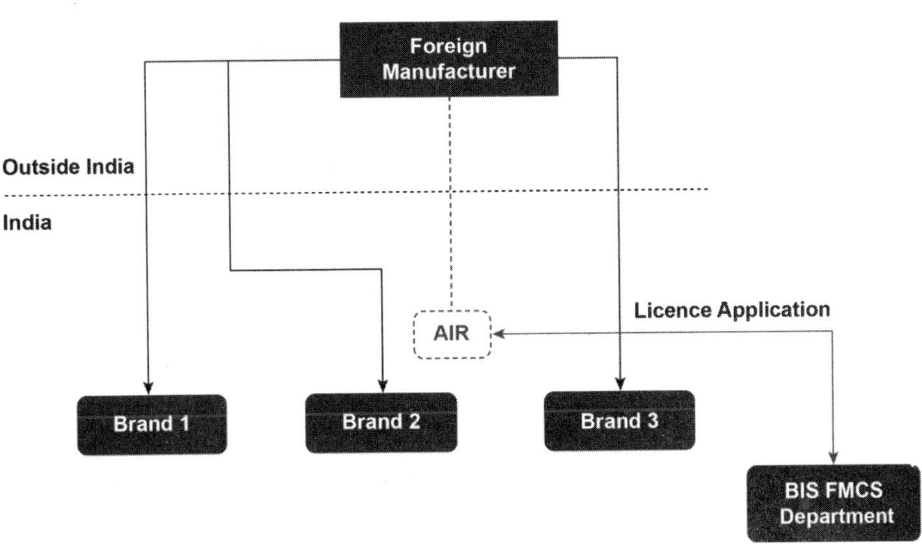

Case snapshot:

Brand 1, Brand 2, and Brand 3 were running their retail businesses in India. Their products were manufactured by a factory located in Country X ('the factory'). Post-manufacturing, the products were imported by the brand companies. The brand companies appropriately engaged with the factory with respect to the terms and conditions of the contractual arrangement and established necessary quality control.

The Ministry of Commerce and Industry (i.e., the relevant line ministry for the above products) issued a Quality Control Order ('QCO') for products covered under a specific IS. The QCO directed the compulsory use of the Standard Mark under a licence issued by BIS in relation to the products covered under the specific IS. The factory was, hence, required to apply for and obtain a licence under the Foreign Manufacturers Certification Scheme ('FMCS') of BIS. The grant of a license would allow the factory to mark the product with the ISI mark and the license number before exporting the products to India.

The brand companies evaluated the new regulatory requirement, its impact on business continuity and their operating model, and the need for setting up a cross-functional team to guide the organisation through the transformation triggered by the QCO.

Uniqueness of Foreign Manufacturer:

1. The vendor had multiple manufacturing locations, i.e., factories, in X country. Each factory was required to seek an independent BIS license under the specific IS.
2. One of the factories manufactured a diverse range of products, which were covered under multiple QCOs.
3. The market positioning of the products did not align with the technical characteristics-based categorization under the QCOs.
4. Among other challenges, the dilemma for brands was whether to continue with a market positioning different from the technical description of the product or change the market positioning to align with the technical characteristics. The latter option could impact the relationship of the product with the consumer and the consumer's loyalty towards the product.

5. The factory's organisational structure was flat, with shopfloor workers and their immediate supervisors. The factory did not have other support functions or such management bandwidth to undertake additional BIS-related compliance activities.
6. The IS mandated an array of quality criteria that required specified testing infrastructure to qualify for a BIS license. The usual business practice did not require the factory to maintain a dedicated testing facility complete with all the testing equipment required under the IS. Testing and quality control were generally housed within the brand companies to ensure consistency in quality.
7. There were sensitivities around additional cost of compliances as the Factory required to upgrade its testing infrastructure, train the quality control staff, and incur the BIS licensing cost.
8. The BIS License was intended to be used for products with respect to multiple brands and importers.
9. FM was required to nominate an Indian resident as an Authorized Indian Representative ('AIR') while submitting the application for a BIS license.

Challenges

1. The factory was required to identify an appropriate AIR to submit and manage the application for a BIS license. The factory, however, was unsure about the requisite qualification of the AIR.
2. The factory also found it challenging to establish mutual accountability with the AIR. The factory was also required to arrange for adequate training and supervision of the AIR throughout the license period.
3. The factory was required to share business-sensitive information related to the manufacturing and quality control processes along with the application for a BIS license.
4. With limited management bandwidth and unfamiliarity with the licensing process, coordination with multiple brands was a challenge.
5. The factory did not have prior experience or familiarity to understand the expectation of the BIS scientist during the factory visit.
6. BIS-approved labs were not available in Country X for conducting such quality tests as were required under the IS.

7. The factory needed to build management capacity and suitably change the SOPs to integrate the BIS-related activities.

Approach and outcome:

1. Brand companies struggled to develop the co-opetition operating model required to collaborate amongst themselves and with the factory for obtaining and using a shared BIS license number on products competing in the market.
2. Brand companies offered additional management bandwidth and advisory support to the Factory for managing the transition. Cross-functional teams were pulled to contribute to the project, involving multiple workstreams supervised by the steering committee.
3. Brand companies and the factory discussed and agreed on the cost sharing and responsibilities in relation to the lifecycle of BIS compliance.
4. The factory volunteered to be under India's regulatory jurisdiction for the limited purpose of licensing and extended an invitation for BIS scientist to visit its factory premises for inspection.
5. Extensive trainings were conducted with respect to the process and testing in the local language. In this regard, the factory appointed a dedicated local resource for coordination with multiple brands, advisors, and the BIS.
6. Brand companies and the factory required strategic organisational transformation to develop the licensing support function to coordinate with other functions like supply chain, manufacturing, compliance, merchandising, etc., all of which were impacted by the BIS requirement.
7. While all this was being done, the brand companies internally deliberated upon the external engagement with the market, consumer, and Regulator in:
   a. Repositioning of the products as per consumer preference.
   b. Assessing the impact of quality control regulations on sales, revenue, and market share.
   c. Re-assessing their sourcing and manufacturing footprint in the short and long term.
   d. Considering the need for policy and administration-level advocacy on the following accounts:

i. *De-minimus* exception to products imported in limited quantities.

ii. Self-certification is subject to risk-based review by the BIS scientist.

iii. Adhoc certification based on desk review followed by a factory visit by the scientist.

SCENARIO 2: Foreign manufacturing location for multiple brands

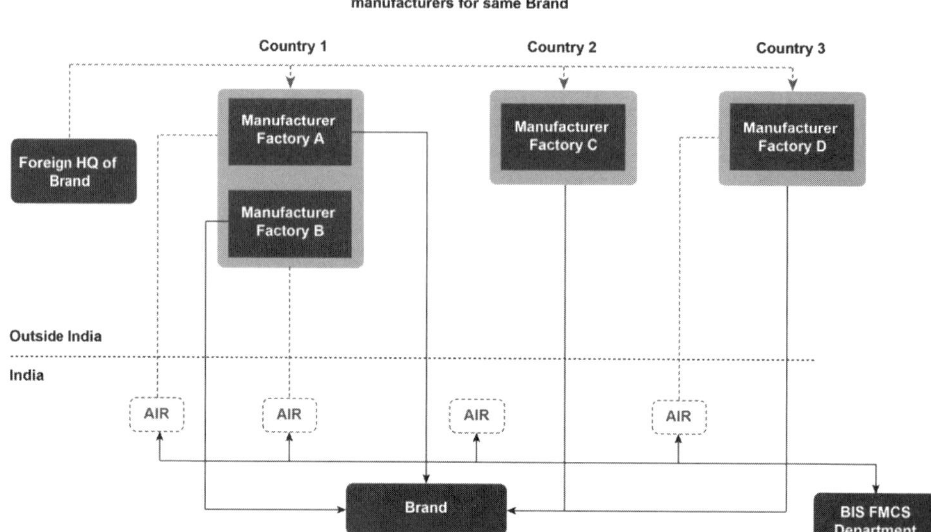

Case snapshot:

The brand company was running its retail business in India. Their products were manufactured by foreign manufacturers located in multiple countries ('the factories'). The finished products were imported by the brand company in India.

In a similar regulatory situation as seen in Scenario 1, the factories were required to apply for and obtain a licence from BIS under FMCS.

The brand company's Foreign Headquarter supported India operations by acting as their buying agent for sourcing the products from a diverse base of manufacturers, keeping in consideration the production capacity, execution capability, quality standards, and the delivery schedule.

Uniqueness of foreign manufacturer under this Scenario:

1. Multiple factories were engaged in manufacturing products for a single brand. Other factors remained the same as in Scenario 1, and the factories were not in compliance with the requirements under the IS.
2. Each factory located in multiple countries was required to obtain their respective BIS license in order to continue doing business with the brand company in India.

3. Each factory was required to nominate an Indian resident as an AIR while submitting their respective application for a BIS license.

Unique challenges under this Scenario:

1. Besides the other challenges listed in Scenario 1, maintaining the consistency of the BIS license application and running the process in a seamless manner were challenging.
2. Each factory was required to appoint an appropriate AIR to sign the application for a BIS license and assume the obligations therein. Besides other challenges, since a designated AIR cannot concurrently act on behalf of another foreign manufacturer, appointing appropriate persons for each factory was a challenge.
3. Each factory needed to understand the contours of the BIS scientist visit and build management capacity for BIS-related ongoing compliance.
4. Although BIS-approved labs were available in Country 2, they were not available in Country 1 or Country 3 for conducting such tests that were permitted to be outsourced.
5. BIS Scientists visited the premises of Factory C and Factory D before the effective date of QCO. However, there was an inordinate delay in organising a scientist's visit to Country 1 due to logistical constraints.

Approach and outcome:

1. Although efforts were made to coordinate with and integrate multiple factories into the ecosystem, only Factory C and Factory D got the BIS license after the factory visit and review of their applications. Factory A and Factory B could not obtain the license by the effective date of the QCO. As a result, the sourcing footprint for the brand company was required to change until Factory A and Factory B obtained their license.

2. Brand Companies offered additional management bandwidth and advisory support to the Factory for managing the transition. Brand company extended management bandwidth and advisory support to the Factory A and Factory B for managing the transition. Factory C and Factory D, on the other hand, opted to navigate through the process on their own.

3. The delay in ability to obtain the BIS license on time forced the brand company to source from domestic manufacturers and supply its existing customers. The delay further caused undue stress on the supply chain, besides loss of business and operational inefficiencies from a factory and brand perspective.

4. Factory A and Factory B managed to obtain a scientist's visit, although 60 days after the effective date. After several rounds of deliberations and technical alignment, both the factories were granted BIS licenses based on a satisfactory review of their applications.

SCENARIO 3: Brand-owned manufacturing facilities outside India

Case study 3 – Brand-owned factories outside India

Country 1

Related Factory A

Related Factory B

Country 2

Related Factory C

Outside India

India

AIR

Separate Licence Applications for each Factory

India Company

BIS FMCS Department

Case snapshot:

A brand company was running its retail business in India. Their products were manufactured by foreign-related factories located in multiple countries ('the related factories'). In a similar regulatory situation as seen in Scenario 1, the RMs were required to apply for and obtain a licence from BIS under FMCS.

Uniqueness of related (intragroup) manufacturer under this Scenario:

1. The related factories were engaged in manufacturing a variety of products for their related entities, including the brand company in India. Other factors remained the same as in Scenario 1, but not all the related factories were in compliance with the requirements under IS:XXXX.
2. There were minimal business sensitivities between the brand company in India and the factories, as they were under the same group of companies. However, all the factories located in different countries were required to obtain their respective BIS license in order to continue supplying manufactured products to India.
3. Since the entities were part of the same group, a suitable in-house official (Indian Resident) was appointed as the common AIR for their respective applications to the FMCS Department.

4. Being part of the same group, managing the BIS license application process internally was possible and efficient.

Approach and outcome:

1. Brand Company, with the support and guidance of their foreign headquarters, adapted the licensing requirement to the dynamism of business operations with focused efforts to coordinate with related factories.
2. Factory A and Factory B were able to procure the requisite test equipment without delay. They also upgraded manufacturing machinery wherever the need was felt. A BIS Scientist visit was successfully organized for them. After the due application process, Factory A and Factory B were granted BIS licenses.
3. However, in the case of Factory C in Country 2, there was an inordinate delay in setting up the in-house testing infrastructure. Although orders were placed for the procurement of the requisite test equipment, there were multiple commercial and logistical hurdles to be addressed. Without the said test equipment, it was not possible to complete the application process or facilitate the scientist's visit to their factory premises. As a result, Factory C could not obtain the license by the effective date of QCO.
4. Besides other approach steps listed in Scenario 1, the entities being part of the same group of companies enabled sharing of management bandwidth, advisory support, and resources for managing the transition.

SCENARIO 4: Manufacturing in India

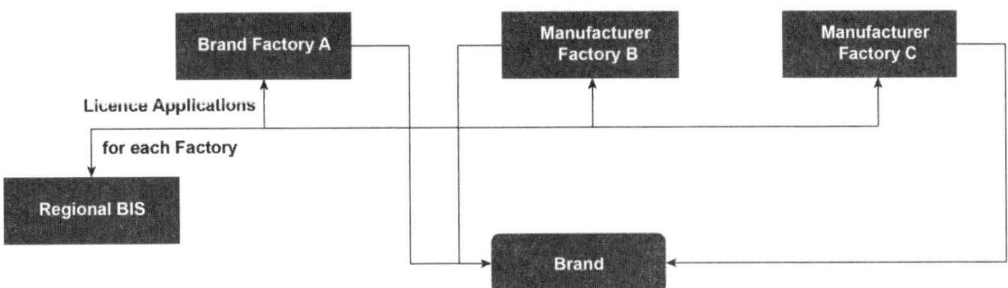

Case snapshot:

Brand company was running its retail business in India and had its own manufacturing facility there. Their products were also manufactured by two other unrelated factories ('the domestic factories'). In a similar regulatory situation as seen in Scenario 1, the brand factory and domestic factories were required to apply for and obtain a licence from BIS.

Uniqueness of domestic related and unrelated manufacturer under this Scenario:

1. Unlike in the other scenarios where manufacturers were located in foreign countries, all related and unrelated manufacturing facilities were in India.
2. Instead of applying for a BIS license to the FMCS, Indian factories have to apply to the regional BIS offices in India. It was a simpler process as compared to FMCS.
3. In the case of Indian manufactures, there was no requirement to appoint an AIR.
4. Since the brand company was to obtain a BIS license for its own manufacturing facility, supervision of the BIS license application process at the domestic factories was well organized.

Approach and outcome:

1. Brand company complied with the licensing requirement for its manufacturing facility and was able to coordinate with the unrelated domestic factories to obtain the BIS license in a time-bound manner so as to avoid any supply chain disruption.

2. As the scientist's visit to the factories didn't require foreign travel, there was less coordination required from a travel and logistics perspective.
3. The brand company is excited to gain market share for its products in India as the foreign factories have not been able to obtain the license in time.
4. Domestic factories are also excited about their increased ability to win government procurement process in India, where the tender conditions included BIS licenses and minimum value addition.

CASE STUDY – INTERMEDIATE/INDUSTRIAL GOODS

Business problem statement:

The government introduced mandatory implementation of Indian Standard IS:XXYY applicable to specific intermediate/industrial goods. Given the IP-intensive manufacturing process, the degree of control, and the substantial involvement of internal resources, the business is dependent on manufacturing undertaken by group entities outside India. It is important that the BIS license be obtained in a timely manner to avoid losing business to competitors and protect the market share in India.

Case study 5 – Intermediate goods

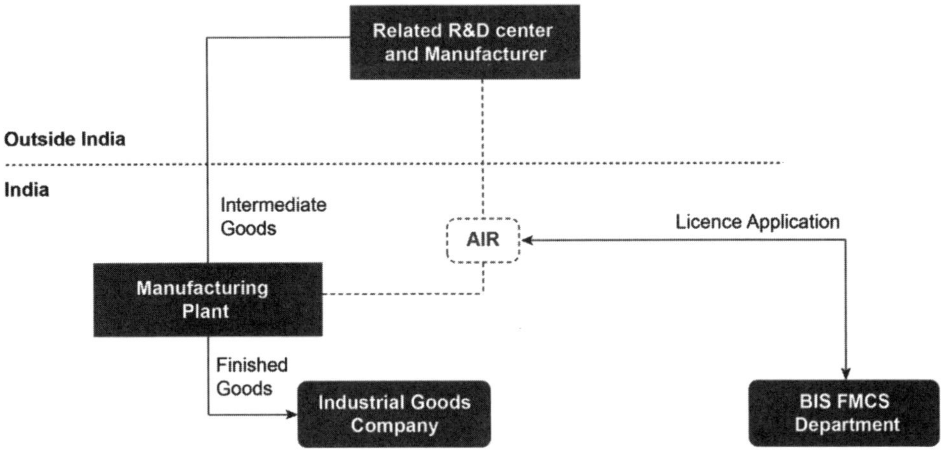

Related R&D center and Manufacturer
Outside India
India
Intermediate Goods
AIR
Licence Application
Manufacturing Plant
Finished Goods
Industrial Goods Company
BIS FMCS Department

Case snapshot:

An industrial goods company was running its manufacturing and wholesale/retail businesses in India. In this regard, a specific type of product ('Product A') was required as an intermediate good for the manufacture of finished goods. Product A was being manufactured by a related factory in Country X. In the past, Product A had been rigorously evaluated by multiple foreign regulatory/certification bodies and found to have no environmental or health concerns.

The Ministry of Chemicals and Fertilizers (i.e., the relevant line ministry for the above products) issued a QCO that directs the compulsory use of the Standard Mark under a licence from BIS on Product A. The related factory was, therefore, required to apply for and obtain a licence from BIS under

FMCS. The license would allow the factory to append the ISI mark on the containers in which Product A is packed and imported to India.

Challenges

1. Compliance with the BIS licensing requirement was critical for business continuity. Any delay would have caused disruptions in the supply chain and production output. However, it was challenging to find alternatives to the foreign intermediate goods that were IP-sensitive.
2. Product A was produced using secret formulations. Sharing such IP-intensive information with the Indian regulatory authorities, i.e., BIS, became a sensitive issue.
3. Ensuring alignment with multiple disclosures made before regulatory authorities, including the BIS authorities, was also challenging. The tax positions adopted in this regard by the company lacked clarity and certainty and were required to be tested.

Approach and outcome:

1. The company was required to make changes to the packaging process to be able to add the printing of BIS-related disclosures.
2. Disclosures in the BIS licensing application were carefully reviewed to ensure that only information that was necessary to know was included and that no business/IP sensitive information inadvertently slipped in.
3. The company moved quickly to ensure that it could receive the BIS license at the earliest and use the 'early mover advantage' to gain market share from the competition.
4. There were travel restrictions to the country where the competitor's factory was located, which created an opportunity for the company to win some clients who were facing disruption because of the competitor's inability to comply with the licensing requirement on time.
5. The company adapted the licensing requirement to the dynamism of business operations and appointed in-house personnel as the AIR for the foreign RM.
6. Appropriate SOPs and internal trainings were organised for seamless management of the process.

APPENDICES

Appendix - 1

THE BIS ACT, 2016

(Bare Text)

THE BUREAU OF INDIAN STANDARDS ACT, 2016 NO. 11 OF 2016

[21*st March*, 2016.]

An Act to provide for the establishment of a national standards body for the harmonious development of the activities of standardisation, conformity assessment and quality assurance of goods, articles, processes, systems and services and for matters connected therewith or incidental thereto.

BE it enacted by Parliament in the Sixty-seventh Year of the Republic of India as follows:—

CHAPTER I PRELIMINARY

1. Short title, extent and commencement.

(*1*) This Act may be called the Bureau of Indian Standards Act, 2016.

(2) It extends to the whole of India.

(3) It shall come into force on such date as the Central Government may, by notification in the Official Gazette, appoint.

2. Definitions.

In this Act, unless the context otherwise requires,—

(1) "article" means any substance, artificial or natural, or partly artificial or partly natural, whether raw or partly or wholly processed or manufactured or hand- made within India or imported into India;

(2) "assaying and hallmarking centre" means a testing and marking centre recognised by the Bureau to determine the purity of precious metal articles and to apply hallmark on the precious metal articles in a manner as may be determined by regulations;

(3) "Bureau" means the Bureau of Indian Standards established under section 3;

(4) "certification officer" means a certification officer appointed under sub-section (*1*) of section 27;

(5) "certified body" means a holder of certificate of conformity or licence under sub-section (*2*) of section 13 in relation to any goods, article, process, system or service which conforms to a standard;

(6) "certified jeweller" means a jeweller who has been granted a certificate by the Bureau to get manufactured for sale or to sell any precious metal article after getting the same hallmarked in a manner as may be determined by regulations;

(7) "conformity assessment" means demonstration that requirements as may be specified relating to an article, process, system, service, person or body are fulfilled;

(8) "conformity assessment scheme" means a scheme relating to such goods, article, process, system or service as may be notified by the Bureau under section 12;

(9) "consumer" means a person as defined in the Consumer Protection Act, 1986 (68 of 1986.);

(10) "covering" includes any stopper, cask, bottle, vessel, box, crate, cover, capsule, case, frame, wrapper, bag, sack, pouch or other container;

(11) "Director General" means the Director General appointed under sub-section (*1*) of section 7;

(12) "Executive Committee" means the Executive Committee constituted under sub-section (*1*) of section 4;

(13) "fund" means the fund constituted under section 20;

(14) "goods" includes all kinds of movable properties under the Sale of Goods Act, 1930 (3 of 1930.), other than actionable claims, money, stocks and shares;

(15) "Governing Council" means a Governing Council constituted under sub-section (*3*) of section 3;

(16) "Hallmark" means in relation to precious metal article, the Standard Mark, which indicates the proportionate content of precious metal in that article as per the relevant Indian Standard;

(17) "Indian Standard" means the standard including any tentative or provisional standard established and published by the Bureau, in relation to any goods, article, process, system or service, indicative of the quality and specification of such goods, article, process, system or service and includes—

(i) any standard adopted by the Bureau under sub-section (*2*) of section 10; and

(ii) any standard established and published, or recognised, by the Bureau of Indian Standards established under the Bureau of Indian Standard Act, 1986 (63 of 1986.), which was in force immediately before the commencement of this Act;

(18) "Indian Standards Institution" means the Indian Standards Institution registered under the Societies Registration Act, 1860 (21 of 1860.);

(19) "jeweller" means a person engaged in the business to get manufactured precious metal article for sale or to sell precious metal articles;

(20) "licence" means a licence granted under section 13 to use a specified Standard Mark in relation to any goods, article, process, system or service, which conforms to a standard;

(21) "manufacturer" means a person responsible for designing and manufacturing any goods or article;

(22) "mark" includes a device, brand, heading, label, ticket, pictorial representation, name, signature, word, letter or numeral or any combination thereof;

(23) "member" means a member of the Governing Council, Executive Committee or any of the Advisory Committee;

(24) "notification" means a notification published in the Official Gazette and the expression "notify" or "notified" shall be construed accordingly;

(25) "person" means a manufacturer, an importer, a distributor, retailer, seller or lessor of goods or article or provider of service or any other person who uses or applies his name or trade mark or any other distinctive mark on to goods or article or while providing a service, for any consideration or gives goods or article or provides service as prize or gift for commercial purposes including their representative and any person who is engaged in such activities, where the manufacturer, importer, distributor, retailer, seller, lessor or provider of service cannot be identified;

(26) "precious metal" means gold, silver, platinum and palladium;

(27) "precious metal article" means any article made entirely or in part from precious metals or their alloys;

(28) "prescribed" means prescribed by rules made under this Act;

(29) "process" means a set of inter-related or interacting activities, which transforms inputs into outputs;

(30) "recognised testing and marking centre" means a testing and marking centre recognised by the Bureau under sub-section (*5*) of section 14;

(31) "recognised testing laboratory" means a testing laboratory recognised by the Bureau under sub-section (*4*) of section 13;

(32) "registering authority" means any authority competent under any law for the time being in force to register any company, firm or other body of persons, or any trade mark or design, or to grant a patent;

(33) "regulations" means regulations made by the Bureau under this Act;

(34) "sale" means to sell, distribute, hire, lease or exchange of goods, article, process, system or service for any consideration or for commercial purposes;

(35) "seller" means a person who is engaged in the sale of any goods, article, process, system or service;

(36) "service" means the result generated by activities at the interface between an organisation and a customer and by organisation's internal activities, to meet customer requirements;

(37) "specification" means a description of goods, article, process, system or service as far as practicable by reference to its nature, quality, strength, purity, composition, quantity, dimensions, weight, grade, durability, origin, age, material, mode of manufacture or processing, consistency and reliability of service delivery or other characteristics to distinguish it from any other goods, article, process, system or service;

(38) "specified" means specified by the regulations;

(39) "standards" means documented agreements containing technical specifications or other precise criteria to be used consistently as rules, guidelines, or definitions of characteristics, to ensure that goods, articles, processes, systems and services are fit for their purpose;

(40) "Standard Mark" means the mark specified by the Bureau, and includes Hallmark, to represent conformity of goods, article, process, system or service to a particular Indian Standard or conformity to a standard, the mark of

which has been established, adopted or recognised by the Bureau and is marked on the article or goods as a Standard Mark or on its covering or label attached to such goods or article so marked;

(41) "system" means a set of inter-related or interacting elements;

(42) "testing laboratory" means a body set up for the purpose of testing of goods or article against a set of requirements and report its findings;

(43) "trade mark" means a mark used or proposed to be used in relation to goods or article or process or system or service for the purpose of indicating, or so as to indicate, a connection in the course of trade of goods, article, process, system or service, as the case may be, and some person having the right, either as proprietor or as registered user, to use the mark, whether with or without any indication of the identity of that person.

CHAPTER II

BUREAU OF INDIAN STANDARDS

3. Establishment of Bureau and Constitution of Governing Council.

(*1*) With effect from such date as the Central Government may, by notification in the Official Gazette, appoint in this behalf, there shall be established a national body for the purposes of this Act, a Bureau, to be called the Bureau of Indian Standards.

(2) The Bureau shall be a body corporate by the name aforesaid, having perpetual succession and a common seal, with power, subject to the provisions of this Act, to acquire, hold and dispose of property, both movable and immovable, and to contract and shall by the said name sue and be sued.

(3) The members of the Governing Council shall constitute the Bureau and general superintendence, direction and management of the affairs of the Bureau shall vest in the Governing Council, which shall consist of the following members, namely:—

(a) the Minister in-charge of the Ministry or Department of the Central Government having administrative control of the Bureau who shall be *ex officio* President of the Bureau;

(b) the Minister of State or a Deputy Minister, if any, in the Ministry or Department of the Central Government having administrative control of the Bureau who shall be *ex officio* Vice-President of the Bureau, and where there is no such Minister of State or Deputy

Minister, such person as may be nominated by the Central Government to be the Vice-President of the Bureau;

(c) the Secretary to the Government of India of the Ministry or Department of the Central Government having administrative control of the Bureau, *ex officio*;

(d) the Director General of the Bureau, *ex officio*;

(e) such number of other persons to represent the Government, industry, scientific and research institutions, consumers and other interests, as may be prescribed, to be appointed by the Central Government.

(4) The term of office of the members referred to in clause (*e*) of sub-section (*3*) and the manner of filling vacancies among, and the procedure to be followed in the discharge of their functions by the members, shall be such as may be prescribed:

Provided that a member, other than an *ex officio* member of the Bureau of Indian Standards constituted under the Bureau of Indian Standards Act, 1986 (63 of 1986.), shall, after the commencement of this Act, continue to hold such office as member till the completion of his term.

(5) The Governing Council may associate with itself, in such manner and for such purposes as may be prescribed, any person whose assistance or advice it may desire in complying with any of the provisions of this Act and a person so associated shall have the right to take part in the discussions of the Governing Council relevant to the purposes for which he has been associated but shall not have the right to vote.

(6) The Governing Council may, by general or special order in writing, delegate to any member, the Director General or any other person subject to such conditions, if any, as may be specified in the order, such of its powers and functions under this Act except the powers under section 37 as it may deem necessary.

4. Executive Committee of Bureau.

(*1*) The Governing Council may, with the prior approval of the Central Government, by notification in the Official Gazette, constitute an Executive Committee which shall consist of the following members, namely:—

(a) Director General of the Bureau, who shall be its *ex officio* Chairman; and

(b) such number of members, as may be prescribed.

(*2*) The Executive Committee constituted under sub-section (*1*) shall perform, exercise and discharge such functions, powers and duties of the Bureau, as may be delegated to it by the Governing Council.

5. **Advisory Committees of Bureau.**

(*1*) Subject to any regulations made in this behalf, the Governing Council may, from time to time and as and when it is considered necessary, constitute the following Advisory Committees for the efficient discharge of the functions of the Bureau, namely: —

(a) Finance Advisory Committee;

(b) Conformity Assessment Advisory Committee;

(c) Standards Advisory Committee;

(d) Testing and Calibration Advisory Committee; and

(e) such number of other committees as may be specified by regulations.

(*2*) Each Advisory Committee shall consist of a Chairman and such other members as may be specified by regulations.

6. **Vacancies, etc., not to invalidate act or proceedings.**

No act or proceedings of the Governing Council, under section 3 shall be invalid merely by reason of—

(a) any vacancy in, or any defect in the constitution of the Governing Council; or

(b) any defect in the appointment of a person acting as a member of the Governing Council; or

(c) any irregularity in the procedure of the Governing Council not affecting the merits of the case.

7. **Director General.**

(*1*) The Central Government shall appoint a Director General of the Bureau.

(2) The terms and conditions of service of the Director General of the Bureau shall be such as may be prescribed.

(3) Subject to the general superintendence and control of the Governing Council, the Director General of the Bureau shall be the Chief Executive Authority of the Bureau.

(4) The Director General of the Bureau shall exercise and discharge such of the powers and duties of the Bureau as may be specified by regulations.

(5) The Director General may, by general or special order in writing, delegate to any officer of the Bureau subject to such conditions, if any, as may be specified in the order, such of his powers and functions as are assigned to him under the regulations or are delegated to him by the Governing Council, as he may deem necessary.

8. Officers and employees of Bureau.

(*1*) The Bureau may appoint such other officers and employees as it considers necessary for the efficient discharge of its functions under this Act.

(*2*) The terms and conditions of service of officers and employees of the Bureau appointed under sub-section (*1*) shall be such as may be specified by regulations.

9. Powers and functions of Bureau.

(*1*) The powers and duties as may be assigned to the Bureau under this Act shall be exercised and performed by the Governing Council and, in particular, such powers may include the power to—

(a) establish branches, offices or agencies in India or outside;

(b) recognise, on reciprocal basis or otherwise, with the prior approval of the Central Government, the mark of any international body or institution, on such terms and conditions as may be mutually agreed upon by the Bureau in relation to any goods, article, process, system or service at par with the Standard Mark for such goods, article, process, system or service;

(c) seek recognition of the Bureau and of the Indian Standards outside India on such terms and conditions as may be mutually agreed upon by the Bureau with any corresponding institution or organisation in any country or with any international organisation;

(d) enter into and search places, premises or vehicles, and inspect and seize goods or articles and documents to enforce the provisions of this Act;

(e) provide services to manufacturers and consumers of goods or articles or processes for compliances of standards on such terms and conditions as may be mutually agreed upon;

(f) provide training services in relation to quality management, standards, conformity assessment, laboratory testing and calibration, and any other related areas;

(g) publish Indian Standards and sell such publications and publications of international bodies;

(h) authorise agencies in India or outside India for carrying out any or all activities of the Bureau and such other purposes as may be necessary on such terms and conditions as it deems fit;

(i) obtain membership in regional, international and foreign bodies having objects similar to that of the Bureau and participate in international standards setting process;

(j) undertake testing of samples for purposes other than for conformity assessment; and

(k) undertake activities relating to legal metrology.

(2) The Bureau shall take all necessary steps for promotion, monitoring and management of the quality of goods, articles, processes, systems and services, as may be necessary, to protect the interests of consumers and various other stake holders which may include the following namely:—

(a) carrying out market surveillance or survey of any goods, article, process, system or service to monitor their quality and publish findings of such surveillance or surveys;

(b) promotion of quality in connection with any goods, article, process, system or service by creating awareness among the consumers and the industry and educate them about quality and standards in connection with any goods, article, process, system and service;

(c) promotion of safety in connection with any goods, article, process, system or service;

(d) identification of any goods, articles, process, system or service for which there is a need to establish a new Indian Standard, or to revise an existing Indian Standard;

(e) promoting the use of Indian Standards;

(f) recognising or accrediting any institution in India or outside which is engaged in conformity certification and inspection of any goods, article, process, system or service or of testing laboratories;

(g) coordination and promotion of activities of any association of manufacturers or consumers or any other body in relation to improvement in the quality or in the implementation of any quality assurance activities in relation to any goods, article, process, system or service; and

(h) such other functions as may be necessary for promotion, monitoring and management of the quality of goods, articles, processes, systems and services and to protect the interests of consumers and other stake holders.

(3) The Bureau shall perform its functions under this section through the Governing Council in accordance with the direction and subject to such rules as may be made by the Central Government.

CHAPTER III

INDIAN STANDARDS, CERTIFICATION AND LICENCE

10. Indian Standards.

(*1*) The standards established by the Bureau shall be the Indian Standards.

(2) The Bureau may—

(a) establish, publish, review and promote the Indian Standard, in relation to any goods, article, process, system or service in such manner as may be prescribed;

(b) adopt as Indian Standard, any standard, established by any other Institution in India or elsewhere, in relation to any goods, article, process, system or service in such manner as may be prescribed;

(c) recognise or accredit any institution in India or outside which is engaged in standardisation;

(d) undertake, support and promote such research as may be necessary for formulation of Indian Standards.

(3) The Bureau, for the purpose of this section, shall constitute, as and when considered necessary, such number of technical committees of experts for the formulation of standards in respect of goods, articles, processes, systems or services, as may be necessary.

(4) The Indian Standard shall be notified and remain valid till withdrawn by the Bureau.

(5) Notwithstanding anything contained in any other law, the copyright in an Indian Standard or any other publication of the Bureau shall vest in the Bureau.

11. Prohibition to publish, reproduce or record without authorisation by Bureau.

(*1*) No individual shall, without the authorisation of the Bureau, in any manner or form, publish, reproduce or record any Indian Standard or part thereof, or any other publication of the Bureau.

(*2*) No person shall issue a document that creates, or may create the impression that it is or contains an Indian Standard, as contemplated in this Act:

Provided that nothing in this sub-section shall prevent any individual from making a copy of Indian Standard for his personal use.

12. Conformity Assessment scheme.

(*1*) The Bureau may notify a specific or different conformity assessment scheme for any goods, article, process, system or service or for a group of goods, articles, processes, systems or services, as the case may be, with respect to any Indian Standard or any other standard in a manner as may be specified by regulations.

(*2*) The Bureau may establish a Standard Mark in relation to each of its conformity assessment schemes, which shall be of such design and contain such particulars as may be specified by regulations to represent a particular standard.

13. Grant of licence or certificate of conformity.

(*1*) A person may apply for grant of licence or certificate of conformity, as the case may be, if the goods, article, process, system or service conforms to an Indian Standard.

(2) Where any goods, article, process, system or service conforms to a standard, the Director General may, by an order, grant—

(a) a certificate of conformity in a manner as may be specified by regulations; or

(b) a licence to use or apply a Standard Mark in a manner as may be specified by regulations, subject to such conditions and on payment of such fees, including late fee or fine, before or during the operation of the certificate of conformity or licence, and as determined by regulations.

(3) While granting a certificate of conformity or licence to use a Standard Mark, the Bureau may, by order, specify the marking and labelling requirements that shall necessarily be affixed as may be specified from time to time.

(4) The Bureau may establish, maintain or recognise testing laboratories for the purposes of conformity assessment and quality assurance and for such other purposes as may be required for carrying out its functions.

14. Certification of Standard Mark of jewellers and sellers of certain specified goods or articles.

(*1*) The Central Government, after consulting the Bureau, may notify precious metal articles or other goods or articles as it may consider necessary, to be marked with a Hallmark or Standard Mark, as the case may be, in a manner as specified in sub-section (*2*).

(2) The goods or articles notified in sub-section (*1*) may be sold through retail outlets certified by the Bureau after such goods or articles have been assessed for conformity to the relevant standard by testing and marking centre, recognised by the Bureau and marked with Hallmark or Standard Mark, as the case may be, as specified by regulations.

(3) The Central Government may, after consulting the Bureau, by an order published in the Official Gazette, make it compulsory for the sellers of goods or article notified under sub-section (*1*) to be sold only through certified sales outlets fulfilling such conditions as may be determined by regulations.

(4) The Bureau may, by an order, grant, renew, suspend or cancel certification of Standard Mark or Hallmark of a jeweller or any other seller for sale of goods or articles notified under sub-section (*1*) in such manner as may be determined by regulations.

(5) The Bureau may establish, maintain and recognise testing and marking centres, including assaying and hallmarking centres, for conformity assessment and application of Standard Mark, including Hallmark, on goods or articles notified under sub-section (*1*), in a manner as may be specified by regulations.

(6) No testing and marking centre or assaying and hallmarking centre, other than the recognised by the Bureau, shall with respect to goods or articles notified under sub-section (*1*), use, affix, emboss, engrave, print or apply in

any manner the Standard Mark, including the Hallmark, or colourable imitation thereof, on any goods or article; and make any claim in relation to the use and application of a Standard Mark, including the Hallmark, through advertisements, sales promotion leaflets, price lists or the like.

(7) Every recognised testing and marking centre, including assaying and hallmarking centre, shall use or apply Standard Mark on good or articles notified under sub-section (*1*), including Hallmark on precious metal articles, after accurately determining the conformity of the same in a manner as may be specified.

(8) No recognised testing and marking centre, including assaying and hallmarking centre, shall, notwithstanding that it has been recognised under sub-section (*5*), use or apply in relation to any goods or article notified under sub-section (*1*) a Standard Mark, including Hallmark, or any colourable imitation thereof, unless such goods or article conforms to the relevant standard.

15. Prohibition to import, sell, exhibit, etc.

(*1*) No person shall import, distribute, sell, store or exhibit for sale, any goods or article under sub-section (*1*) of section 14, except under certification from the Bureau.

(2) No person, other than that certified by the Bureau, shall sell or display or offer to sell goods or articles that are notified under sub-section (*3*) of section 14 and marked with the Standard Mark, including Hallmark and claim in relation to the Standard Mark, including Hallmark, through advertisements, sales promotion leaflets, price lists or the like.

(3) No certified jeweller or seller shall sell or display or offer to sell any notified goods or articles, notwithstanding that he has been granted certification, with the Standard Mark, including Hallmark, or any colourable imitation thereof, unless such goods or article is marked with a Standard Mark or Hallmark, in a manner as may be specified by regulations, and unless such goods or article conforms to the relevant standard.

16. Central Government to direct compulsory use of Standard Mark.

(*1*) If the Central Government is of the opinion that it is necessary or expedient so to do in the public interest or for the protection of human, animal or plant health, safety of the environment, or prevention of unfair trade practices, or national security, it may, after consulting the Bureau, by an order published in the Official Gazette, notify—

(a) goods or article of any scheduled industry, process, system or service; or

(b) essential requirements to which such goods, article, process, system or service,

which shall conform to a standard and direct the use of the Standard Mark under a licence or certificate of conformity as compulsory on such goods, article, process, system or service.

Explanation.—For the purpose of this sub-section,—

(i) the expression "scheduled industry" shall have the meaning assigned to it in the Industries (Development and Regulation) Act, 1951(65 of 1951.);

(ii) it is hereby clarified that essential requirements are requirements, expressed in terms of the parameters to be achieved or requirements of standard in technical terms that effectively ensure that any goods, article, process, system or service meet the objective of health, safety and environment.

(*2*) The Central Government may, by an order authorise Bureau or any other agency having necessary accreditation or recognition and valid approval to certify and enforce conformity to the relevant standard or prescribed essential requirements under sub-section (*1*).

17. Prohibition to manufacture, sell, etc., certain goods without Standard Mark.

(*1*) No person shall manufacture, import, distribute, sell, hire, lease, store or exhibit for sale any such goods, article, process, system or service under sub-section (*1*) of section 16—

(a) without a Standard Mark, except under a valid licence; or

(b) notwithstanding that he has been granted a license, apply a Standard Mark, unless such goods, article, process, system or service conforms to the relevant standard or prescribed essential requirements.

(2) No person shall make a public claim, through advertisements, sales promotion leaflets, price lists or the like, that his goods, article, process, system or service conforms to an Indian standard or make such a declaration on the goods or article, without having a valid certificate of conformity or licence from the Bureau or any other authority approved by the Central Government under sub-section (*2*) of section 16.

(3) No person shall use or apply or purport to use or apply in any manner, in the manufacture, distribution, sale, hire, lease or exhibit or offer for sale of any goods, article, process, system or service, or in the title of any patent or in any trade mark or design, a Standard Mark or any colourable imitation thereof, except under a valid licence from the Bureau.

18. Obligations of licence holder, seller, etc.

(*1*) The licence holder shall, at all times, remain responsible for conformance of the goods, articles, processes, systems or services carrying the Standard Mark.

(2) It shall be the responsibility of the distributor or the seller, as the case may be, to ensure that goods, articles, processes, systems or services carrying the Standard Mark are purchased from certified body or licence holder.

(3) It shall be the responsibility of the seller before the goods or article is sold or offered to be sold or exhibited or offered for sale to ensure that—

- (a) goods, articles, processes, systems or services carrying the Standard Mark bear the requisite labels and marking details, as specified by the Bureau from time to time;
- (b) the marking and labelling requirements on the product or covering is displayed in a manner that has been specified by the Bureau.

(4) Every certified body or licence holder shall supply to the Bureau with such information and with such samples of any material or substance used in relation to any goods, article, process, system or service, as the case may be, as the Bureau may require for monitoring its quality and for the recovery of the fee as may be prescribed in the certificate of conformity or the licence.

(5) (*a*) The Bureau may make such inspection and take such samples of any material or substance as may be necessary to see whether any goods, article, process, system or service, in relation to which a Standard Mark has been used, conforms to the requirements of the relevant standard or whether the Standard Mark has been properly used in relation to any goods, article, process, system or service with or without a licence.

(*b*) The Bureau may publicise the results of its findings and the directions given in pursuance thereof.

(6) If the Bureau is satisfied under the provisions of sub-sections (*4*) and (*5*) that the goods, articles, processes, systems or services in relation to which a

Standard Mark has been used do not conform to the requirements of the relevant standard, the Bureau may direct the certified body or licence holder or his representative to stop the supply and sale of non- conforming goods or articles and recall the non-conforming goods or articles that have already been supplied or offered for sale and bear such mark from the market or any such place from where they are likely to be offered for sale or prohibit to provide the service.

(7) Where a certified body or licence holder or his representative has sold goods, articles, processes, system or services, which bear a Standard Mark or any colourable imitation thereof, which do not conform to the relevant standard, the Bureau shall direct the certified body or licence holder or his representative to—

- (a) repair or replace or reprocess the standard marked goods, article, process, system or service in a manner as may be specified; or
- (b) pay compensation to the consumer as may be prescribed by the Bureau; or
- (c) be liable for the injury caused by non-conforming goods or article, which bears a Standard Mark, as per the provisions of section 31.

CHAPTER IV

FINANCE, ACCOUNTS AND AUDIT

19. Financial Management of Bureau of Indian Standards.

The Central Government may, after due appropriation made by Parliament by law in this behalf, make to the Bureau grants and loans of such sums of money as the Government may consider necessary.

20. Fund of Bureau.

(*1*) There shall be constituted a fund to be called the Bureau of Indian Standards fund and there shall be credited thereto—

- (a) any grants and loans made to the Bureau by the Central Government;
- (b) all fees and charges received by the Bureau under this Act;
- (c) all fines received by the Bureau;
- (d) all sums received by the Bureau from such other sources as may be decided upon by the Central Government.

(2) The fund shall be applied for meeting—

(a) the salary, allowances and other remuneration of the members, Director General, officers and other employees of the Bureau;

(b) expenses of the Bureau in the discharge of its functions under the Act; and

(c) expenses on objects and for purposes authorised by this Act:

Provided that the fines received in clause (*c*) of sub-section (*1*) shall be used for consumer awareness, consumer protection and promotion of quality of goods, articles, processes, system or services in the country.

21. Borrowing powers of Bureau.

(*1*) The Bureau may, with the consent of the Central Government or in accordance with the terms of any general or special authority given to it by the Central Government, borrow money from any source as it may deem fit for discharging all or any of its functions under this Act.

(*2*) The Central Government may guarantee in such manner as it thinks fit, the repayment of the principal and the payment of interest thereon with respect to the loans borrowed by Bureau under sub-section (*1*).

22. Budget.

The Bureau shall prepare, in such form and at such time in each financial year as may be prescribed, its budget for the next financial year, showing the estimated receipts and expenditure of the Bureau and forward the same to the Central Government.

23. Annual report.

(*1*) The Bureau shall prepare, in such form and at such time in each financial year as may be prescribed, its annual report, giving a full account of its activities during the previous financial year, and submit a copy thereof to the Central Government.

(*2*) The Central Government shall cause the annual report to be laid, as soon as may be after it is received, before each House of Parliament.

24. Accounts and audit.

(*1*) The Bureau shall maintain proper accounts and other relevant records and prepare an annual statement of accounts, in such form as may be prescribed by the Central Government in consultation with the Comptroller and Auditor-General of India.

(2) The accounts of the Bureau shall be audited by the Comptroller and Auditor-General of India at such intervals as may be specified by him and any expenditure incurred in connection with such audit shall be payable by the Bureau to the Comptroller and Auditor- General of India.

(3) The Comptroller and Auditor-General of India and any person appointed by him in connection with the audit of the accounts of the Bureau shall have the same rights and privileges and the authority in connection with such audit as the Comptroller and Auditor- General of India generally has in connection with the audit of Government accounts and, in particular, shall have the right to demand the production of books, accounts, connected vouchers and other documents and papers and to inspect any office of the Bureau.

(4) The accounts of the Bureau as certified by the Comptroller and Auditor-General of India or any other person appointed by him in this behalf together with the audit report thereon shall be forwarded annually to the Central Government and that Government shall cause the same to be laid before each House of Parliament.

CHAPTER V
MISCELLANEOUS

25. Power of Central Government to issue directions.

(*1*) Without prejudice to the foregoing provisions of this Act, the Bureau shall, in the exercise of its powers or the performance of its functions under this Act, be bound by such directions on questions of policy as the Central Government may give in writing to it from time to time:

Provided that the Bureau shall, as far as practicable, be given an opportunity to express its views before any direction is given under this sub-section.

(2) The decision of the Central Government whether a question is one of policy or not shall be final.

(3) The Central Government may take such other action as may be necessary for the promotion, monitoring and management of quality of goods, articles, processes, systems and services and to protect the interests of consumers and various other stakeholders and notify any other goods, articles, processes, systems and services for the purpose of sub-section (*1*) of section 16.

26. Restriction on use of name of Bureau and Indian Standard.

(*1*) No person shall, with a view to deceive or likely to deceive the public, use without the previous permission of the Bureau,—

(a) any name which so nearly resembles the name of the Bureau as to deceive or likely to deceive the public or the name which contains the expression "Indian Standard" or any abbreviation thereof; or

(b) any title of any patent or mark or trade mark or design, in relation to any goods, article, process, system or service, containing the expressions "Indian Standard" or "Indian Standard Specification" or any abbreviation of such expressions.

(2) Notwithstanding anything contained in any law for the time being in force, no registering authority shall—

(a) register any company, firm or other body of persons which bears any name or mark; or

(b) register a trade mark or design which bears any name or mark; or

(c) grant a patent, in respect of an invention, which bears a title containing any name or mark,

if the use of such name or mark is in contravention of sub-section (*1*).

(3) If any question arises before a registering authority whether the use of any name or mark is in contravention of sub-section (*1*), the registering authority may refer the question to the Central Government whose decision thereon shall be final.

27. Appointment and powers of certification officers.

(*1*) The Bureau may appoint as many certification officers as may be necessary for the purpose of inspection whether any goods, article, process, system or service in relation to which the Standard Mark has been used conforms to the relevant standard or whether the Standard Mark has been properly used in relation to any goods, article, process, system or service with or without licence, and for performing such other functions as may be assigned to them.

(2) Subject to any rules made under this Act, a certification officer shall have power to—

(a) inspect any operation carried on in connection with any goods, article, process, system or service in relation to which the Standard Mark has been used; and

(b) take samples of any goods or article or of any material or substance used in any goods, article, process, system or service, in relation to which the Standard Mark has been used.

(3) Every certification officer shall be furnished by the Bureau with a certificate of appointment as a certification officer, and the certificate shall, on demand, be produced by the certification officer.

(4) Every certified body or licence holder shall—

(a) provide reasonable facilities to certification officer to enable him to discharge the duties imposed on him;

(b) inform certification officer or the Bureau of any change in the conditions which were declared or verified by the certification officer or the Bureau at the time of grant of certificate of conformity or licence.

(5) Any information obtained by a certification officer or the Bureau from any statement made or information supplied or any evidence given or from inspection made under the provisions of this Act shall be treated as confidential:

Provided that nothing shall apply to the disclosure of any information for the purpose of prosecution and protection of interest of consumers.

28. Power to search and seizure.

(*1*) If the certification officer has reason to believe that any goods or articles, process, system or service in relation to which the contravention of section 11 or sub-sections (*6*) or (*8*) of section 14 or section 15 or section 17 has taken place are secreted in any place, premises or vehicle, he may enter into and search such place, premises or vehicle for such goods or articles, process, system or service, as the case may be.

(2) Where, as a result of any search made under sub-section (*1*), any goods or article, process, system or service has been found in relation to which contravention of section 11 or sub-sections (*6*) or (*8*) of section 14 or section 15 or section 17 has taken place, the certification officer may seize such goods or article and other material and documents which, in his opinion will be useful for, or relevant to any proceeding under this Act:

Provided that where it is not practicable to seize any such goods or article or material or document, the certification officer may serve on the owner an order that he shall not remove, part with, or otherwise deal with, the goods or article or material or document except with the previous permission of the certification officer.

(3) The provision of the Code of Criminal Procedure, 1973(2 of 1974.), relating to searches and seizures shall, so far as may be, apply to every search or seizure made under this section.

29. Penalty for contravention.

(*1*) Any person who contravenes the provisions of section 11 or sub-section (*1*) of section 26 shall be punishable with fine which may extend to five lakh rupees.

(2) Any person who contravenes the provisions of sub-sections (*6*) or (*8*) of section 14 or section 15 shall be punishable with imprisonment for a term which may extend to one year or with fine which shall not be less than one lakh rupees, but may extend up to five times the value of goods or articles produced or sold or offered to be sold or affixed or applied with a Standard Mark including Hallmark, or with both:

Provided that where the value of goods or articles produced or sold or offered to be sold cannot be determined, it shall be presumed that one year's production was in such contravention and the annual turnover in the previous financial year shall be taken as the value of goods or articles for such contravention.

(3) Any person who contravenes the provisions of section 17 shall be punishable with imprisonment for a term which may extend up to two years or with fine which shall not be less than two lakh rupees for the first contravention and not be less than five lakh rupees for the second and subsequent contraventions, but may extend up to ten times the value of goods or articles produced or sold or offered to be sold or affixed or applied with a Standard Mark, including Hallmark, or with both:

Provided that where the value of goods or articles produced or sold or offered to be sold cannot be determined, it shall be presumed that one year's production was in such contravention and the annual turnover in the previous financial year shall be taken as the value of goods or articles for such contravention.

(4) The offence under sub-section (*3*) shall be cognizable.

30. Offences by companies.

Where an offence under this Act has been committed by a company, every director, manager, secretary or other officer of the company who, at the time the offence was committed, was in charge of and was responsible to the company for the conduct of the business of the company, or authorised representative of the company as well as the company, shall be deemed to be guilty of the offence and shall be liable to be proceeded against and punished accordingly, irrespective of the fact that the offence has been committed with or without the consent or connivance of, or is attributable to any neglect on the part of any director, manager, secretary or other officer of the company, or authorised representative of the company.

Explanation.—For the purposes of this section,—

(a) "company" means a body corporate and includes a firm or other association of individuals; and

(b) "director", in relation to a firm, means a partner in the firm.

31. Compensation for non- conforming goods.

Where a holder of licence or certificate of conformity or his representative has sold any goods, article, process, system or service, which bears a Standard Mark not conforming to the relevant standard, or with colourable imitation, the certified body or licence holder or his representative shall be liable to compensate the consumer for the injury caused by such non-conforming goods, article, process, system or service in such manner as may be prescribed.

32. Cognizance of offence by courts.

(*1*) No court inferior to that of a Metropolitan Magistrate or a Judicial Magistrate of the first class, specially empowered in this behalf, shall try any offence punishable under this Act.

(2) No court shall take cognizance of any offence punishable under this Act save on a complaint made by—

(a) or under the authority of the Bureau; or

(b) any police officer, not below the rank of deputy superintendent of police or equivalent; or

(c) any authority notified under sub-section (*2*) of section 16; or

(d) any officer empowered under the authority of the Government; or

(e) any consumer; or

(f) any association.

(3) Any police officer not below the rank of deputy superintendent of police or equivalent, may, if he is satisfied that any of the offences referred to in sub-section (*3*) of section 29 has been, is being, or is likely to be, committed,

search and seize without warrant, the goods, die, block, machine, plate, other instruments or things involved in committing the offence, wherever found, and all the articles so seized shall, as soon as practicable, be produced before a Magistrate as prescribed under sub-section (*1*).

(4) The court may direct that any property in respect of which the contravention has taken place shall be forfeited to the Bureau.

(5) The court may direct that any fine, in whole or any part thereof, payable under the provisions of this Act, shall be payable to the Bureau.

33. Compounding of offence.

(*1*) Notwithstanding anything contained in the Code of Criminal Procedure, 1973 (2 of 1974.), any offence committed for the first time, punishable under this Act, not being an offence punishable with imprisonment only, or with imprisonment and also with fine, may, either before or after the institution of any prosecution, be compounded by an officer so authorised by the Director General, in such manner as may be prescribed:

Provided that the sum so specified shall not in any case exceed the maximum amount of the fine which may be imposed under section 29 for the offence so compounded; and any second or subsequent offence committed after the expiry of a period of three years from the date on which the offence was previously compounded shall be deemed to be an offence committed for the first time.

(2) Every officer referred to in sub-section (*1*) shall exercise the powers to compound an offence, subject to the direction, control and supervision of the Bureau.

(3) Every application for the compounding of an offence shall be made in such manner as may be prescribed.

(4) Where any offence is compounded before the institution of any prosecution, no prosecution shall be instituted in relation to such offence against the offender in relation to whom the offence is so compounded.

(5) Where the composition of any offence is made after the institution of any prosecution, such composition shall be brought to the notice of the court in which the prosecution is pending in writing by the officer referred to in sub-section (*1*), and on such notice of the composition of the offence being given and its acceptance by the court, the person against whom the offence is so compounded shall be discharged.

34. Appeal.

(*1*) Any person aggrieved by an order made under section 13 or sub-section (*4*) of section 14 or section 17 of this Act may prefer an appeal to Director General of the Bureau within such period as prescribed.

(2) No appeal shall be admitted if it is preferred after the expiry of the period prescribed therefor:

Provided that an appeal may be admitted after the expiry of the period prescribed therefor if the appellant satisfies the Director General that he had sufficient cause for not preferring the appeal within the prescribed period.

(3) Every appeal made under this section shall be made in such form and shall be accompanied by a copy of the order appealed against and by such fees as may be prescribed.

(4) The procedure for disposing of an appeal shall be such as may be prescribed:

Provided that before disposing of an appeal, the appellant shall be given a reasonable opportunity of being heard.

(5) The Director General may *suo motu* or on an application made in the manner prescribed review the order passed by any officer to whom the power has been delegated by him.

(6) Any person aggrieved by an order made under sub-section (*1*) or sub-section (*5*) may prefer an appeal to the Central Government having administrative control of the Bureau within such period as may be prescribed.

35. Members, officers and employees of Bureau to be public servants.

All members, officers and other employees of the Bureau shall be deemed, when acting or purporting to act in pursuance of any of the provisions of this Act, to be public servants within the meaning of section 21 of the Indian Penal Code (45 of 1860.).

36. Protection of action taken in good faith.

No suit, prosecution or other legal proceeding shall lie against the Government or any officer of the Government or any member, officer or other employee of the Bureau for anything which is in done or intended to be done in good faith under this Act or the rules or regulations made thereunder.

37. Authentication of orders and other instruments of Bureau.

All orders and decisions of, and all other instruments issued by, the Bureau shall be authenticated by the signature of such officer or officers as may be authorised by the Bureau in this behalf.

38. Power to make rules.

The Central Government may, by notification in the Official Gazette, make rules for carrying out the purposes of this Act.

39. Power to make regulations.

The Executive Committee may, with the previous approval of the Central Government, by notification in the Official Gazette, make regulations consistent with this Act and the rules to carry out the purposes of this Act.

40. Rules and regulations to be laid before Parliament.

Every rule and every regulation made under this Act shall be laid, as soon as may be after it is made, before each House of Parliament, while it is in session, for a total period of thirty days which may be comprised in one session or in two or more successive sessions, and if, before the expiry of the session immediately following the session or the successive sessions aforesaid, both Houses agree in making any modification in the rule or regulation or both Houses agree that the rule or regulation should not be made, the rule or regulation shall thereafter have effect only in such modified form or be of no effect, as the case may be; so, however, that any such modification or annulment shall be without prejudice to the validity of anything previously done under that rule or regulation.

41. Act not to affect operation of certain Acts.

Nothing in this Act shall affect the operation of the Agricultural Produce (Grading and Marking) Act, 1937 (1 of 1937.) or the Drugs and Cosmetics Act, 1940 (23 of 1940.), or any other law for the time being in force, which deals with any standardisation or quality control of any goods, article, process, system or service.

42. Power to remove difficulties.

(*1*) If any difficulty arises in giving effect to the provisions of this Act, the Central Government may, by order, published in the Official Gazette, make such provisions not inconsistent with the provisions of this Act as may appear to be necessary for removing the difficulty:

Provided that no order shall be made under this section after the expiry of two years from the commencement of this Act.

(*2*) Every order made under this section shall be laid, as soon as may be after it is made, before each House of Parliament.

43. Repeal and savings.

(*1*) The Bureau of Indian Standards Act, 1986 (63 of 1986.) is hereby repealed.

(2) Notwithstanding such repeal, anything done or any action taken or purported to have done or taken including any rule, regulation, notification, scheme, specification, Indian Standard, Standard Mark, inspection order or notice made, issued or adopted, or any appointment, or declaration made or any licence, permission, authorisation or exemption granted or any document or instrument executed or direction given or any proceedings taken or any penalty or fine imposed under the Act hereby repealed shall, insofar as it is not inconsistent with the provisions of this Act, be deemed to have been done or taken under the corresponding provisions of this Act.

(3) The mention of particular matters in sub-section (*2*) shall not be held to prejudice or affect the general application of section 6 of the General Clauses Act, 1897 (10 of 1897.) with regard to the effect of repeal.

Appendix - 2

BIS Locations

(As extracted from BIS Annual Report 2021-22)

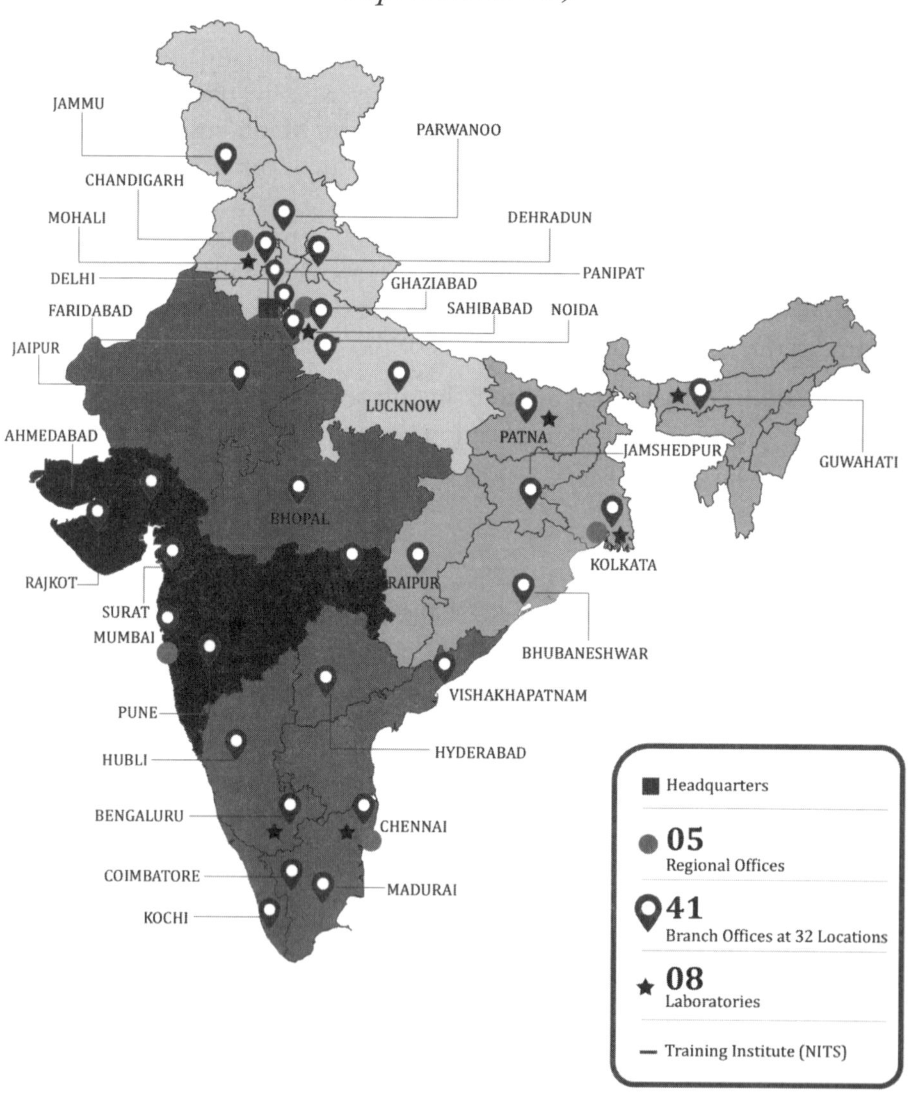

Appendix - 3

BROAD PILLARS OF QUALITY

(As extracted from Indian National Strategy for Standardization - INSS document)

Pillar 1

Pillar 2

Pillar 3

Pillar 4

Appendix - 4

KEY STANDARDIZATION AREAS

(As extracted from Standards National Action Plan - SNAP 2022-27)

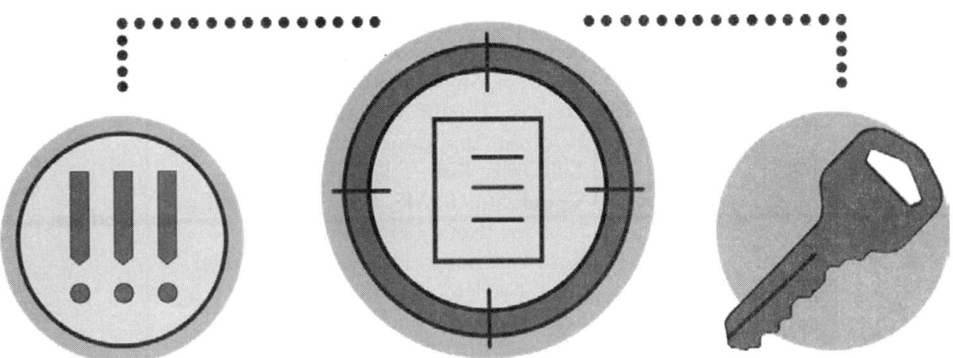

Taking into account the outcome of various stakeholder consultations undertaken while framing the Standards National Action Plan 2022, inputs from the Strategic Road Maps of each of the Division Councils of BIS, the identified sectoral priorities and analysis of the national socio- economic requirements, key subject areas of national standardisation to be taken up by BIS in the next five years along with their priorities have been identified and given in **Annex A**.

Important sectors of the national economy were analysed on the basis of their contribution to national GDP and to trade and various policy level imperatives set by NITI Aayog and Central Ministries were examined to define sector-wise national economic priorities. To set the social priorities, a study of the NITI Aayog reports, various developmental programmes and policy directives of Central Ministries, world body reports on India and UN SDG 2030 was carried out along with the impact of these on various aspects like sustainability, health, safety, environment, security, population, employment, social empowerment and inclusivity, gender equality, consumer protection, etc. Based on the above, combined socio-economic priorities as applicable were then arrived at. The priority of a standardisation subject has been identified as high, medium and low and has been arrived at depending on socio-economic priority of the relevant sector and the transcending priority considerations as defined in this document.

Detailed work programmes would be prepared by the concerned technical committees elaborating the specific subjects from these identified standardisation areas. Where necessary and based on a comprehensive assessment by technical committees, other subjects of standardisation to supplement these would also be identified and progressively included in the work programme and executed through Annual Action Plans.

SECTOR	FIELD	SUBJECT AREA	PRIORITY
Agriculture	Agricultural Equipment and Machinery	Drones used in agriculture (Spraying, Yeild Estimation, Nutrient Application, Seeding and Irrigation)	High
		Use of Artificial Intelligence (AI) / Internet of Things (IoT) in agriculture, Block Chain in agriculture	High
		Test procedures for Potato Combine Harvester, Trash Multure, Trash Shredder, Sugarcane Ratoon Management Devices, Tractor Mounted Sprayers, Fertilizer Applicator for Sugarcane, Strip Till Drills, Roto Till Drills, Happy Seeder, Super SMS, Power Harrow (Rice Harrow), Rotary Plow/Puddler, Roto Cultivator, Heavy Duty Puddlers, Super Seeder, Self-Propelled Weeders, Self-Propelled Forage Harvester (3/4 Wheels), Ridger Tiller, Disc Mower, Electrostatic Sprayer, Soil Scanner and Pest Scanner	Medium
		Performance requirement and test methods for electrical tractors	Medium
		Performance requirement standards for alternate fuel and dual fuel use in tractors	Medium
		Testing procedure and performance parameters related to HST /CVT /IVT Transmissions	Medium
		Functional safety standard on agriculture machines	Medium
		Conversion of AIS published under CMVR and OECD standards into Indian Standards	Medium
	Agricultural Management	Guidelines for contract farming and commercial farming	Medium
		Guidelines for Hydroponic Farming	High
		Guidelines for Vertical Agriculture	Medium
	Agriculture Inputs	New pesticide formulations	Medium
		Bio- pesticides	High
		Botanical Pesticides	High

SECTOR	FIELD	SUBJECT AREA	PRIORITY
		Nano Fertilizer	Medium
		Bio-stimulants	Medium
		Label claim based innovative fertilizer formulations	Medium
		Chemically inert, environmentally safe, chelated micronutrients for use in agriculture	Medium
Audio Visual Services	Media and Entertainment Services	Cinema Theatres	Low
		Radio Stations	Low
		Event Management	Low
		Sound and Music in M&E Sector	Low
		New Media Services	Low
Basic Services	Basic Standards on Services	Service Classification	Low
		Service Communication	Low
		Service Contract	Low
		Service Monitoring	Low
		Service performance indicators and measurements	Low
		Customer expectation and perception measurement	Low
		Service use/Perception data analytics	Low
		Service Delivery Channels – Modes of communication / delivery/customer interaction	Low
		Service process risks	Low
		Service Level Agreements	Low
		Use of ICT in services	High
		Customer data security	High
		Human Resource – Specific skill/attributes requirements for services	Low
		Template for vertical services standards	Low
Building, Constructi	Building Materials and Components	New and innovative building materials (including	Medium

SECTOR	FIELD	SUBJECT AREA	PRIORITY
on and Urban Development		their test methods)	
		New water proofing compounds and techniques	Medium
		New plastic piping materials	Medium
		Laboratory furniture	Low
		Clinker from alternate sources	Medium
		Performance based approach in doors and windows	Low
		Pervious concrete	Low
		Soil testing and test equipment	High
		Hand book on water proofing	Low
		Tactile Ground Surface Indicator (TGSI)	High
		Metal framing components	High
		Reinforcing and prestressing steel including fibre reinforced polymer bars and galvanized steel bars	High
		Water storage tanks	Medium
		Sewerage ancillary structures like manholes, gratings, etc.	Medium
Building, Construction and Urban Development	Building Materials and Components	Sanitary appliances and water fittings	High
		Updation of standards for lignocellulosic panel products	Low
	Construction Practices	Mechanization in construction (mechanized tunneling, trenchless technology)	Low
		Geophysical investigation including sonic logging and cross-hole seismic tomography	Low
		Ground improvement techniques	High
		Restoration and maintenance of stone masonry, heritage and other structures	Medium
		Safety during construction	Medium
		Safety in demolition	High

SECTOR	FIELD	SUBJECT AREA	PRIORITY
		Contract management	Medium
	Construction Technologies	Prefabricated construction including 3D printing, Prefabricated and Prefinished Volumetric Construction and Design for Manufacturing and Assembly	Medium
		Digital technologies in construction including Building Information Modelling	Medium
		Tensile fabric/membrane structures	Medium
		Pre-engineered building	High
	Fire Safety	Fire and life safety audit	High
		Fire safety in hospitals, hotels and shopping malls	High
		Fire safety in various manufacturing industries (e.g. pharmaceutical, electrical and electronics, automobile, etc)	High
		Inspection, testing and maintenance of fire protection systems	High
	Planning and Housing	Urban and rural habitat planning	Medium
		Development control rules	Medium
	Public Health Engineering	Updation of standards for public health engineering	Medium
	Structural Design and Safety	Assessment, rehabilitation and maintenance (structural health monitoring) of buildings and structures including seismic instrumentation and testing	Medium
		Safety of external building fabric impacted by wind borne debris	High
Building, Constructi on and Urban Developme nt	Structural Design and Safety	Structural design using stainless steel	Low
		Updation of structural design codes (concrete, steel, cold-formed light gauge steel, tall buildings, shallow and pile foundations, transmission line towers and their foundation)	High
		Updation of standards relating to	High

SECTOR	FIELD	SUBJECT AREA	PRIORITY
		earthquake resistant design based upon revised Probabilistic Seismic Hazard Map (PSHM) of India	
		Static and dynamic tests for pile foundations	Medium
		Foundation for solar PVs	Medium
		New foundation systems (for example combined piled raft system)	High
		Design of breakwater structures; components of ports and harbours	Medium
		Universal design for accessibility	High
		Guidelines on sustainable materials/solutions and green and net zero buildings	Medium
		Sustainable water supply and sanitation including non-sewered sanitation system	Medium
Business and Legal Services	Business Services	Security services	Medium
		Business Process Management	Medium
		Business consultants	Medium
		Ageing societies / Senior care	High
		Management consultancy	Medium
Chemicals and Petro-chemicals	Dyes and Dyestuff	Dyestuff	Medium
	Environmental labelling	Green labelling of soaps and detergents	High
	Inorganic chemicals	Speciality chemicals	Medium
	Printing Inks	Inks for sensitive applications like pharma/hygiene products/cosmetics /toys /diapers	Medium
		Eco-friendly inks	Medium
		Non-Intentionally Added Substances (NIAS) in inks	Low
		Positive list of constituents for inks	Low
	Surface Protection	Fluororesin based coatings	Low

SECTOR	FIELD	SUBJECT AREA	PRIORITY
	Coatings	Fire retardant paint coatings	Low
		Nano composite material based paints	Low
		Coatings and varnishes	Medium
	Thermal insulation	New age thermal insulation materials	Medium
Constructi on and related Services	Construction and related Engineering Services	Geotechnical investigation services	Medium
		Project management services	Medium
		Valuation of immovable properties	Medium
		Construction and demolition waste management services.	High
		Conservation of heritage structures	Medium
		Facility management of buildings	Medium
		Structural design and proof checking consultancy services.	Medium
		Structural auditing, maintenance and retrofitting services	Medium
Education Services	Higher Educational, Skill Development and related Services	Coaching centre services	Medium
		Campus facilities and accommodation services	Medium
		Skill development services	Medium
	School Education and related Services	E- Learning services	Medium
		Foundational learning services	Medium
Electrical Appliances, Equipment and Lighting	Appliances	Washing machines	Medium
		Induction hobs	Medium
		Various fans and regulators (revision)	Medium
	Equipment	Welding Additive Equipment	Medium
	Luminaries	Ultra-Violet germicidal devices	High
		Grounded recessed luminaries	Medium
		Luminaries for specific application (e.g. swimming pool, clinical areas of hospitals, etc)	Medium
		Extra-Low-Voltage lighting systems for	Medium

SECTOR	FIELD	SUBJECT AREA	PRIORITY
		ELV light sources.	
		National Lighting Code (revision)	High
		Drone lighting	Medium
		Guidelines for lighting specific locations (e.g. interior illumination, public thoroughfares, etc)	Medium
	Switchgear	LV switchgear & Controlgear	Medium
		DC switchgears	Medium
Electrical Energy and Power	Batteries	Secondary batteries - Reuse of secondary batteries	High
	Grid Integration	Interconnection and interoperability of Distributed Energy Resources	Medium
	Smart Grid	Cyber security (Security risk assessment and industrial automation and control system security)	High
	Transformers	Guidelines for repairing transformers	Medium
		Converter Transformers	Medium
		Transformer for solar application.	High
SECTOR	**FIELD**	SUBJECT AREA	PRIORITY
Electrical Energy and Power	Transformers	Voltage regulation distribution transformers.	Medium
		Transformer installation, commissioning and maintenance (revision)	Medium
Electronics	Electronics Products and Manufacturing	PCB	Medium
		Energy consumption rating	High
		Component manufacturing	High
		Semiconductor manufacturing	High
		Wearable devices	High
		E-waste management	High
Environm-ent	Carbon Accounting	GHG emission estimation and Carbon Footprint of specific sectors	Medium
	Carbon Capture	Carbon capture, use and storage	Medium

SECTOR	FIELD	SUBJECT AREA	PRIORITY
	and Sequestration		
	Circular Economy	Guidance for specific sectors on Circular Economy	High
	Environment Management	Guide for implementation of EMS	Medium
		EMS related tools.	Medium
	Environmental Rating	Product Category Rules	Medium
	Nuclear materials for peaceful application	Naturally occurring radioactive materials and contaminants in geological, biological and environmental matrices (water, soil, etc)	Medium
		Limits of radioactive materials	Medium
	Packaging - Sustainable packaging	Safe, secure and sustainable paper packaging	Medium
		LCA of packaging materials	Medium
	Waste Management	Guidelines on discharge effluents from various sources	Medium
		Guidelines on important discharge parameters	Medium
		Reuse/recycling of treated used water	Medium
		Residue management in treatment plants	Medium
		Zero Liquid Discharge	Medium
		Guidelines for discharge of emerging contaminants	Medium
		Discharge standards for sewage	Medium
	Water Quality	Safe drinking water for travel	Medium
		IoT based smart water quality monitoring and management	Medium
		Source water quality monitoring (Online)	Medium
		Water quality monitoring network	Medium
		Non-potable use of water	Medium
		Water standards – updating limits of radioactivity	Medium

SECTOR	FIELD	SUBJECT AREA	PRIORITY
Environm-ental and Related Services	Biodiversity	Biodiversity assessment	Medium
		Traditional knowledge including Ayush	Medium
		Biological invasive	Medium
		Sustainable forest management	Medium
		Ecosystem services and valuation	Low
		Protection of aquatic ecosystem	Medium
	Drinking Water Supply, Wastewater and Storm Water Systems & Services	Management of assets of water utility	High
		Emergency/Disaster management system in water utility	High
		Water loss investigations in drinking water supply system	High
		Provision for alternate water supply during crisis	High
	Environmental Services	Greenbelt development and management	Medium
		Assessment of environmental monitoring services	Medium
		Street and public facility cleaning services	Medium
		Forest fire management	Medium
Ferrous and Non-Ferrous Metals	Aluminium and Aluminium alloys	Aluminium stock	Medium
		Aluminium hard alloy plates, sheets and coils	Medium
	Feedstock for Iron	Feedstock for Iron	Medium
	Pipes, Tubes and Sections	Electric Fusion Welded stainless pipes for high temperature applications	Medium
		Stainless steel pipes and tubes for various applications	Medium
		Single wall copper and zinc coated steel refrigerator condenser tubes	Medium
		Pipes and tubes for transportation of Bio-PNG	High
		Steel sections for architectural applications	Medium
		Steel pipes and tubes for solar applications	High

SECTOR	FIELD	SUBJECT AREA	PRIORITY
		Fire resistant steel pipe and tubes	Medium
	Powder Metallurgy	Tungsten base heavy alloys	Medium
		Powder Additive Manufacturing (3D Printing)	Medium
		Un-notched Charpy Impact Test for powder metallurgy products	Low
		Molybdenum specific material for high temperature sintering furnace	Low
	Refractories	Carbon bricks refractories	Low
		Silica refractory ramming mass	Low
	Stainless Steel	Triply material for utensils	Medium
		Stainless steel structural steel	Medium
		Stainless steel ingots/billets/blooms for re-rolling	Medium
	Steel and Alloys Steels	Zn-Al-Mg coated steels	Medium
		Wear and abrasion resistant steel	Medium
		Hot rolled steels for Line Pipes	Medium
		Continuous Galvanizing Grade (CGG) Zinc alloys	Medium
		Induction tempered spring steel wire	Medium
Ferrous and Non-Ferrous Metals	Test Methods	Eddy current testing of steel wires	Low
		Test methods for mechanical property evaluation using miniature specimens at ambient and high temperature conditions under static and acyclic loading	Low
		Characterization of Intrinsic Threshold Stress Intensity Range	Low
		Gammatographic evaluation of integrity of shielding structures	Low
		Non-Destructive fineness confirmation of precious metal by ED-XRF	Medium
		Chemical analysis by instrumental methods	Medium
	Welding Electrodes	Flux cored (Tubular) electrodes and rods	Medium

SECTOR	FIELD	SUBJECT AREA	PRIORITY
		for Metal Arc Welding of stainless steel, Heat resisting steel and Low alloy steel	
Financial Services	Banking and Financial Services	Interfaces of digital financial service providers	Medium
		Fintech services	Medium
		Insurance policy documents and declarations	Medium
Food and Food Processing	Food Analysis	Test method for identification of constituent oils in blended oil	Medium
		Methodology for manufacturing of biomolecules (in food and agriculture) using genetically modified microorganisms	Medium
		Test methods for detection of microplastics in food items	High
		Molecular based methods for food safety	Low
		Validation of rapid testing kits through specified criteria/ SoP for formulation of standards	Medium
	Food Processing Equipment and Machinery	Test code of equipment and machinery related to Cold Plasma Technology	Medium
		Horizontal standards on energy efficient food processing equipment and machinery	Medium
	Food Products	Minimally processed fruits and vegetables	Medium
		Traditional food products manufactured by MSME sector	Medium
		Emerging packaged waters in the form of alkaline water, black water, fortified water, copper+, sparkling water, flavoured water etc.	Medium
		Fortified foods/ Enriched foods	High
		Fish cutlet and fish momo	Medium
		Virgin coconut oil	Medium
		Coconut copra	Medium
		Preserved chapatti	Medium

SECTOR	FIELD	SUBJECT AREA	PRIORITY
		Ripening chamber for fruits	Medium
		3-D printed food products	Medium
Food & Food Processing	Food Quality Assurance	GMP/ Food safety guidelines for tea, coffee & cocoa	High
		Food fraud - Pre-emptive methodologies	Medium
Health and Safety	Chemical Hazard	Guidelines on chemical hazards	Medium
	Occupational Health and Safety	Hazard identification and Risk assessment	Medium
		Quantitative risk assessment for chemical industries	Medium
		Computer risk model assessment	Medium
Healthcare	Forensic Sciences	Protocol for examination of a victim and accused of sexual assault	Medium
		Autopsy table	Low
	Health Informatics	Remote care monitoring	Medium
		Randomized Clinical Trials (RCT) of software as device	Medium
		Digital therapeutics	Medium
		Gene, Genome, Proteonics, Epigenetics	Medium
		Aayush (Process and RCT)	Medium
	Hospital Equipment	Sterilization processes	Medium
	Hospital Planning and Management	Hand hygiene performance and compliance	Medium
		Collection and transport of samples by medical laboratories	Medium
		Maintenance management of medical devices	Medium
		Medical air-conditioning systems	Medium
	Medical Biotechnology	Nanoparticle characterization systems	Low
	Medical Devices	Anaesthetic and resuscitation equipment (respiratory gas monitors, voice prostheses)	High

SECTOR	FIELD	SUBJECT AREA	PRIORITY
		Rehabilitation appliances and equipment (Club foot braces, folding cane, therapeutic footwear, standing frame, spinal and ankle foot orthoses, pressure relief cushions)	High
		Medical diagnostic kits (general and disease specific diagnostics)	High
		Dentistry equipment (cements, spoons and bone cutters, diamond rotary cutters, scalers and excavators, intra oral camera)	High
		ENT Instruments (ossicular reconstruction prosthesis, VNG machine)	High
		Neurosurgery instruments (Digital Reaction Time Apparatus, Algometer)	High
		Obstetric instruments (menstrual cups, IUCD, Biomarkers for semen exposure)	High
		Ophthalmic instruments (glaucoma drainage devices, Microsurgical Keratome Blade, ocular prosthesis), AR/VR in ophthalmic diagnostics and therapy	High
Healthcare	Medical Devices	Orthopaedic instrument and implants (arthroscopy system, non-active surgical implants, osteosynthesis implants, metal intramedullary nailing systems)	High
		Surgical instrument and implants (surgical mesh implants for hernia, surgical ligation devices, liposuction devices used in plastic surgery, cryoablation for cancer therapy, robotic surgical devices, AR/VR for surgical planning, electrosurgical unit, surgical training devices)	High
		Cardiovascular equipment (cardiac occluders, pericardial patch)	High
	Medical Laboratory Instruments	Laboratory ware (glass and plastic)	Low
		Medical laboratory analytical equipment and culture preparation instrument	Low

SECTOR	FIELD	SUBJECT AREA	PRIORITY
		Medical laboratory furniture	Low
		Ultrapure water purification system	Low
	Veterinary Science	Planning considerations for veterinary hospital and clinics	Low
		Veterinary instrument (catheter, IV cannula, endometrial forceps)	Low
Informat-ion Technology	Digital Technologies	Artificial Intelligence	Medium
		Internet of Things	Medium
		Blockchain and DLT	Medium
		Big Data	Medium
		Geographic Information System	Medium
	ICT	Metaverse	Medium
		Smart cities ICT aspects	Medium
	IT Security Techniques	Data privacy	High
		Cyber security	High
		Mobile security guidelines	High
	IT Services	Data maturity assessment and data governance	Medium
		Trustworthiness	Medium
		Digitally delivered services	Medium
		Natural Language Processing	Medium
		RFID/ Geo-tagging	Medium
IT and IT Enabled Services	IT and IT Enabled Services	Cloud services	Medium
		Digital signature services	Medium
	Retail, E-commerce and E-payments Services	E-commerce - principles and guidelines for self-governance	Medium
		E- subscription	Medium
Jute and Jute Products	Jute	Jute and allied fibres (ramie, hemp, flax, sunn, sisal, banana etc) and their related products	Low

SECTOR	FIELD	SUBJECT AREA	PRIORITY
	Jute Products	Jute sacking bags for various applications	Low
Leather and Leather Products	Footwear	Standards on therapeutic footwear	High
	Leather Materials and Allied Products	Sustainable manufacture of leather	High
		Carbon Foot Print of leather and tanning materials	High
		Leather - vocabulary	Medium
		Shorter-term biodegradability test	High
Machinery, Engineering and Manufactu-ring	Abrasives	Safety requirements for coated abrasive products	High
		Safety requirements for super abrasive products	Medium
	Arms and Ammunitions	12 bore breech loading shot gun single and double barrel including semi-sutomatic and 12 bore pump action gun	Medium
		0.25" bore revolver/ pistol	High
	Conveyor Belts	Pipe conveyor belts	High
		Energy saving conveyor belts	Medium
		Light weight conveyors and flat conveyor belts	High
		Hybrid conveyor belts	High
	Fuel Related Products	Green energy generation and storage related equipment (e.g. green hydrogen, green ammonia, bio-diesel)	Medium
		Performance requirement standards for hydrogen fuel cell used in mobile machinery	High
		Performance requirement standards for alternate fuel and dual fuel use in mobile machinery	Medium
		Cryogenics container and its components	Medium
		Cryogenics operational requirements	Low
	Household Products	Lock cartridge	Medium
		Gas stoves of non-metallic body	Medium
		Gas hobs	Medium

SECTOR	FIELD	SUBJECT AREA	PRIORITY
		Burning appliances for clean and bio-based fuels	High
	Industrial Automation	Model-Based Standards Authoring	Medium
		Nuclear Digital Ecosystems	Medium
	Industrial Production	Anchor fastener	Medium
		Railway bearings	Medium
	Machine and Machine Tools	Hydraulic torque wrench	Medium
		Safety of press brakes	High
	Machinery	Safety of mobile machines working underground	High
		Adoption of functional safety standard for earth moving machines	Medium
		Paver machines	Medium
Machinery, Engineering and Manufactu-ring	Material Handling Equipment and Ropeways	Balance ropes in mines	Medium
		Electromagnetic examination of ferromagnetic steel wire rope	Medium
		Safety in rides	High
	Metal Cutting	Metal cutting bandsaw blades bimetallic	Low
	Metrology	Gas flow meters	Low
		Evaluation of uncertainties in fluid flow	Medium
	Pressure Vessels	Unfired Pressure Vessels Code (Revision)	Medium
	Printing Machinery	Colour printing machines - commissioning, operation and testing	Medium
		Digital printing machinery	Medium
	Pumps	Horizontal split case pumps	Medium
		Vertical turbine pumps	Medium
	Refrigeration and Air-conditioning	Cold chain equipment	Medium
	Robotics	Exoskeleton robots	Medium
		Legged robots including bipods	Medium
	Smart Manufacturing	Cyber-physically controlled smart machine tool systems	Medium

SECTOR	FIELD	SUBJECT AREA	PRIORITY
	Sports Goods	Protective equipment for sports	Medium
		Physical training equipment	Medium
	Toys	Toy safety standards	Medium
Managem-ent and Systems	Environmental Social Governance (ESG's)	Internal investigation	Medium
		Fraud Control Management Systems — Guidance for organizations responding to the risk of fraud	Medium
		Efficiency measurement	Medium
		Promotion and implementation of gender equality	Medium
		Performance indicator for Enviro-Economic-Social- Governance benefits and impact assessment for Environmental Social Governance (ESG's)	Medium
	Management Techniques	Facility management - Role in sustainability and resilience	Low
		Facility management - Existing performance management in facility management organizations – State of the industry	Medium
		Life Cycle Costing in procurement	Low
		Technology in facility management	Medium
		Asset Management - Guidance on the alignment of financial and non-financial functions	Medium
		Principles and guidelines for development and implementation of sustainable finance products and services	Medium
		Sustainable Human Resource Management	Low
		Guidelines for the application of ISO 9001 in policing organization	Medium
		Indicators/Template for impact assessment for SDGs	Low
		Rating for tourism city	Medium
Managem-	Risk and Resilience	Risk Maturity Model	Medium

SECTOR	FIELD	SUBJECT AREA	PRIORITY
ent and Systems		Cyber resilience	Medium
		Guideline for the implementation of IS/ISO 31000 amongst Indian industries	Medium
		Risk management for corporates	Medium
		Energy Resilience	Low
	Statistical Techniques	Quality of measurement results - Criteria for repeat/replicate testing	Low
		Guidelines on statistical software	Medium
		Data Ethics	Medium
Medical Value Travel Services	Health, Fitness and Sports Services	Yoga services	Low
		Gym services	Low
		Physical activity, sports and injury management	Medium
		Healthcare services	Low
	Medical Value Travel Services and Wellness Services	Medical value travel services	Low
		Wellness services	Low
Petroleum, Polymers and Related Products	Coal and Related Products	Ash fusion temperature for biomass	Medium
		Biomass for steelmaking	Medium
		Safety of solid biofuels	Medium
	Cosmetics	Horizontal Standards in Cosmetics	Medium
		Testing of cosmetics - Alternate methods	Medium
	Fragrance and Flavour	Synthetic menthol	Medium
	Petroleum and Related Products	New generation fuels – EBMS, E20, M15, H-CNG, B10, ATF	High
		Flash point of diesel, Methanol (M100) and MD95 fuel, motor gasoline - RON95, pyrolysis oils	High
		Categorization of products having similar specifications with customs department	Medium
		Lubricants based on trends in engine design/ hardware change, metallurgy change, regulations on emission norms,	Medium

SECTOR	FIELD	SUBJECT AREA	PRIORITY
		injection technology, after treatment devices (SCR, DPF, DOC, CatCon, Etc.), alternate fuels, and advancements in industrial lubricants, including dedicated lubricants, high performance lubricants	
		Auto and industrial lubes and greases (revisions)	Medium
		Test methods of lubricants	Medium
		Additive label for lubricants	Medium
		Natural / Green lubricants	High
	Polymer - Rubber	Safe handling practices for the rubber raw materials	Medium
		Guidelines/Protocols/Good practices for packing, storing and handling of cup lump.	Medium
		Raw materials and identification of hazardous substances.	High
		EOLT (End of Life Tyres)	High
Petroleum, Polymers and Related Products	Polymer - Rubber	Recovered carbon black	High
		White/Latex reclaimed rubber	Medium
		Characterisation of polymer bound rubber chemicals	Medium
Textiles including Technical Textiles	Agrotech	Nets, mats and fabric for various agro applications	Medium
		Silage bags/grow bags & barrier packaging bags	Medium
		Coir root trainer pots	Medium
	Aquaculture	Polyester/nylon fish cage	Medium
	Buildtech	Gym services	Medium
		Fabrics for architectural applications	High
		Scaffolding nets	Medium
		Awning and canopies	Medium
		Inflatables	Medium
		Woven and nonwoven wall coverings	Medium

SECTOR	FIELD	SUBJECT AREA	PRIORITY
		Fabric for signage and hoarding	Low
	Clothtech	Laces and tapes of narrow fabrics/braids	Low
		Elastic narrow fabric	Low
		Labels and badges	Low
	Coir and Coir Products	Coir products for horticultural applications	Low
		Coir brushes	Medium
	Geotextiles	Geocomposite strips	High
		Woven and knitted geotextiles for all subgrade stabilisation	High
		Geosynthetics clay liners	Medium
		Drainage composites	High
		Rockfall protection nets	High
		GeotubesGeotextiles for bituminous layer	Medium
		Erosion control coir mat	High
		Textiles fabric impregnated with cement for erosion control	High
	Industrial Textiles	Fabrics and products of industrial applications (filters, pipes and hoses, belts and conveyors, webbings & slings, abrasive cloth, industrial wipes, etc)	Medium
	Manmade Fibre Yarns	Yarns and filaments of nylon and polyester	Low
	Medtech	Community mask and medical respirator	High
		Guidelines for reprocessing of healthcare textile	High
		Dressings, paddings and other products for surgical applications	High
		Dental floss	High
		Scrub suit/Patients clothing	High
		Products for maternity applications	High
		Burn sheet	High
		Products for orthopaedic applications	High

SECTOR	FIELD	SUBJECT AREA	PRIORITY
		Leukodepletion filter or textiles used for blood purification	High
Textiles including Technical Textiles	Mobiltech	Polyester tyre cord	Medium
		Fabrics, felts and other products for automobiles	Medium
	Oekotech	Test method for Volatile Halogenated Organics, Volatile Hydrocarbons (Nonhalogens)	Medium
		Test method for chlorinated organic carriers, Polycyclic Aromatic Hydrocarbons (PAHS)	Medium
		Indian green textile standards	High
	Packtech	Packs and bags of PP/HDPE for various applications	Medium
		Woven / nonwoven laminated or coated fabric, waterproof, rain gowns	Medium
	Physical Methods of Test	Smoothness test for fabrics	Low
	Protech	Clothing for defence personnel	High
		Clothing for other use	High
		Sleeping bags and rucksack	High
		Protective nets	Medium
	Ready Made Garments (Man-Made Apparel)	Kids wear safety requirements	High
		Apparels for women and girls	Medium
		Apparels for men and boys	Medium
		Various woven fabrics of nylon and polyester	Medium
		FR treated nonwoven fabric based disposable bed sheets, bed rolls, curtains and pillow covers for hotels, hospitals, railways and other travel industry	Medium
	Rope and Net	Helideck net	Low
	Silk and Silk Products	Grading of Eri and Muga silks	Medium
		Spun silk	Medium

SECTOR	FIELD	SUBJECT AREA	PRIORITY
	Speciality Fibre	Fibres and filaments of new age materials (aramid, basalt, carbon, pre-oxidized, glass, UHMWPE, etc)	Medium
	Sportech	Sport nets	Medium
		Fabrics for sports application	Medium
		Artificial sports turfs	Medium
		Conductive textiles/Smart textiles/E-textiles for different applications in sportech, medtech, protech and indutech etc.	Medium
	Textiles Floor covering	Woven and non-woven carpet backing cloth	High
		Artificial grass made of synthetic yarn for landscape	Low
	Textiles Machinery and Accessories	Carding (specifically metallic staves), drawing and spinning (e.g., Baxter Flyer)	Low
		Spare parts of jute machinery	Low
Tourism and Hospitality Services	Travel, Tourism and Hospitality Services	Sustainable tourism	Low
		Hospitality	Medium
Transport and Logistics Services	Supply Chain Management	Warehouse management	Low
		Logistics services for high value goods	Medium
	Transport Services	Cold chain logistics	Medium
		Transportation of dangerous goods	Medium
Transport and Logistics Services	Transport Services	Public transport services	Medium
		Cargo transportation services	Medium
		Packers and movers services	Medium
		Courier services	Medium
		Multimodal transportation services	Medium
Transportation including e-mobility	Aerospace	Aero engine components and testing	Medium
		Aircraft safety equipment/Sensors,	Medium
		Titanium fasteners used in aircraft	Medium
	Automobiles	Clean energy transition and integration in automobiles	High

SECTOR	FIELD	SUBJECT AREA	PRIORITY
		Fire mitigation requirements	High
		Green economy through recycled content, EPR, waste disposal and resource efficiency	High
		Airbags	High
		Child restraint system	High
	Bicycle	Aluminium alloy, carbon fibre and titanium bicycles	Medium
		E-bicycles	Medium
		Critical components of bicycles	Medium
	Drone	Drone	High
	Electromobility	EV Battery Swap	High
		Dual gun charging of heavy electric vehicles	High
		BMS for electric vehicles	High
		Cloud based charging system	High
		High capacity EV chargers	High
		Safety of EV charging charging infrastructure	High
		Safety of EV batteries	High
		Recycling of EV batteries and reuse of EV battery system in stationery storage	High
		Batteries including transportation of batteries	High
	Marine	Battery used for marine propulsion	Low
	Navigation	Navigation of aircraft to satellite	Low
	Packaging Logistics	Handling and storage of hazardous material	High
		Composite drum used In chemical industry	Medium
		Slip sheet	Medium
		Multi-model container for transportation of vehicle	Medium

SECTOR	FIELD	SUBJECT AREA	PRIORITY
	Road Safety	Safety installations (crash barriers, bollard's etc)	High
		Safety - Critical components of vehicles	High
	Transportation	Transportation of specially abled people	High
Water Resources	Coastal Zone Water Management	Control of salt water intrusion	High
		Preventions of coastal hazards	Medium
		Coastal erosion protection	Medium
		Anti-erosion works in coastal area	Medium
	Disaster Mitigation and Management	Glacial Lakes Outburst Floods	Medium
		Anti-erosion works on river course	Medium
		Design and construction of fuse plug to facilitate breaching	Medium
		Flood forecasting using real time reservoir Inflow	Medium
		Flood map of India	Medium
		River morphology and flood plain study	Medium
Water Resources	Environment Impact Assessment	Environment and social impact on river training works	Medium
		Climate resilient water security	Medium
		Assessment of environmental flow	Medium
		Conservation of aquatic ecosystems in reservoirs and lakes	Medium
	Ground Water	Aquifer storage and recovery techniques	Medium
		Guidelines for aquifer mapping	Medium
		Impact assessment techniques for artificial recharge structures	Medium
		Guidelines for surface runoff harvesting using small structures	Medium
		Ground water harvesting using unconventional measures	Medium
		Groundwater flow monitoring	Medium
	Hydro Structure Construction,	standardisation on dams safety management, planning and rehabilitation	High

SECTOR	FIELD	SUBJECT AREA	PRIORITY
	Operation and Maintenance	Life Cycle Assessment of dams	High
		Sediment management and disposal	Medium
		Guidelines on performance of old or existing hydraulic structures	Medium
		Guidelines on treatment of defects in the foundation of masonry and concrete dam	Medium
		Optimization and simulation of reservoir operation	Medium
		Dam safety protocol and retrofitting	High
		Dam break analysis	High
		Roller compacted dams	Medium
		Rubber dams	Medium
		Adit gates design	Medium
		Ventilation of underground power houses	Medium
		Performance monitoring of hydraulic structures	Medium
		Piano key weirs	Medium
		Installation, maintenance and operation of instruments in tunnels	Low
		Standards on geological investigations in himalayan region	Low
	Water Resources Management	Efficient use of water resources	High
		Interlinking of rivers	High
		Standards on artificial ponds/ lakes	Medium
		Canal automation	Medium
		Water use efficiency	High
		Inland water transportation design	Medium
		Rejuvenation of traditional water resources	High
		Water audit	Medium

SECTOR	FIELD	SUBJECT AREA	PRIORITY
		Piped irrigation network	Medium
		Seepage losses in reservoirs	Medium
		Evaporation control in canals	Medium
		Integrated Watershed Management	Medium

Appendix - 5

BUREAU OF INDIAN STANDARDS CITIZEN'S CHARTER

(As published by BIS)

This Charter is a declaration of our commitment to achieve excellence in the formulation of Indian standards, implementation of the Product Certification Scheme, Management Systems Certification Scheme, Training Services, Information Services, Sale of Standards and other BIS Publications and Standards Promotion and Consumer

Awareness for the benefit of consumers and the public at large. The Charter has been prepared in consultation with all stakeholders including customers of the Bureau. This Charter is also available in regional languages.

1. OUR VISION

The Bureau of Indian Standards (BIS), the National Standards Body of India, resolves to be the leader in matters concerning Standardization, Certification and Quality.

2. OUR OBJECTIVES

- ☐ To provide harmonious development of standards
- ☐ To satisfy the customer's need for quality and safety of goods and services through operation of Certification schemes.
- ☐ To generate awareness on standards, standard mark, and safety and quality of products through seminars, awareness programmes and publicity Campaigns.
- ☐ To provide effective and timely services.

3. OUR MISSION

3.1 BIS Act 1986 provides for the establishment of a Bureau for the harmonious development of the activities of standardization, marking and quality certification of goods and for matters connected therewith or incidental thereto.

3.2 We dedicate ourselves to achieve excellence through effective implementation of Bureau of Indian Standards Act, 1986 and Rules and Regulations framed there under and provide prompt and efficient services to all concerned.

4. OUR KEY SERVICES

4.1 Formulation of Indian Standards

4.2 Certification Schemes

4.2.1 *Product Certification Schemes*

i) Scheme for Domestic Manufacturers

ii) Scheme for Foreign Manufacturers

iii) ECO Mark Scheme

iv) Halmarking of Gold and Silver jewellery & artefacts

v) Registration Scheme

4.2.2 *Management Systems Certification*

i) Quality Management Systems Certification scheme (QMS)

ii) Environmental Management Systems Certification scheme (EMS)

iii) Occupational Health & Safety Management Systems Certification scheme (OHSMS)

iv) Food Safety Management Systems Certification scheme (FSMS)

v) Service Quality Management Systems Certification scheme (SQMS)

vi) Hazard Analysis Critical Control Point certification scheme (HACCP)

vii) Energy Management System (EnMS)

viii) Integrated(QMS and HACCP)

4.3 Training Services

i) Open Programmes ii)In-house programmes

iii) International Training Programmes for developing countries in the fields of Standardization and Quality Assurance, Laboratory Quality Management Systems and Management Systems.

4.4 Information Services

i) Library Services

ii) SSI Facilitation Cell has been set up at BIS HQs. At regional and branch offices, information/assistance is provided by Head of Regional/Branch Office as per **Annex I**.

iii) Technical Information services at HQs.

iv) WTO-TBT Enquiry Point

4.5 Sale of Indian and Overseas Standards and BIS Publications

4.5.1 *E-sale of Indian Standards*

4.6 Standards Promotion through

i) Consumer Awareness Programmes

ii) Educational Utilization of Standards Programmes

iii) Industrial Awareness Programmes

iv) Publicity through Press and Media

5. IDENTIFICATION OF LEVELS & CONTACT POINTS FOR OBTAINING SERVICE

The organization Chart of BIS is given at our website www.bis.gov.in. Nodal Officer as mentioned in **Annex-I** may be contacted for further details.

6. CLIENT GROUPS/STAKEHOLDERS/USERS

Our clients include Government organizations, Public Sector Undertakings, Industry and Consumers.

7. TIME NORMS FOR THE KEY SERVICES

Time Norms for the key services are given in **Annex II**. In case of noncompliance, the PGO in the respective office of BIS may be contacted (as given in **Annex I**).

8. SERVICE QUALITY & SERVICE DELIVERY STANDARDS

BIS is committed to provide quality service as per service delivery norms prescribed in **Annex II**.

9. PROCESS/PROCEDURES TO ACCESS SERVICE BENEFITS

9.1 **Formulation of National Standards**

BIS formulates Indian Standards for various sectors that have been grouped under 14 Departments like Chemical, Food and Agriculture, Civil, Electro Technical, Electronics & Information Technology, Mechanical Engineering, Management & Systems, Metallurgical Engineering, Petroleum Coal & Related Products, Medical Equipment and Hospital Planning, Textile, Transport Engineering, Production & General Engineering and Water Resources. Any query/proposal on Standards formulation can be made to DDG (Standardization) or Head of the concerned Technical Department at Headquarters, New Delhi.

9.2 **Certification Schemes**

The Bureau operates a Product Certification Scheme, which is governed by The Bureau of Indian Standards Act, 1986 and Rules and Regulations framed there under. The BIS Product Certification Scheme operates in an impartial, non-discriminatory and transparent manner and aims at providing quality products to the consumer. Presence of BIS Standard Mark on a product indicates conformity to the relevant Indian Standard and before granting licence to any manufacturer, it is ensured that the applicant has all required manufacturing, testing facilities to manufacture and test product through competent technical person as per relevant Indian Standard.

Any query/proposal on Product Certification Scheme can be made to DDG(Certification) or DDG of the region or, Head of the concerned Branch office. For queries relating to Hallmarking, it can be made to DDG (HM) or Head Hallmarking Department in the Hqrs or to concerned Head of the Branch Office.

9.3 Training Services

Bureau of Indian Standards has set up National Institute of Training for Standardization (NITS) to meet the training needs of industry, Government and Service sector. The Institute is operating from its campus at NOIDA. It also has six training centres at the BIS offices in Kolkata, Mumbai, Chennai, Jaipur, Bhopal and Bangalore

Any query/proposal relating Training Services can be made to Deputy Director General, Training or, Head, NITS, Noida.

9.4 Information Services

9.4.1 BIS provides Technical Information Services to Industry, importers, exporters, individuals and government agencies in response to their enquiries.

All details relating to above services are available at BIS web site; www.bis.gov.in

9.4.2 At BIS Head Quarters, SSI facilitation Cell performs as Information facilitation counter. In Regional and Branch offices, Head or Nodal officer (as per **Annex. I**) performs this job.

10. PUBLIC GRIEVANCES REDRESSAL MECHANISM

10.1 All complaints against poor quality of ISI marked products/Hallmarked jewellery and artefacts, or Services provided by BIS can be sent to Public Grievance Officers (PGOs) appointed by BIS at all locations where BIS offices exist. The PGOs after necessary verification of supporting documents forward the complaint to Consumer Affairs Department (CAD) at Head Quarters for recording of the complaint centrally. The addresses, telephone/fax nos. and emails of Nodal officer and Public Grievance officers (PGOs) are given in **Annex I**.

10.2 Complaints against ISI marked products/Hallmarked jewellery and artefacts or for services provided by BIS, can be lodged in writing or online on BIS website www.bis.gov.in.

10.3 All recorded complaints relating to ISI marked products/Hallmarked jewellery and artefacts will be redressed within a period of three months of their recording. In case of complaints for services provided by BIS relating to its activities such as Product Certification, Standard Formulation, Management System Certification, Compulsory Registration Scheme, Sale of Standards and Publications, Training etc, redressal will be done within one month of recording of the complaint.

10.4 Monitoring of complaints is done centrally by CAD on monthly basis through Management Control Report (MCR).

10.5 The procedure for complaint redressal in respect of ISI marked products/hallmarked jewellery/artefacts is given in **Annex IIIA** and that in respect of services provided by BIS is given in **Annex IIIB**.

10.6 In case, complainant is not satisfied with the redressal of the complaint, he/she may prefer an appeal before ADG, BIS within 30 days time.

11. WEBSITE AND RELEVANT INFORMATION

11.1 BIS has website www.bis.gov.in in which forms, processes, procedures in respect of various BIS activities are available. Besides, The BIS Act, Rules and Regulations etc. are also available on the web site.

12. ONLINE CHARTER

12.1 **BIS Citizen's Charter is hosted on BIS website.**

13. RIGHT TO INFORMATION ACT

13.1 BIS is implementing The RTI Act 2005 and has appointed Central Public Information Officers (CPIOs) and Appellate Authorities at different Regional Offices/Branch Offices throughout the country. The information relating to RTI is available on BIS website www.bis.gov.in.

14. OUR EXPECTATIONS

a) **Standard Formulation**

i) Any proposal for formulation of Indian Standard on new subject should be accompanied by adequate justification and relevant document(s) with essential requirements stating therein the other national and international standards on the subject, if available. Additionally, such proposals should be accompanied by duly filled in proforma available on BIS web site for proposing new subject for national standardization.

ii) Views of all members of the concerned technical committees are sought by circulation of documents. It is expected that the members of Technical Committees send their comments within the given time frame. The comments forwarded on the circulated document by the members should be clear and without any ambiguity. It is also expected that members attend the Technical Committee meetings regularly and effectively contribute in time bound manner.

iii) BIS expects that other technical experts/stakeholders to comment on the draft Indian Standard, when put in public domain through BIS website.

b) **Certification**

All applicants are expected to ensure that the applications for the grant of licences under Certification Schemes are complete in all respects for speedy processing.

i) In case of Product Certification, the applicant is expected to have the complete infrastructure to manufacture and test the product as per relevant Indian standard. The applicant shall be ready for BIS visit to his manufacturing unit, pay required charges and ensure timely compliance to BIS instructions issued from time to time.

ii) For Management System Certification, the organization shall be ready for the audit and give compliance report on the non-conformities issued to them within the stipulated time frame.

Annex I

LIST OF NODAL OFFICER AND PUBLIC GRIEVANCE OFFICER (PGOS)

Sl. No.	Nodal Officer	EPABX	Head of HQ/RO /BO	FAX No.	E MAIL
1	Head (Consumer Affairs Department), Bureau of Indian Standards, ManakBhavan, 9, Bahadur Shah Zafar Marg New Delhi-110002	STD-011 23230131, 23233375, 23239402	23235069	23235069	cad@bis.gov.in
2	Deputy Director General CENTRAL REGIONAL OFFICE, Bureau of Indian Standards, Manakalaya 9, Bahadur Shah Zafar Marg New Delhi-110002	STD-011 23230131, 23233375, 23239402	23237617	23238911	cro@bis.gov.in
3	Deputy Director General EASTERN REGIONAL OFFICE, Bureau of Indian Standards 1/14, C.I.T. Scheme VII M, V.I.P. Road, Kankurgachi, Calcutta-700054	STD-033 23208499, 23208561-62, 23208662, 23202910	23209474	23209474	ero@bis.gov.in
4	Deputy Director General NORTHERN REGIONAL OFFICE Bureau of Indian Standards Plot No. 4-A, Sector 27-B, Madhya Marg, Chandigarh - 160 019.	STD-0172 2650206, 2650290	0172-2650259	0172-2650259	nro@bis.gov.in
5	Deputy Director General SOUTHERN REGIONAL OFFICE Bureau of Indian Standards CIT Campus, IV Cross Road, Chennai-600113	STD-044 22542519, 22541216, 22541442	22542365	22541087	sro@bis.gov.in

Sl. No.	Nodal Officer	EPABX	Head of HQ/RO /BO	FAX No.	E MAIL
6	Deputy Director General WESTERN REGIONAL OFFICE, Bureau of Indian Standards Manakalaya, E-9, MIDC Behind Marol Telephone Exchange Andheri (East), Mumbai-400093	STD:0 22 283278 91- 92, 28329295	28218093	28253433	wro@bis.gov.in
7	Head AHMEDABAD BRANCH OFFICE Bureau of Indian Standards 3rd Floor,Navajivan Amrut Jayanti Bhavan, Behind Gujarath Vidya pith, Off. Ashram road, Ahmedabad 380014	STD-079 27540317, 27540318, 27540319, 27540320	27540314	079-27540636	ahbo@bis.gov.in
8	Head BANGALORE BRANCH OFFICE, Bureau of Indian Standards Peenya Industrial Area, 1st Stage, Bangalore-Tumkur Road, Bangalore-560058	STD-080 283949 55- 56, 28396324 28398860 28392296	28395604	28398841 28395604	bnbo@bis.gov.in
9	Head BHOPAL BRANCH OFFICE Bureau of Indian Standards Comercial-Cum Office Complex, Opposite Dushera Maidan, E-5, Arera Colony, Bittan Market, Bhopal-462016	STD: 0755 2423449, 2423452, 2420493 2423454 2442550	2423453	2423451	bplbo@bis.gov.in

Sl. No.	Nodal Officer	EPABX	Head of HQ/RO /BO	FAX No.	E MAIL
10	Head BHUBANESHWAR BRANCH Bureau of Indian Standards OFFICE, 6t Flor, Gruha Nirman Bhawan (OSHB Building), Sachivalaya Marg Bhubaneshwar- 751001	STD-0674 2394193 2391727	2390847	0674- 2393039	bhbo@bis.gov.in
11	Head COIMBATORE BRANCH OFFICE Bureau of Indian Standards 5th Floor, Kovai Tower, 44 BalaSundaram Road, Coimbatore-641018	STD-0422 2240141, 2245622, 2249016	2248892	2246705	ctbo@bis.gov.in
12	Head, DEHRADUN BRANCH OFFICE, Bureau of Indian Standards C-43, Sector 1, Defence Colony, Dehradun	0135- 2665129, 2665130	0135- 2665071	2665272	dhbo@bis.gov.in
13	Head FARIDABAD BRANCH OFFICE, Bureau of Indian Standards SCO – 21, Sector 12, Faridabad-121001	STD-0129 2292175, 2292179	2292173	2291860	frbo@bis.gov.in
14	Head GHAZIABAD BRANCH OFFICE, Bureau of Indian Standards Savitri Complex 116,G.T.Road, Ghaziabad-201001	STD-0120 2861175, 2861498	2861174	2862195	gzbo@bis.gov.in

Sl. No.	Nodal Officer	EPABX	Head of HQ/RO /BO	FAX No.	E MAIL
15	Head GUWAHATI BRANCH OFFICE, Bureau of Indian Standards 2nd Floor, West End Block HOUSEFED Building Complex Last Gate, Dispur Guwahati 781 006	STD-0361-2224670	2224670	2525937	ghbo@bis.gov.in
16	Head HYDERABAD BRANCH OFFICE, Bureau of Indian Standards Plot no 1, Sy no 367/1 Industrial Development Park, Moulaali, Hyderabad -500 040	STD-040 27249993, 27249996, 27249997, 27249998	27249993	27249993	hbo@bis.gov.in
17	Head JAIPUR BRANCH OFFICE Bureau of Indian Standards Prithavi Raj Road Opp-Bharat Overseas Bank Limited C-Scheme Jaipur 302 001	STD-0141 2223281, 2223282, 2223283	2223286	2223281	jpbo@bis.gov.in
18	Head JAMSHEDPUR BRANCH OFFICE Bureau of Indian Standards F/10-A, Namdih Road P.O. Burmamines, Jamshedpur - 831007 (Jharkhand)	0657- 2345481, 2345498	0657- 2345481, 2345498	0657- 2345498	jdbo@bis.gov.in
19	Head LUCKNOW BRANCH OFFICE	STD-0522 2306664	2306664	2306664	lkbo@bis.gov.in

Sl. No.	Nodal Officer	EPABX	Head of HQ/RO /BO	FAX No.	E MAIL
	Bureau of Indian Standards 4th Floor, B-2 Block PICUP BHAWAN Gomti Nagar Lucknow - 226 010				
20	Head NAGPUR BRANCH OFFICE Bureau of Indian Standards NIT Building II Floor Gokul Path Market Nagpur-440010	STD-0712 2565171, 2554268	2540807	2554267	ngbo@bis.gov.in
21	Head PARWANOO BRANCH OFFICE Bureau of Indian Standards House no. 15, Sec 3 District Solan – 173 220	STD-01792 235437,23 5 338 235439	235436	235435	nlbo@bis.gov.in
22	Head PATNA BRANCH OFFICE Bureau of Indian Standards Patliputra Industrial Estate, Patna800013	STD-0612 2262808 2271625	2275342	2275342	ptbo@bis.gov.in
23	Head PUNE BRANCH OFFICE Bureau of Indian Standards MAIDC Building, First Floor, Plot No. 657-660, Market Yard, Gultekdi, PUNE –411037	STD-020 24274803, 24274806	24264911	24268659	pnbo@bis.gov.in
24	Head RAJKOT BRANCH OFFICE	STD-0281 2385157 2385160	0281- 2563981 2563982	0281- 2563981	rjbo@bis.gov.in

Sl. No.	Nodal Officer	EPABX	Head of HQ/RO /BO	FAX No.	E MAIL
	Bureau of Indian Standards F P No. 364/P, Ward no. 13, Opposite Crystal Mall, Next to Bharat Petrol Pump, Kalawad Road, Rajkot- 360005	2384042	2563984 2563978		
25	Head, KOCHI BRANCH OFFICE, Bureau of Indian Standards Vankarath Towers, 2nd Floor N. H. Bye - Pass Road, Signal Junction Palarivattom, Kochi 682024	STD-0484-2341174/75/ 76	2341066	0484-2341176	kobo@bis.gov.in
26	Head VISHAKHAPATANAM BRANCH OFFICE Bureau of Indian Standards 'C' Block, First Floor, UdyogBhawan, VUDA Complex, Siripuram Vishakhapatanam-530003	STD-0891-2712833, 0891-2712834	2712833	2712837	vzbo@bis.gov.in
27	Head National Institute of Training for Standardization (NITS) Bureau of Indian Standards Plot No.A-20-21, Institutional Area, Sec 62 Gautam Budh Nagar NOIDA-201307	STD-0120-4670232	0120-4670232	0120-4670227	nits@bis.gov.in
28	Head JAMMU & KASHMIR BRANCH OFFICE Bureau of Indian Standards	01923-222690, 222696	01923-222690, 222696	01923-222690, 222696	jkbo@bis.gov.in

Sl. No.	Nodal Officer	EPABX	Head of HQ/RO /BO	FAX No.	E MAIL
	Lane No. 4, SIDCO Industrial Complex, Bari Brahmana, Jammu – 181133 (J&K)				
29	Head, HARYANA BRANCH OFFICE Bureau of Indian Standards Plot No. 4-A, Sector 27-B, Madhya Marg, Chandigarh - 160 019.	2659065 (Telefax)	2659065 (Telefax)	2659065 (Telefax)	mdch1@bis.gov.in
30	Head, CHANDIGARH BRANCH OFFICE-I Bureau of Indian Standards Plot No. 4-A, Sector 27-B, Madhya Marg, Chandigarh - 160 019.	2659072 (Telefax)	2659072 (Telefax)	2659072 (Telefax)	mdch2@bis.gov.in
31	Head, CHANDIGARH BRANCH OFFICE-II Bureau of Indian Standards Plot No. 4-A, Sector 27-B, Madhya Marg, Chandigarh - 160 019.	2659021 (Telefax)	2659021 (Telefax)	2659021 (Telefax)	mdch3@bis.gov.in
32	Head, DELHI BRANCH OFFICE-I Bureau of Indian Standards Manakalaya 9, Bahadur Shah Zafar Marg, New Delhi-110002	23237401	23237401		dlbo1@bis.gov.in
33	Head, DELHI BRANCH OFFICE-II Bureau of Indian Standards Manakalaya,	23232922	23232922		dlbo2@bis.gov.in

Sl. No.	Nodal Officer	EPABX	Head of HQ/RO /BO	FAX No.	E MAIL
	9, Bahadur Shah Zafar Marg, New Delhi-110002				
34	Head, CHENNAI BRANCH OFFICE-I Bureau of Indian Standards CIT Campus, IV Cross Road, Chennai-600113	044-22541220	044-22541220	044-22541220	cnbo1@bis.gov.in
35	Head, CHENNAI BRANCH OFFICE-II Bureau of Indian Standards CIT Campus, IV Cross Road, Chennai-600113	044-22541076	22541076	22541076	cnbo2@bis.gov.in
36	Head, MUMBAI BRANCH OFFICE-I Bureau of Indian Standards E9, Behind Marol Telephone Exchange, Andheri (East), Mumbai 400 093.	022-28327893	28327893	28327893	mubo1@bis.gov.in
37	Head, MUMBAI BRANCH OFFICE-II Bureau of Indian Standards Manakalaya, E9, Behind Marol Telephone Exchange, Andheri (East), Mumbai 400 093.	022-28235680	28235680	28235680	mubo2@bis.gov.in
38	Head, KOLKATA BRANCH OFFICE Bureau of Indian Standards 1/14 CIT Scheme VII M, V.I.P. Road, Kankurgachi, Kolkata 700 054.	23208373	23208373	23208373	kkbo@bis.gov.in

Sl. No.	Nodal Officer	EPABX	Head of HQ/RO /BO	FAX No.	E MAIL
39	Head, RAIPUR BRANCH OFFICE Bureau of Indian Standards GovindSarang Complex 2nd Floor, New Rajendra Nagar Raipur - 492006 (Chhattisgarh)	0771-2419404, 2412235	0771-2419404	0771-2419404	hrpbo@bis.gov.in
40	Head, DURGAPUR Bureau of Indian Standards Technical Block Building Adjacent to Research & Control Laboratory, Durgapur Steel Plant Durgapur – 713203	0343-2583178	0343-2583178	0343-2583178	dpbo@bis.gov.in

Annex II

Time Norms for Key Services

Sl. No.	ACTIVITY	TIME
1	FORMULATION OF INDIAN STANDARDS	Priority1: 12 months Priority 2: 24 months Normal : 28 months
2.	CERTIFICATION SCHEMES	
	a) **Product Certification** i) Scheme for Domestic Manufacturers	Normal procedure:4 months Simplified procedure:1 month
	ii) Scheme for Foreign Manufacturers	6 months
	iii) ECO Mark Scheme	4 months
	iv) Hallmarking of Gold and Silver Jewellery & artefacts	7 Working days
	v) Registration Scheme	20 Working days
	b) **Management System Certification** i) Quality Management Systems (QMS) ii) Environmental Management Systems (EMS) iii) Occupational Health & Safety Management Systems (OHSMS) iv) Food Safety Management System (FSMS) v) Service Quality Management Systems (SQMS) vi) Hazard Analysis Critical Control Point certification scheme (HACCP) vii) Energy Management System (EnMS) viii) Integrated(QMS and HACCP)	3 months for all
3	TRAINING SERVICES	
	a) Open Programmes	As per Training Calendar of NITS
	b) In-House Programmes	Within one month from date of receipt of request
	c) International training programme in the field of standardization , Quality and Laboratory, Management Systems for Developing Countries	As per training calendar of NITS

4	**INFORMATION SERVICES** a) **Library Services** i) Issue of standards/books ii) To become Member of Library b) **Single Window Facilitation Cell** c) **WTO Enquiry Point** i) Acknowledgement of an enquiry ii) Dissemination of TBT(Technical Barrier to Trade) notification	Across the counter 15 Working days Across the counter 5 Working days 5 Working days from date of hosting on WTO website
5	**SALE OF STANDARDS AND PUBLICATIONS** (*see* Note 1)	Across the counter By Post : Within 2 weeks
6	**STANDARDS PROMOTION** through a) Consumer Awareness Programmes b) Educational Utilization of Standards Programmes c) Industrial Awareness Programmes	Within 15 days from the date of receipt of request.
7	**GRIEVANCES REDRESSAL**	Three months
8	**IMPLEMENTATION OF RTI ACT' 2005**	Within 30 days of receipt of request.

Note 1 – For sale of standards time norms may vary depending upon the availability, which will be informed to the purchaser.

Note 2 – Under Certification scheme, the actual time taken may exceed if some actions are pending on the part of the applicant. Further, in case of Foreign Manufacturers scheme, getting visa and other clearances may take additional time.

Annex IIIA

PROCEDURE FOR COMPLAINT REDRESSAL IN RESPECT OF ISI MARKED PRODUCTS/HALLMARKED JEWELLERY/ARTEFACTS

Complaints can be lodged online at BIS website www.bis.gov.in, complaints@bis.gov.in, or through mobile application. Alternately, complaint can be sent in writing to BIS Hqs/Regional offices/Branch offices. In case of online complaint,complaints through mobile application acknowledgement is sent immediately assigning a complaint number.

- Written complaints are recorded centrally by Consumers Affairs Department (CAD) at BIS Head Quarters. Therefore any complaint sent to Branch office or Regional office is also recorded centrally. A Complaint number is given and the complaint is acknowledged by CAD.
- Complainant should give his/her contact details along with details of product and problem encountered and remedy requested to facilitate recording of the complaint and for investigation thereof. If the complaint is lacking in some required information, the complainant will be requested by the concerned office of BIS (Hqs/Regional/Branch Office) to furnish additional details required for recording of the complaint.
- Action on the complaint will be made by contacting the complainant (by concerned Branch office at complainant end) and carrying out investigation at licensee end (i.e. manufacturer of the product) by concerned Branch Office
- In case of violation of BIS Act, Rules, Regulations, actions such as; stop marking, deferment of renewal of licence, cancellation of licence will be taken against the licensee as per prescribed procedures.
- All recorded complaints will be redressed in 3 months time.
- To know the status of complaint, the complainant may contact CAD at Head Quarters or, concerned BIS office (Regional office or, Branch office). For complaints registered online, the status of complaint will be available on BIS website and can be seen by logging in complaint No. and e mail id of the complainant.
- In case, complainant is not satisfied with the redressal of the complaint, he/she may prefer an appeal before ADG, BIS within 30 days time.

Contact details Head

Consumer Affairs Department, Bureau of Indian Standards, Manakalaya 9 Bahadur Shah Zafar Marg, New Delhi-2

Tel. No: 23235069 **E mail:** cad@bis.gov.in, complaints@bis.gov.in

Annex IIIB

PROCEDURE FOR COMPLAINT REDRESSAL IN RESPECT OF BISSERVICES

Complaints can be lodged online at BIS website www.bis.gov.in, complaints@bis.gov.in, or through mobile application. Alternately, complaint can be sent in writing to BIS Hqs/Regional offices/Branch offices. In case of online complaint, complaints through mobile applicationacknowledgement is sent immediately assigning a complaint number.

- Written complaints are recorded centrally by Consumers Affairs Department (CAD) at BIS Head Quarters. Therefore any complaint sent to Branch office or Regional office is also recorded centrally. A Complaint number is given and the complaint is acknowledged by CAD.
- Complainant should give specific complaint with necessary details to facilitate its recording.
- The complaint will be investigated/Inquired and remedial action will be taken accordingly.
- All recorded complaints will be redressed in one month's time.
- In case, complainant is not satisfied with the redressal of the complaint, he/she may prefer an appeal before ADG, BIS within 30 days time.

Contact details Head

Consumer Affairs Department, Bureau of Indian Standards, Manakalaya 9 Bahadur Shah Zafar Marg, New Delhi-2

Tel. No: 23235069 **E mail:** cad@bis.gov.in, complaints@bis.gov.in

- If the complaint is related to allegations of corruption on the part of officers/staff, the same can be registered online under the category;

Lodge complaints pertaining to BIS officer/staff (Vigilance related).

Such complaints can also be registered directly to Chief Vigilance Officer, Manakalya, 4th Floor, Bureau of Indian Standards, 9, Bahadur Shah Zafar Marg, New Delhi-110 002, Telephone No. 23235336.

Appendix - 6

BIS GUIDANCE ON QUALITY CONTROL ORDERS

(As published by BIS)

1. **Overview of QCO**

1.1 Bureau of Indian Standards (BIS), the National Standards Body of India is engaged in the activities of Standardization, Conformity Assessment and Quality Assurance of goods, articles, processes, systems and services. The Indian Standards established by BIS forms the basis for the Product Certification Schemes, which provides Third Party Assurance of Quality, Safety and Reliability of products to consumers.

1.2 *Thrust on Mandatory Certification*

1.2.1 BIS certification scheme is basically voluntary in nature. However, for a number of products compliance to Indian Standards is made compulsory by the Central Government under various considerations viz. public interest, protection of human, animal or plant health, safety of environment, prevention of unfair trade practices and national security. For such products, the Central Government directs mandatory use of Standard Mark under a Licence or Certificate of Conformity (CoC) from BIS through issuance of QCOs.

2. **Provisions of the BIS Act**

2.1 The Central Government, after consulting BIS, publishes QCOs in exercise of the powers conferred by sub-sections (1) and (2) of section 16 read in conjunction with section 17 and sub- section (3) of section 25 of the BIS Act, 2016 thereby bringing the products under BIS Mandatory Certification.

3 **Conformity to Indian Standard and Compulsory use of Standard Mark**

3.1 The products under QCOs shall conform to corresponding Indian Standard(s) mentioned in the QCO and shall bear the Standard Mark under a Licence or CoC from BIS as per the relevant Scheme of BIS (Conformity Assessment) Regulations, 2018 as notified in the Order.

4. **Date of commencement**

4.1 QCOs are issued by various Line Ministries (Regulators) under the Central Government depending upon the product(s)/ product categories being regulated through the Order, after having stakeholder consultations.

4.2 The date of commencement of the QCO is clearly emphasized in the Order itself so that the stakeholders are well aware of the timelines for its implementation in terms of necessary manufacturing and testing infrastructure and compliance of the product to the requirements of the relevant Indian Standard.

5. **Prohibition Orders**

5.1 After the date of commencement of the QCO, no person shall manufacture, import, distribute, sell, hire, lease, store or exhibit for sale any product(s) covered under the QCO without a Standard Mark except under a valid Licence or CoC from BIS.

6. **Applicability on Imported Goods**

6.1 Domestic Laws / Rules / Orders / Regulations applicable to domestically produced goods shall apply, *mutatis mutandis*, to imports, unless specifically exempted. If domestic product(s) are subjected to mandatory compliance with Indian Standards, such product(s) if imported would also need to comply with Indian Standards compulsorily. Thus, for these products, the manufacturer in foreign country will be required to obtain a Licence or CoC from BIS under the Foreign Manufacturers Certification Scheme (FMCS) of BIS.

7. **Penalty for contravention of the provisions of QCO**

7.1 Any person who contravenes the provisions of the Order shall be punishable under the provisions of sub-section (3) of section 29 of the BIS Act, 2016 with imprisonment or with fine or with both.

8. **Exemptions from applicability of the Order**

8.1 Any exemptions like non-applicability of the Order on specific product(s), product(s) meant for export etc. come under the purview of the Line Ministry (Regulator) who has issued the QCO. Wherever exemptions are permitted, these are clearly brought out in respective QCO itself.

9. **Amendment / Revision of Indian Standards covered under QCO**

9.1 The latest version of Indian Standards including the amendments issued thereof shall apply for implementing the provisions of QCOs. Whenever any amendment or revision is made to an Indian Standard covered under the QCO, such amendment or revision shall apply to the provisions of the QCO with effect from the date notified by BIS.

9.2 In such cases, BIS provides sufficient period for concurrent running of both the versions of Indian Standard (existing as well as revised). The licensee manufacturer shall changeover to the revised version of Indian Standard within the timelines notified by BIS from time to time.

10. **Clarifications on QCO**

10.1 If any person is having issues/queries/clarifications related to applicability of QCO on a particular product or implementation of QCO or any matters connected therewith or incidental thereto like extension in the date of implementation of QCO, exemptions, stock-in-hand as on the date of implementation of the Order etc., they may approach the concerned Line Ministry/Department of the Central Government that has issued the QCO.

10.2 If any person is having queries/clarifications related to coverage of any product under Indian Standard covered under QCO, they may approach BIS.

11. Role of BIS in implementation of QCOs

11.1 For the purpose of facilitating the Central Government in issuance of QCOs, BIS regularly interacts with Line Ministries/ Departments and provides technical inputs related to Indian Standards, appropriate Conformity Assessment Scheme etc. and also participates in stakeholder's consultation meeting.

11.2 Further, for implementation of the provisions of QCO, BIS acts as the Certification Authority and grants Licence or CoC to manufacturers as per relevant Conformity Assessment Scheme. BIS also acts as the Enforcement Authority for the products specified in the QCO.

12. Information on QCOs

12.1 The information on QCOs issued by the Central Government can be obtained from BIS website under the following link **Conformity Assessment -> Product Certification -> Products under Compulsory Certification.**